DEADLINE

Judah Knight

GREENTREE
PUBLISHERS

Deadline
© 2024 by Judah Knight
Library of Congress Control Number: 2024922483

Published by Greentree Publishers
Newnan, Georgia
Greentreepublishers.com

Printed in the United States of America
ISBN: 978-1-944483-62-3

Library of Congress Control Number: 2024922483

Cover Design: 100Covers.com

Follow Judah Knight:
Website: Judahknight.com
Facebook: facebook.com/authorjudahknight
Twitter: @judahknight

Greentree Publishers
www.greentreepublishers.com

Contents

GIFT...

As a way of saying thanks for your interest in the "Deadline Series," we are offering a gift. Request a free copy of Judah Knight's novella entitled *Captive* by visiting Judah's website:

judahknight.com/free-gift/.

Captive is a suspenseful story that fits neatly in Judah Knight's "Davenport Series." The story is set during the Christmas season but can be enjoyed year around. The same book is for sale with the title *Christmas Captive*, but you can download it for free! You could read it as the seventh book of the series or enjoy it as a standalone book. We will send you a free copy in a pdf format. We respect your privacy and will not share your e-mail with anyone else.

Now, we hope you enjoy the first book in the "Deadline Series."

GreenTree Publishers

CHAPTER ONE

A New Chapter

"He looks so natural," the old blue-haired woman muttered as she patted Erin's hand.

Natural would be laughing or cursing, criticizing, or barking orders. Natural would have been asking Erin when she'd go back to school or marry someone with a real future.

Her father didn't look natural. He looked dead.

The chairs surrounding the room appeared to be a haven of safety, so Erin moved from her father's side and found a quiet place to process the ridiculousness of this night.

Guests walked up to the casket with bowed heads like in church. They viewed the corpse of a man they never bothered to visit when he was alive, made a banal comment about how wonderful he looked, and spent the rest of the time laughing with their friends and spreading the latest gossip. Georgia funerals were big social events, at least they were in this town.

Maybe the well-wishers would forget Erin existed. Why wouldn't they? For twenty-four years, no one realized Big Fred Douglas had a daughter.

Even lying in the casket, her father seemed to call, "Come on, Erin. Hold your shoulders back. How will you ever succeed if you can't stand up straight? At least you've got Greg."

The room shrank, and Erin's breath came in short gasps. She didn't have Greg and never would.

He saw nothing in me, so he left, Daddy. I didn't have the guts to tell you.

Two weeks earlier, Erin had pulled into the hospital parking lot and planned to go to her dad's room to tell him the news. The wedding was off. She'd rehearsed her lines on the way to the hospital. "Greg left, Dad. You said I was lucky to have gotten a husband. Well, I wasn't so lucky."

The two-timer had been seeing Julie Harwood for a month or two. Why had Erin cried for a solid hour for a loser like Greg Sessions? Or was she the loser? Telling her father about the breakup would have been the most logical thing to do.

Erin glanced at her father's lifeless body, dressed for a wedding that wouldn't happen. It was best he never knew. She didn't have to listen to his rants and see his familiar headshake. Another tear rolled down her cheek, but she knew this tear was for herself.

"Hey, Buttercup."

Erin didn't have to look up to know Ryan Jeffries had decided to grace her with his presence for the second time that day. She knew he would come because he always showed up. He was like the refinancing emails she kept getting even though she didn't own a house.

Ignoring him seemed like the best option, but could Ryan ever be ignored? "My name's not Buttercup."

"I like Buttercup."

"I don't." Erin picked at her nails. "You were here earlier. You didn't have to come back."

"Just checking on you and your mom. How's she holding up?"

Erin peered across the room at her mother's pale, pinched face. Francine Douglas had aged ten years in two days. At least the Xanax had kicked in.

"She's okay. It's not like we didn't know this was about to happen." Erin looked back at the casket before closing her eyes. "We still weren't ready for it."

"You can't ever be ready."

"Guess not," Erin agreed. "Mom's so drugged up she won't remember Dad died. She's going to have a hard time. He was always in charge. She's never paid a single bill."

"Have you?"

Erin snorted and reached for a tissue. "My dad didn't trust me with money or anything else. When I got paid, I always gave him most of my paycheck, and he took care of everything. I don't even know how to...to do whatever you're supposed to do with a checking account."

"You mean write checks or balance the account?"

"Both, though I don't guess people write checks anymore. Mom and I are pathetic. I've never paid the rent. Greg did it. He thought I would let him move in with me before the wedding, so he always paid it."

"What a jerk. He was sleeping with Julie and wanted to move in with you."

Erin's eyes roamed to her lap, heat rising up her neck. Small pieces of tissue fell to the floor like snowflakes as Erin worked through a box of Kleenex. Hot tears dripped from her face as she reached for a fresh tissue.

"Erin, I'm sorry. I shouldn't have said that."

"It's okay." Erin dabbed her cheeks. "It's best. I wouldn't have made him happy."

"Give yourself a break, Erin. Greg's a jerk. You're too good for him."

Erin sighed. "I don't think that was the problem. It's over, and it's for the best. Moving back in with Mom is looking more inevitable every day. It's time we learn how to be grown-ups for a change."

"Don't do anything yet, Erin. Better to let things settle a bit. In the meantime, I'll teach you how to balance your checking account and pay your bills. We'll figure out your next steps when the funeral's behind us."

The day of the funeral was exhausting and surprising. If Erin hadn't known better, she would have thought she was at the wrong service.

The eulogy proved Pastor Brant didn't know her father. Saying kind things at a funeral was normal, but in this case, they weren't true. Brant was *her* minister. She supposed someone told him positive things about her dad and forgot the rest. Her father was a good man in his own way, but she'd always heard that even being good wasn't good enough when it came to eternity.

Why were her memories of her father always of him correcting her or pointing out one of her many mistakes?

"Erin, you've got to quit snorting when you laugh. No wonder you don't have a boyfriend."

"Clean your glasses. It's a wonder you're not bumping into things."

"Erin, if you slump your shoulders any more, they're going to be dragging the ground."

No wonder Greg left. Why had he been interested in her in the first place?

Family and a few friends gathered at her mother's house that evening for a meal. The ladies from the Baptist church she attended had provided a feast, and Erin wondered what she and her mom would do with the extra food. Maybe she could take it to the fire station. She sat at her mom's kitchen table and tried to eat, but all she could do was move the food around on her plate.

Ryan sat beside her. "You better eat, Butter...uh, Erin."

"I'm not hungry. Where's Stacy? I didn't see her with you at the funeral. Or is it Megan? Aren't you two permanent fixtures?"

"They're both old news."

"No way. Stacy and Megan are gorgeous."

"They may be hot, but they were high maintenance. The cost of taking care of them was breaking the bank. Lying low for a while is a better option. You going back to work tomorrow? The women's department at Regis is not the same without you."

Erin nearly choked. "I'm sure they're getting along just fine without me. Besides, what do you know about the women's department?"

"You'd be surprised."

"Never mind. Let's change the subject."

"How about the subject of your job? Why don't you apply for another one? You hate working at Regis."

Erin thought about her hours putting out clothing and dealing with irate customers. Convincing plus-sized women they couldn't squeeze into a size ten or twelve had become so commonplace that HR should have included the task in the job description. She hated dealing with grumpy people all the time. Nothing she said or did made them happy. Then, there was the store manager, who always had an attitude.

"So, Regis isn't my favorite place in town, but I won't be able to get a job anywhere else. The fact is I was lucky to get that job."

Ryan reached for her roll and took a bite. "You're signing your own death certificate. Oh, sorry. I'm being insensitive. That's what my mom used to say."

"Signing my death certificate?"

"Planning your own demise. It's a dumb saying. I tell you what you ought to do!" He returned the roll to her plate and crossed his arms.

"This ought to be rich. What?"

"You sure are becoming snappy in your old age."

"I'm not snappy. What were you about to say?"

"You should go back to school. Really, Erin, a college degree would open many opportunities for you."

"Do you know how ridiculous that idea is, Ryan?" Erin realized her loud volume when she noticed her mom's next-door neighbor gaping at her from the other side of the dining room.

"To start with," Erin lowered her voice, "no college in the world would accept me. The last time I tried was a disaster. Besides, I can't afford it."

"Don't sell yourself short. You're smarter than you realize."

"Reality to Ryan. Hello. Are you forgetting I've already tried the college path once?"

Erin's Aunt Martha sat beside her and began prattling on about the funeral service and the wonderful eulogy. Without stopping to breathe, she moved from the service to Erin's botched wedding to the reading of her brother's will. Erin hadn't given much thought to the will, though she knew her father had one. Fred Douglas never had many material things.

Aunt Martha thought Erin's mother would be okay, and Erin knew her father's insurance would cover the funeral cost but probably not much else. When she didn't eat the rest of her food, her aunt pulled the plate across the table and stuffed her mouth as she mumbled something about children in Africa.

At 10:00, Erin left her childhood home and drove across town to the three-bedroom ranch she rented from Mr. Bosely. She kicked off her shoes at the door and tossed her socks into the laundry room. The green shag carpet slipped through her toes, and she focused on the mauve-colored walls. The colors were horrendous. Would her landlord install new carpet or let her paint?

Her real dream was to buy her own house, but that would never happen. What she wanted now more than anything was to be in bed, but she had to shower first.

A black blur darted through the kitchen, and Erin marveled at how such a huge cat could move so fast. She glanced toward Daphne's bowls and decided she'd have to quit feeding her so much. "Time to put you on a diet, girl."

Thirty minutes later, Erin stepped from the bathroom and dressed for bed. She crawled under her sheets and fluffed her pillow. She replayed the funeral through her mind and couldn't believe her father was gone.

Reaching for the other pillow, Erin pulled it close to her chest. Was she going to spend the rest of her life hugging a pillow? So pitiful. Pillows were always faithful, however. Men, not so much.

Her conversation with Ryan came to mind. He was insane. Going back to school was not an option, but getting a new job was something worth considering.

Erin had the next day off, but the thoughts of job hunting made her head spin. Regis Department Store wasn't so bad, and her routine had become familiar. She was fortunate to have a job, so she should be content. Besides, what choice did she have?

A loud yawn escaped as her mind drifted back to her father. Would his absence ever feel normal? He'd been hard on her, but he loved her. Right? Somehow, she had to quit thinking and go to sleep.

Ryan's stupid, quirky grin flashed through her mind. Go back to school. He was nuts.

CHAPTER TWO

The Early Bird

W hen the blaring alarm clock jolted Erin from a deep sleep, she reached to pound it to silence. Her fist caught more of the table than the clock, however, and pain shot up her hand. The clock slid off the table and onto the floor.

The three weeks since her father's funeral had been filled with mistakes and stupid mess-ups. She'd broken the glass pitcher from her grandmother, bent the blade on her lawnmower by running over a dumb root in the backyard, and locked her keys in her car three times. She peered over the edge of the bed at her most recent screwup and saw the remains of her clock scattered across the floor.

"Crap. That clock's brand new."

Her mind fastened onto something her father had said years earlier. "Erin, when you use words like crap, you're only making people think you have a limited vocabulary."

"I do have a limited vocabulary, Dad," she said.

"It's better to remain silent and let someone think you're stupid than to open your mouth and remove all doubt."

He'd laughed so hard at his comment that he failed to realize she wasn't laughing.

Erin laid her head back on the pillow and closed her eyes. Chirping birds outside her window told her she was fighting a losing battle. Days off were like glimmers of sunshine on rainy days, and she considered rolling over, covering her head with the pillow, and going back to sleep. The image of her bike leaning against the outside wall came to mind. Putting in a few miles would make her feel better.

Erin roused herself and threw back the covers. She stepped into a pair of sweatpants and pulled on a T-shirt before glancing out the window. The mailbox caught her attention, and she thought of the cycling gloves she'd ordered. She eyed the blisters on her hands. Maybe the gloves would solve her problem. Did UPS come the previous day? Padding to the front door, she peered through the window to the porch. Nothing.

Gloves were small enough to fit into a mailbox. She pulled open the door and headed outside.

Sure enough, someone had crammed the package into the mailbox with an assortment of bills, flyers, and junk mail. Erin pulled everything from her mailbox.

Walking back to the house, she fingered through the mail. Electric bill. Kohl's credit card bill. Using a credit card for clothes was not a good idea. And what was up with these real-tors? They wanted to buy her house, and she didn't own it.

A final envelope from a lawyer caught her eye. Surely, an ambulance chaser. Things were getting bad when lawyers started sending out circulars.

Erin tossed the mail onto the kitchen counter. She gasped as two envelopes fell into the crack between her stove and the countertop.

"No, no, no!"

Why did stuff like that always have to happen to her? Now, she'd have to pull the whole stove out to retrieve two pieces of trash. It could wait.

She scanned the remaining mail on the counter and found the two bills. The crack between the stove called to her. It was junk mail, so why bother? She turned toward her bedroom.

Erin's thoughts drifted back to her mom. Ryan had helped them sign up for online bill pay. Erin didn't mind using the internet for the payments, but she preferred sending each payment online one at a time. The only problem was that her mom couldn't remember how to do it from week to week.

Fred Douglas had put all his accounts in order and left his wife plenty of money to take care of herself. Erin thought back to the reading of her father's will three weeks earlier. Her mother had gotten everything, but Erin had been shocked he had enough money so her mom wouldn't have to get a job after all. Plus, he had a two-million-dollar life insurance policy.

Her father had always been so secretive, so she shouldn't be surprised he had such a large insurance policy. At least her mom's needs were met. Her Aunt Martha was miffed she'd been left out of the will. She disguised her feelings by commenting that Erin also hadn't gotten anything.

Erin turned toward the window. She should go for a bike ride, but she had all day. The call of the bed was too much. Her down comforter welcomed her as it embraced her like an old friend. After a few minutes, she adjusted her black, plastic glasses and reached for her phone as it buzzed with a text.

"Sent you an email. Read it and call me when you're ready to talk. Taking the day off."

Ryan took the day off? He took more days off than he worked.

She placed her pillows behind her back and opened her laptop. Scrolling through her daily emails, she saw several promoting discounted eBooks. Kohl's was having a sale next weekend. Erin paused to read her daily horoscope. Why had she signed up to receive such trash? It wasn't even true, but she couldn't help but read it every day.

> Your man is lucky to have you, but don't be too full of yourself. Humility is never a bad path. The celestial lineup is totally in your favor, and you can expect romance and perfect nights for the next week. Get your candles and music ready!

Erin snorted and reached for the toilet paper roll on the bedside table to blow her nose.

"You sound like a sick goose," her father once said.

Readjusting the pillows behind her back, Erin reread her horoscope. "What man? No celestial lineup can turn my life into romance and perfect nights. Who writes this dribble? My best opportunity for romance is reading Francine Rivers."

Erin eyed her bookshelf and thought about Francine Rivers. *Redeeming Love* was outstanding. Was it really a modern-day version of a Bible story? A girl at work had mentioned that, but Erin was unsure. What must it be like to write a novel? How often had she read a book and wished to be a writer? There's no way she could write anything anyone would want to read. She'd have to be content to be a reader. Thanks to Mrs. Kitchens, reading had become her passion.

Thoughts of third grade flooded her mind. She'd always been at the bottom of her class. She'd almost failed third grade because she didn't know how to read. It was a wonder she made it that far.

Faking it had been a snap for her first two years of school, but her third-grade teacher discovered Erin couldn't read. Mrs. Kitchens would always be Erin's hero. How many other teachers would have worked so hard to help a slow kid learn basic phonetics? The persistent teacher kept telling Erin she was going to be an expert reader.

Erin looked at the drawer of her bedside table where she kept the yellow star Mrs. Kitchens had given her at the end of the year. Most improved. Erin would love to be a teacher like Mrs. Kitchens and help kids who otherwise didn't have a chance.

Third-grade teachers didn't usually spend hours tutoring students after school to help them learn to read, so Mrs. Kitchens was a real superstar and deserved a medal.

The glint from a picture frame on the table caught her attention. Her father was so young and vibrant, and her mom and brother appeared so happy. She wore a yellow jumper, which had been her favorite in fourth grade. Erin frowned as she stared at herself. If Worth Elementary School had given out an award for the ugliest girl, she would have won it. Her red hair practically glowed in the dark, and her freckled face made her look like an imp. She was more freckle than face.

Middle school and high school had been disasters. She could have been mistaken for a boy until eleventh grade, except for her long, frizzy hair. The new ninth-grade coach assigned her a locker in the boys' locker room. *Didn't he realize Erin is a girl's name?*

Erin pressed her camera app and turned the phone around as a mirror. She recoiled at what she saw.

Although her hair had darkened and she finally bloomed, no one would want this flower in their bouquet.

Her mother had told her many times that her hair would darken. She reviewed her reflection on the phone and knew it would take a lot more than auburn hair to bring ugly to plain. *Plain would be a wonderful change of pace.*

At least she wasn't overweight. Riding her bike each morning before work kept her in shape, and she found true solace pedaling down a country road while watching the sun peek over the horizon. The thought of her bike leaning against the wall under the carport came to mind, but her bed sure felt comfortable. Maybe she'd skip today.

Erin returned to her emails, and her eyes landed on Ryan's. The subject alone made her want to delete it: "Let's find a new job."

Why won't he mind his own business? Every woman Ryan dated had been blonde and beautiful. *He needs to find another beautiful, blonde bimbo and quit worrying about me.*

Her eyes scanned down to the content of the email.

"Rise and shine, sleepyhead."

Erin turned toward her windows. Were her shades pulled down? Could he see into her room? After studying the top of the email, she saw he'd sent the thing at 5:00. *Of course, I'd still be asleep. He's insane. Why wasn't he sleeping instead of worrying about my employment?*

She returned her attention to the email. "The early bird gets the worm, and in this case, the new job. I've scanned a few options I found online. Check out the links and tell me what you think. You may have to join jobhunter.com first so you can have access to the content. Barnes & Noble is hiring. You love to read, right? Call me when you're up."

Erin slid out of bed and headed to the bathroom. On the way, she stubbed her toe on the dresser's edge. She leaned over and grabbed her throbbing toe.

"Dang. I've got to quit doing that."

Thirty minutes later, with a cup of coffee steaming in front of her on the kitchen table, she opened Gmail on her laptop computer and found Ryan's note. "Okay, Ryan. Whatever it takes to make you happy. I'll join this stupid job site."

The *join* button glared at her from the screen, taunting and calling. She reached out a shaky finger and let it hover above the touchpad. She clicked it.

Ryan's suggestions flashed before her eyes in no time. Barnes & Noble was indeed hiring. What would it be like to work at her favorite store? A post for a nanny popped up, but she'd rather pull out her fingernails than take care of someone's bratty kids.

When she clicked on the last link in Ryan's email, her computer hummed for a second before the website for the local community college opened. "Cute, Ryan. I hate to tell you, but when you drop out of college because you flunked your classes, they won't let you come back."

She clicked on the degree tab and scanned the options. Teaching third grade would be rewarding, but teaching literature to high school students would be a dream.

After studying the page on her computer screen, she sighed and closed her eyes. If she walked into Perimeter College, the people in the admissions office would hurt themselves laughing at her.

The chorus of "How to Disappear Completely" sounded from her phone. Stupid song. She needed to change her ringtone.

"Are you stalking me, Ryan Jeffries?"

"Good morning to you, too, Buttercup. Are you always this cheerful in the mornings? No, I'm not stalking you. Stalking would mean I'm following or harassing you."

Erin's eyes scanned the living room and landed on the front window, which was not covered by a window shade. "I'd say you're harassing me. I finished reading your email and closed my computer right before you called. Doesn't that sound a little coincidental?"

"Not to me," Ryan chuckled. "I've been waiting until I thought you'd had enough beauty sleep."

"Why aren't you at Gatner doing whatever you do to make all that money you throw around? You have more to worry about than hassling me."

Erin had never been inside his home, but she knew it had to cost a bundle, as did his brand-new BMW. He was loaded. No wonder he always had beautiful women hanging all over him.

"How many times do I have to tell you? I'm not hassling you, Buttercup. I'm just helping out an old friend."

"So, now I'm old?"

"You're incorrigible."

"You're right. I'm hopeless."

"That's not what I meant," Ryan interrupted. "I'll pick you up in thirty minutes, so be ready."

"Where are we going?"

"I'm taking you to meet the manager at Barnes & Noble and then to lunch."

"Assuming I want a new job at Barnes & Noble, I'd have to apply online."

"It never hurts to meet the manager. It'll help him connect a face to an application."

"Connecting this face to my application is not a good idea."

"Oh, Buttercup. What am I going to do with you? I have another surprise stop for you, too. I'll be there at half past nine."

"But..." Erin pulled the phone away from her ear and eyed the screen. "He hung up on me. The nerve."

Erin groaned and threw the phone into her pillow. "He's the one who's incorrigible. Why won't he leave me alone?"

Friends for Life

E rin plopped onto her overstuffed Goodwill bargain couch and managed to spill coffee on her shirt. Figures. About half of her shirts had stains of some kind on them. Groaning, she thought about how her day was already spinning out of control.

Why was Ryan such a pain? Why did he even bother trying to be her friend? He had worked off his debt to her. As she reached for a clean top in her closet, her mind drifted back thirteen years.

Erin had to go to the restroom so badly that day that if Mrs. Jenkins hadn't given her a hall pass, she would have been in big trouble. Her fifth-grade teacher never offered a pass without asking questions, but this time, she'd relented. Erin's desperation must have been written all over her freckled face.

"Thanks," Erin blurted as she hurried out of the room and down the hall.

Rushing into the restroom, she took care of her business but chose not to be in a hurry to return to the discussion on converting fractions to decimals. She preferred being alone.

The writing on the restroom walls always intrigued her. Why would girls write such messages? As she approached the sink moments later, she washed her hands and face as if she could somehow wash off the freckles. After a quick glance in the mirror, she still looked like a clown.

Pushing open the door, Erin walked to the water fountain between the girls' and boys' restrooms and heard a stall door bang closed in the boys' room. The familiar voice of the school bully echoed into the hallway—Barry Goldstein.

A shiver ran down her spine. Barry was mean to everyone. Even the teachers avoided him.

"Ryan, Ryan, Ryan," Barry said. "Thought you could slip off without giving me my money?"

Ryan Jeffries. They weren't exactly friends, but he went to her church. He was a nice enough boy, but she knew him only from a distance. In fact, she knew everyone from a distance, like she had a contagious disease or something.

"Please, Barry," Erin heard Ryan whine. "I won't be able to eat today if I give you my money again."

"Are you talking back to me, Dork? Do you think I care if you eat?"

Erin heard a thud and figured Barry had pushed Ryan against the wall. Then, she heard the sounds of a scuffle.

Was Ryan fighting Barry? No way.

SMACK! Ryan began to cry, and she bolted into the boys' bathroom.

Barry sat on top of Ryan in the middle of the floor. The bully raised his hand, ready to punch Ryan's already glowing cheek. Without thinking, Erin kicked Barry in the head. The bully howled, grabbed his ear, and rolled off Ryan.

This overgrown fifth grader had picked on everyone, and Erin was sick of it. When Barry scrambled off the floor, she balled up her fist and punched him in the nose. Blood gushed down his shirt as he stood in horror. He covered his nose and ran out of the restroom.

"You al right?" She eyed the boy on the floor, who jumped up and hurried into a stall.

Erin leaned against the stall door. "It's okay to cry. I cry all the time."

"I'm not crying," came the muffled reply.

Too late. She'd already seen the tears running down his cheeks, but she knew better than to correct him. Boys never wanted to admit to crying.

Erin's eyes roamed the dingy room. Four stalls and two strange things hanging on the wall.

Erin jiggled the door. Locked. "Want me to check out your face? We've got lunch, and if I get caught in the boys' bathroom..."

The stall door cracked open and then squeaked as Ryan walked out, staring at his feet. Erin counted the specks in the square of linoleum at her feet.

"Uh, well," Erin stammered, "we need to go. I'll...uh...You want me to help you clean up your face?"

She pulled his chin up to inspect his wet cheek. The right side of his face was red where Barry had punched him. Erin put a paper towel under the cold water and wiped his face. Nothing she could do about the shiner.

"There," she announced. "Good as new. No one will notice anything. We need to leave. I don't want anyone to see me in here."

When Erin walked into the lunchroom, all the kids were abuzz about Barry's bloody nose. One of the boys asked her what happened.

Ryan looked like he wanted to melt into the floor.

"I was at the water fountain," Erin said, "and I saw Barry push Ryan and say he would take his lunch money. Then, Ryan punched him in the nose."

Ryan beamed at Erin as the other boys began to slap him on the back and give him high fives. From that moment, Ryan became Erin's closest friend.

She smiled as she pulled the coffee cup to her lips. Ryan was her only friend. How pathetic. Even after he grew up and became a superstar football player in high school, he never forgot what happened in the boys' room.

The two had become superglued together. Ryan was like the older brother she'd never had, though they were the same age. Right now, he was an annoying big brother.

Erin returned to the couch, opened the favorites tab on her web browser, and clicked on the familiar real estate website. She saw three new houses for sale, and one of them was only a couple of miles away. A fixer-upper, but she wasn't the fixer-upper type. She scanned the other ads and thought one of the houses sounded adorable. *It's like Cinderella's little cottage in the woods. Oh, I wish....*

Even with a glimmer of hope, a wave of helplessness overtook her. She couldn't buy a house right now, so why did she waste her time looking at this stupid website?

Daphne jumped onto the couch and curled up beside Erin. The cat's purring sounded like a tiny hum of contentment.

"Well, good morning, Daffy girl." Erin ran her fingers through the huge cat's black fur. "You'll never guess what I'm doing." She paused as if listening for Daphne's reply. "Oh, excellent guess. You only see me doing it every day. I need to save up another $10,000 for a down payment. Having ten grand by the end of the week should be a breeze."

Erin set her computer beside her, stood, and stretched. "I might have $10,000 by the end of the next decade, but probably not. Then, I'd have to convince a loan officer to give me a loan. Not in this lifetime!" The cat jumped down and curled her tail around Erin's leg. "You care where we live, don't you, girl?"

She glanced at her watch and realized Ryan would soon be there. Not only was he persistent, but he was always punctual. Punctuality was another thing Erin could add to her deficiency list. She was always late, except to work. That was the one exception. In fact, she made it a point to arrive ten minutes or more early to work.

Ryan's shiny black car pulled into her driveway.

Erin looked toward the cabinet where she kept cereal and sighed. She would have enjoyed breakfast, but coffee would have to be good enough. She pulled down her travel mug and filled it before adding plenty of cream.

"Daffy, you be sweet while I'm gone." She hurried out the door and slipped into the front seat of Ryan's slick, black sedan.

New car smell enveloped her, as did the warmth of the leather seat. She thought it odd that the seat was warm even though the morning was a little cool. Heated seats, of course.

"Good morning, Sunshine."

"Why am I getting into the car with you? I'm not sure I want a new job. Why are you concerned about what I'm doing with my life?"

"Aren't you a bouquet of roses this morning! Thorns and all."

"I don't understand why you're so worried about my job."

"I'm not worried about your job, Erin. I know you hate it. I wouldn't be much of a friend if I weren't willing to help you leave something you hate and find something you love."

Erin buckled her seatbelt as Ryan pulled out into the street. "At least you called me Erin." She drew in a deep breath. "I'm sorry I'm in such a bad mood. I just had a hard enough time landing a job at Regis. I don't think I've got it in me to go through the whole process again."

"Applying for a few jobs can't hurt anything, Erin. The job-hunting experience will be beneficial for you."

"Okay, okay. I'll apply for a new job somewhere if it will make you happy. So, where's the mystery stop?"

"Mystery stop?"

"Yeah. You said we had a surprise stop."

"Oh, that. Well, if I told you, it wouldn't be a surprise."

"Where are we going first?"

"I suggest we go big or go home."

"Meaning?"

"Meaning we go to Barnes & Noble first, and you can meet the manager."

"I don't know what to say to the manager at Barnes & Noble."

"Talk with him about his store and how much you love books. Tell him you plan to apply online, but you want to meet him first. He'll love you."

"Right. I've got about as much chance of working for Barnes & Noble as becoming the next CEO of Gatner Enterprises."

"I hadn't heard the CEO was stepping down," Ryan teased. "Erin, you've got nothing to lose. You love Barnes & Noble, and you love to read. I think it's a perfect fit."

As Ryan pulled onto the interstate, Erin watched the passing cars. Her life felt like a blur of cars headed who knows where. She had no clarity in her life and wondered if she was destined to wander through the years until she died, like her father. Didn't life have a grander purpose?

Having someone with whom to share life would be a tremendous start. Her mind returned to Greg, and she couldn't help but wonder what he was doing. He'd probably marry Julie Harwood. She was beautiful and rich, two things Erin would never be.

Oh, well. Maybe this Barnes & Noble thing would work out. Working there would be an improvement. If, by some miracle, she managed to land this job, she'd be in debt to Ryan for the rest of her life.

CHAPTER FOUR

Promptings

Erin entered the side door of her home and flipped the light switch. Her annoying ringtone blasted from her cell phone. Who would be calling? She wanted to disappear completely—into her bed. Her stomach growled, reminding her she was running on empty.

Okay. Food, then bed. Ryan had offered dinner out, but she didn't want to wear out their friendship. He had been with her almost every day since her father passed.

She dug into her purse while the Radiohead ringtone mocked her. *Where's my stupid phone?*

Erin yelped as something brushed her ankle. "Daphne. Silly girl, you scared me." Her fingers wrapped around the phone. *Mom.*

"Hey, Mom. You okay?"

Francine's distant voice sounded more like she was on Mars instead of only fifteen miles away. "No. I'm not okay. I'll never be okay."

"Yes, you will, Mom. You've got all the money you'll ever need. You're going to be fine."

"I'm not talking about money, Erin."

"Yeah." Erin's tone softened. "Mom, it'll take some time, but you'll be fine."

"If I can remember how to pay these bills, I might be okay. I'd also like to understand this mutual fund your dad left."

"I'm sort of clueless, too. I mean, why did he have all this money set aside? Did Dad want us to be in the dark? Maybe he didn't think we could handle financial stuff."

"Don't say hurtful things about your father, Erin."

"Sorry, Mom. Ryan said he would give us all the help we need. He suggested we meet tomorrow night at your house, and he'll help us understand the investment account. You okay with Ryan helping us again?"

"I can't move forward, Erin."

"Yes, you can," Erin responded, "and Ryan wants to make sure you have a usable financial plan and that you understand the mutual fund account. He'll help you figure out how to take care of the basics. He's good with figures, Mom." Stacy Newsome's gorgeous body flashed into her mind, Ryan's most recent flame. "I mean, money and financial stuff is his forte."

"He's such a fine boy. I don't know why he's still single."

"I don't think he's interested in marriage. He can have any woman he wants. Did you need something, Mom?"

"No, dear. I...well, everything's so quiet."

Erin imagined her mother alone in the massive house she had shared with her father for thirty years. Why hadn't she already thought of spending the night with her? *I am so stupid and insensitive. I should have been staying with her some.*

"Mom, I just got home. I thought I'd pick up a few things and come over. You want company? I mean, I could even spend the night and go to work from your house in the morning."

"Erin, you're sweet, but I'll be fine."

"No, Mom. I'll feed Daphne, grab some clothes, and be right over."

After pulling out an overnight bag, she riffled through her drawer and pulled out clothes. Trying to remember what she'd worn recently, Erin studied her dresses in the closet. As she pulled out a dress, her phone buzzed with a text. It had to be Ryan.

"Have you applied at B&N?"

"Leave me alone," Erin shouted at her phone. "I haven't even had time to think about it." Daphne looked up and tilted her head.

Erin's mind went back to her meeting with Mr. Winslow. He was a kind man and told her he still had an opening. He encouraged her to apply online, but he couldn't guarantee anything. *That was his way of saying he was so sorry, and he'd never be able to offer me a job.*

Her phone buzzed with another message. "Helloooo. Anyone home?"

She stabbed in her reply. "Leave me alone. Just got home. Been on the phone with Mom. Heading to her house for the night."

After pounding the send button, she jabbed at her phone a few more times. "I might apply when I get there or not. It's none of your business."

Regret eked into her consciousness as she thought about Ryan waking early that morning to scan the internet so he could help her find a job. He was trying to help her. Why was she so angry?

She began typing another message. "Sorry. I might apply later."

Hurrying into the kitchen, Erin poured food into Daphne's bowl and refilled the water bowl. She had to help her mom figure out what to do, but she needed help herself. Maybe the Barnes & Noble thing would work out. Working there would be wonderful.

The surprise stop with Ryan shouldn't have been a surprise. When he turned into the parking lot of the college, she
wanted to jump from the car and run. Her visit to the school
hadn't been bad. The lady in admissions told her that dropping out didn't mean she couldn't return. She wanted to slap
the smugness off Ryan's face, but deep down, she wondered
if it would be possible to return to school.

Two hours later, after consoling her mother in the living
room, Erin collapsed onto her old bed. Being in her childhood
bedroom brought back bad memories. She remembered hearing her parents argue, but the worst memory was the night her
little brother had been killed. Chills ran down her back.

His death had been her fault. If she had taken him with
her to Steak 'n Shake after the football game, he never would
have been in the car accident. She had lied to her parents, saying she was going with friends when she had wanted some
alone time. Her parents should have known she didn't have
any friends. Though her father didn't say it, she knew he
blamed her for Ricky's death.

Erin's body cried out for sleep, but her dark
thoughts…She had to do something.

She sat on the edge of the bed and picked up her computer. The job hunter site glowed before her, and ten minutes
later, she had completed the Barnes & Noble application.

Before losing her nerve, she went to the Perimeter College
page to apply to go back to school. Halfway down the page, a
question asked if she would be entering as a freshman.

Not a freshman, but a sophomore? Would they make her start
over? She checked the sophomore box, completed the rest of
the application, added her debit card number for the fee, and
hit send.

Erin picked up her phone and sent a message to Ryan. "I did it."

He must have been holding his phone because his reply was instant. "Did what? Got married?"

Does he ever sleep?

"Cute," she typed. "I applied at B&N and Perimeter. Thanks for your help today, even though Perimeter won't accept me, and B&N won't hire someone like me."

"We'll see."

Erin stared at her phone before tapping it a few times. "Goodnight."

Six thirty would come early, so she closed her computer and set the alarm on her phone. Reaching for a tissue, she blew her nose. Ryan was being a real pain in the neck.

As she pulled the covers back and rested her head on the pillow, a silly smile crossed her face. Working at B&N would be cool.

The next morning, Erin woke to the aromas of bacon and coffee. For the last two months, her breakfast had been a Pop-Tart or a banana and coffee on her commute to work.

She normally rode her bike a few miles and then hurried through her morning routine of getting dressed, grabbing breakfast to go, and rushing out the door. She had to leave her home by 8:00 to ensure she had time to get to work by 9:00. What would it be like to live in a small community where she wouldn't have to deal with rush hour traffic?

"Wow, Mom. Scrambled eggs and bacon? Aren't you overdoing it?"

"I cooked this breakfast for your father for years," her mom said.

Erin floundered, unsure of a perfect response. After what could've been a few seconds or a few minutes, she steadied her mom's shoulders and wrapped her in an embrace. "You're going to be okay, Mom. It's going to take time, but you'll see."

"I'm so lost. My whole life revolved around your father."

"Pastor Brant says one of the best ways to overcome grief is to help others. Why don't you think about volunteering somewhere?"

"Volunteer?"

"I'm sure there are plenty of things you could do at my church. I remember seeing a lot of volunteers at the hospital, too."

"I can't go back to the hospital," her mom protested. "Too many bad memories."

"Do you want me to call Pastor Brant and see if there's something you can do?"

"The church isn't ready for me yet," Mom said. "It's too soon." Her mom turned back to the stove and picked up the frying pan. "Grab a plate for your eggs and bacon. I also have biscuits in the oven."

Over breakfast, Erin told her mother about applying for school and the Barnes & Noble possibility. She told her mother she'd love to teach literature one day to high school students, but she didn't think she'd make it out of college. "I doubt they'll let me come back."

"Maybe not, dear. College isn't for everyone."

Erin's phone buzzed, and she eyed the screen. Ryan, of course. No one else texted her.

"Can we postpone financial planning with your mom until Sunday night? Something's come up this evening."

Erin knitted her brows as she wondered about *something*. Did Ryan's something have long, tan legs and a perfect figure? It was Saturday, and she knew Ryan well.

"I think you mean someone has come up." Erin typed into her phone. "Let me guess. You're going out with Stacy."

"Not Stacy. Her roommate, Melissa, called last night, and she needs some help with a project."

"Sure. I've heard that line before. Enjoy your date. Sunday night is fine."

Erin retrieved her coffee tumbler, kissed her mom, and hurried out the door. The snooze button was going to be her undoing, and she spent too much time talking with her mom. If traffic was bad, she'd be late for work.

She ran into the department store two minutes late with a wet coffee stain on the front of her dress. Spilling coffee had been bad enough, but being stopped by the police officer for speeding made this the worst day of her week.

Tears rolled down her cheeks as she threw her purse into the locker in the employees' break room. *What is my deal? So, I got a speeding ticket. It's not my first, and I don't even care about the stupid dress.* She turned around and ran straight into her supervisor.

"Good morning, Erin," Mrs. Boseman said, her eyes focusing on the wet spot on Erin's dress. "Looks like you had a difficult time getting to work today. I'm sure these last few weeks have been a challenge."

Erin's gaze dropped to the evidence of her coffee disaster, which had turned her yellow dress into a lovely shade of brown. She wanted to crawl under the table. "Yes, ma'am. It's been an adjustment."

"Why don't you find a dress off the rack to wear? Don't worry about paying for it, just give me the tags."

"Mrs. Boseman. I can't..."

"I'd rather you choose a new dress than go home to change. We're short-staffed today as it is."

Erin hurried out of the break room and found a light blue dress on purse, desperate to stop the Radiohead ringtone purse, desperate to stop the Radiohead ringtone the sales rack. After changing, she got to her assigned place by 9:20. Regis didn't open until 10:00, so she had plenty of time to prepare her department for the day. Mrs. Boseman was sweet, but her kindness didn't make up for the likelihood of cranky customers.

Maybe Barnes & Noble would work out.

CHAPTER FIVE

Celebration

Over the next month, Erin took as many extra shifts as possible. The weeks after the funeral had been brutal, and she'd missed a lot of work. Regis didn't pay employees for personal time off, and rent wouldn't pay itself.

Erin walked across the Regis' parking lot toward her car that afternoon and heard her phone ringing in her purse. While wiggling the phone from the side pocket, she dropped her purse onto the ground. The rest of the contents spilled across two parking spaces, and a groan slipped from her lips. Clumsy was her middle name. Reaching for her wallet and compact, she eyed the unknown number on her phone.

A sales call?

She started to slide the phone back into her purse but looked at the screen. Erin swiped her finger across the face of the phone.

"Hello?"

Soft music played in the background. "Hello. This is Alfred Winslow from Barnes & Noble. Is this Erin Douglas?"

Erin dropped the phone, and it bounced on the hard pavement. *Aaagghh. Klutz.*

She retrieved the device and gasped when she saw the cracked glass. "Uh…sorry, yes. This is Erin. I'm sorry. I dropped my phone."

"Not a problem, Miss Douglas. I am the manager at Barnes & Noble on Mt. Zion Road in Morrow. I have reviewed your application and would like to ask you to come by this week for an interview."

"Interview? Yes, sir. I'd like that. When would you like me to come?"

"Tomorrow or Wednesday. Two o'clock?"

"I have Wednesday off, so two would be perfect. I'll see you then. Thank you."

Sitting in her driveway forty-five minutes later, Erin didn't remember the drive home. She had an interview at her favorite store in the world. It didn't seem possible.

What was she thinking? An interview would be a disaster. Her heart raced, and she began panicking.

Should she call Ryan? How would he react? Calling him Friday to tell him Perimeter College had accepted her had been both exhilarating and irritating. Nothing short of a miracle, but Ryan had been a little smug. Would a call today be a repeat? Her head pounded.

No, I'll wait until they turn me down for the job before calling Ryan.

Erin retrieved mail from the box and headed into her house. As she dropped everything onto the kitchen table, a letter from Perimeter College caught her attention, and she pulled the stationery from the envelope. It was a repeat of the email she'd already seen, but this one informed her she was only six hours shy of being a junior. Wow! How was she almost a junior? The letter also informed her she had to meet with an advisor.

Her knuckles turned white as she gripped the letter and slumped onto her couch. As she closed her eyes and tried to process the events of the last few weeks, Daphne jumped onto her lap and purred.

"Hello, girl." Erin smiled and stroked the large feline balled on her lap. "You won't believe what happened. I've got a job interview at Barnes & Noble. I know, right? Shocker. So, I find out I'm going back to school, and I'm interviewing for my dream job. They probably won't hire me, but it's still amazing that the manager called."

Erin sighed and tried to imagine what it would be like to leave the department store. Daphne adjusted her position and nuzzled Erin's neck. Erin cuddled the one friend who never let her down.

"Of course, you may love me only because I feed you way too much."

Daphne jumped from Erin's lap when someone knocked on the door. The doorknob jiggled. Thankfully, she'd locked it behind her.

"Who's there?" Erin called out as she moved toward the door.

"The boogeyman," the familiar voice said.

Erin didn't know whether to be happy or annoyed. Why was he so nosy? She unlocked the door and pulled it open. Ryan stood there grinning like a loon. "You're kind of like cobwebs. You keep showing up."

"Ummm. I've been called many things in my life but never a cobweb." Ryan entered the house and plopped onto the recliner in the living room.

"Please, do come in." Erin rolled her eyes. "Would the boogeyman like some tea or water?"

"Tea sounds perfect."

Ryan followed her into the kitchen and sat at the table while Erin rummaged in the refrigerator. She poured a glass of sweet tea and placed it in front of him. His stupid trademark grin covered his face.

"What's with the smile?" Erin crossed her arms.

"You've got a secret."

"No, I don't."

"You're incapable of lying to me, Miss Douglas, and you have something written all over your face. Remind me to say yes if you ever ask me to play poker."

Erin wrapped her arms around herself and blew a stray strand of hair from her face.

"Okay, so maybe I have a secret."

Ryan continued to smile but said nothing.

"Mr. Winslow called from Barnes & Noble and asked me to come for an interview."

"Haha! I knew it. I knew he'd recognize a rising star when he saw one."

"Rising star? Give me a break."

Ryan furrowed his brow. "Aren't you excited? I'd think you'd be jumping up and down, not to mention thanking me for insisting you apply for a new job."

"Ryan, just because someone called me for an interview doesn't mean I'm hired. It means he wants to talk to me. Nothing else. I imagine he has a certain number of people he has to interview before giving the job to someone."

Erin turned to the sink and filled up a glass with water. "I don't think you need to plan a celebration dinner yet."

"When's the interview?"

"Wednesday."

Ryan pulled the phone from his pocket and swiped and tapped the screen a few times before holding the phone to his ear.

Erin moved toward the table. "Who are you calling?"

"Hello?" Ryan said into the phone. "Yes, ma'am. I'd like to make reservations for two, Wednesday night at 7:00." He paused a minute. "My name is Ryan Jeffries, and yes, ma'am, we'll be celebrating a momentous occasion. Thank you very much."

Erin sat at the table and gaped at Ryan pocketing his phone.

"I made reservations for us at Valentino's for Wednesday night. We're going to celebrate."

"You're crazy. I won't get the job, and I've never heard of Valentino's, but it doesn't sound like it's in my price range."

"It's in mine, so don't worry about it. We're going to celebrate your new job."

Erin shook her head. "Don't clear your packed calendar just yet, Mr. Jeffries."

On Wednesday night, Ryan pulled out a chair from a beautifully decorated table. Erin scanned the restaurant and wanted to run out the back door. *This is so out of my league.*

Ryan nodded toward the chair. She sat before her nerves made her unsteady.

Uniformed attendants, well-dressed patrons, expensive bottles of wine... At a nearby table, dessert plates were decorated with chocolate writing beside delectable tiramisu. How could she eat at a place like this?

Why did I let Ryan bring me here? Chick-fil-A would have been fine.

"It's not like I got a contract with some huge firm, Ryan. This place is a little over the top." Erin couldn't hide her grin.

Her day couldn't have gone better, and she was about to burst with excitement about her new job. The soft chair welcomed her like a new friend, and she took in her surroundings. This place was impressive.

"I told you," Ryan beamed. "Mr. Winslow recognizes quality when he sees it."

"I don't know about that." Erin picked up the menu, and her face turned as white as the tablecloth. "Ryan. We can't eat here. These prices!"

"Not only can we eat here, Erin Douglas, but we're going to eat here. Study the menu and figure out what you want. Anything."

Erin scanned the menu again and tried to relax. "I'm sorry, Ryan. I'm not much fun. I do appreciate you bringing me here. I'm a little…a little out of my element."

This new job paid more than Regis and would be a lot more enjoyable. School started soon. She did have something to celebrate.

"Give yourself a break, Erin."

Erin lowered her voice, "I don't even know which fork to use."

"You'll use them both," Ryan laughed. "Start on the outside and move in. The outside fork is for your salad. The inside fork is for your main course."

Erin nodded and placed the napkin onto her lap. "I'm so excited about my new job and returning to school. Two impossibilities, but thanks to you, it's happening."

"No, it's thanks to you, Erin. You're a lot smarter than you think. You're going to be a hit at your new job, and you'll be at the top of your class in no time. Wait and see."

Erin snorted as she was about to take a sip of water. "Don't be so sure, Ryan. I'm happy but nervous about going back."

"You'll be fine. Now, let's order the meal this celebration requires."

CHAPTER SIX

The Message

The colorful spring had been replaced by the heat waves of a Georgia summer. Erin checked her watch as she locked the car and walked toward Howard Hall. One more final exam and her summer term would end.

Where had the time gone? These last few months had been a blur. She couldn't believe two semesters had already passed. Seemed as if she'd just sat at her desk in English literature, marking her first day back to school.

After finishing with two Bs and one C during her first semester, it didn't make sense to take a break for the summer. When she saw the course offerings, she knew she couldn't pass up the creative writing class that had been in Ryan's original email about going back to school. Pulling off an 89 on the final exam would give her an A for the class. Unbelievable! She'd never made an A. She had studied so hard for this exam and felt prepared.

The first part of the final would involve answering questions about English grammar, figures of speech, and symbolism in the books they'd read throughout the semester. The first part would be a cinch, but the second part involved writing a paper in class.

The assistant distributed the exams, and Erin went straight to work. She noticed some of the other students struggling with the test, but she tore through the questions like a hot knife through butter.

When Erin turned in her completed exam, she couldn't help but be nervous about the essay. Her professor displayed five different photographs. She had to choose one and write the first two pages of a story the picture inspired.

Erin chose a lighthouse standing as a sentinel beside the ocean of what had to be a scene in Maine. The thing that caught her attention was a little girl standing at the base of the lighthouse looking back at her dog.

The girl made her think of herself—alone but determined. For Erin, the lighthouse represented the big challenge or adventure that called the girl forward. In her story, the brave girl eagerly embraced her adventure. This point might be where the parallel with herself stopped. She was far from brave. She was, however, grateful for her own lighthouse.

Whether the paper was good or not, Erin had no idea. Just completing the exam filled her with relief. She headed to her car and drove toward home. When she passed Krispy Kreme and saw the *Hot Now* light on, she knew it must be a sign she should stop and celebrate. Two semesters were behind her, and she was ten hours into her junior year of college. Hard to believe. Two hot doughnuts wouldn't hurt her. *I'll work them off in the morning on my bike.*

Erin pulled the door open and inhaled. *I bet I gained a pound by smelling this little piece of heaven.* She saw a couple of college students sitting at a table with their books out and a business-man working on his laptop near the window.

The fresh doughnuts made their decadent processional down the conveyor belt. Erin watched the round treasures drift through the shower of hot, sinful glaze as her stomach did somersaults.

She stepped closer as row after row of hot donuts were crowned with the secret to her greatest weakness. A girl at church once said Krispy Kreme doughnuts would be in heaven. This place had her number.

After paying for her order, Erin lifted the tray of dough-nuts and breathed in the aroma as she hurried toward a table in the corner. She pulled out her phone and saw Ryan had messaged her earlier to wish her luck on the test. "I'm all done." She typed into the phone. "Not bad. Grades won't be posted for a day or two."

Within seconds, Ryan replied, "Melissa and I are going bowling after work. Want to come? We could celebrate."

Erin leaned back in her chair as she read his text for the second time. Was he crazy? Was she so pitiful that she'd go along with him on a date?

I'll die before being a third wheel.

Erin's fingers flew across the face of her phone. "I'm spending the evening with my mom. Maybe some other time.."

Thirty minutes later, Erin pulled into her driveway and left the car running as she hurried across the street to her mailbox. After parking under the carport, she noticed a missed call from a strange number. Someone left a voicemail.

The smell of trash greeted her as she walked into her house. *Idiot. You didn't take out the trash.* Dirty dishes sat in the sink, but the rest of her house was relatively clean. She dropped the mail onto the counter and played the message from her voicemail on speaker as she scanned the mail.

"Miss Douglas. This is Angie Westmoreland from Kirk-land & Williams. We handled your father's last will and testa-ment. I'm calling to confirm that you received our letter a few months ago. It's very important you follow the instructions included in it. If you have any questions, please feel free to give us a call."

Erin's eyes fell onto an old pile of mail lying on the end table by the couch. She inspected each envelope on the counter and the end table. Nothing. *I don't remember a letter from Kirkland & Williams.* A faint memory of two pieces of mail slipping into the crack between the countertop and the stove came to mind. *Oh, no. One of them must have been the letter.*

She hurried to the stove and studied it to see how to pull it out from between the cabinets. It took some work, but she wiggled the appliance out enough so she could see the two envelopes on the floor. The name *Kirkland & Williams* was printed across the top of one. Erin reached for the envelopes and pulled out the letter.

> Miss Douglas. My name is James Williams. I served as your father's attorney. In accordance with your father's wishes, I'm asking you to come for an appointment on August 7, your twenty-fifth birthday. We have a final matter to discuss regarding your father's will. I suggest you not mention this letter to anyone until we can talk. Please call my office for an appointment.

August seventh? My birthday. I'm not supposed to mention this to anyone. Weird.

Her father had been dead a year, and he was still demanding and controlling. She had a vague memory of meeting Mr. Williams, but his name had not registered when she first saw the letter. He was the lawyer who read her father's will to the family after the funeral.

Two weeks dragged by, and the only odd thing was that Ryan Jeffries had been missing from her life. Melissa occupied his time, and they were now an official couple, or, at least, they were the last time she checked Instagram.

Was Melissa the right girl for Ryan? Erin had a hard time imagining him walking the aisle.

A week in the Smoky Mountains had been a pleasant distraction. Gatlinburg was an incredible place, and she enjoyed hiking to Clingman's Dome and Laurel Falls.

Her favorite experience was riding a bike on the eleven-mile loop road through Cade's Cove. The wildflowers called to her, and she'd seen too many deer to count. Watching a mama bear and her cub frolicking had been the highlight. She could go to the cove every day and never tire of it, so returning home days before her birthday was more difficult than she'd anticipated.

Escaping from her mother on the morning of her birthday proved challenging. Her mother insisted on taking Erin to breakfast, and she also wanted to go shopping. Erin was supposed to be at the lawyer's office at 2:00 that afternoon, so shopping was out.

"I can't go shopping, Mom. I have…a…I'm going to see a friend in Decatur."

Her mother stared in disbelief, clearly shocked Erin had a friend.

Unconvinced, she asked, "Really?" Why shouldn't Francine Douglas be surprised? If Erin really had a friend other than Ryan, she would have been surprised, too.

Erin slipped her purse over her shoulder so she could make a quick exit. "Yes. It's someone I met a year or so ago. I appreciate the breakfast, Mom. I'll call you later."

Erin kissed her mom's forehead and hurried out of the restaurant. She had some time to kill before her appointment, so she drove toward Walmart. Her mother went to Walmart all the time, so she detoured to Dunkin' Donuts for coffee. She could camp out there for a while.

The law offices of Kirkland & Williams were on the northeast side of Atlanta, forty-five minutes away. Erin normally preferred to stay south of I-285 and avoid downtown Atlanta as much as possible. However, the unpredictable and often nightmarish traffic was light.

She arrived at the lawyer's office fifteen minutes early and found a parking spot near the front. The brick building loomed before her and morphed into the house of horrors she'd once seen in an old movie.

Erin closed her eyes and opened them again. The building looked like a modern place of business with an aged brick facade. Grabbing her phone, she scrolled through emails and chewed her nails. Her stomach twisted, and she thought she might throw up.

This lawyer thing was such a mystery to her. A year earlier, Mr. Williams read over the will with the family, and it was simple.

The shocker had been the size of the mutual fund her father left in her mother's name. It would provide her mom with about $50,000 a year. How did he have that kind of money?

Big Fred Douglas also had a two-million-dollar life insurance policy, and Mr. Williams had offered the name of a financial advisor who helped Erin's mom invest it wisely. Mr. Williams read the will, and her mother got everything. The whole stressful event only lasted about ten minutes.

Erin pulled the letter from her purse. She'd almost memorized the words. We have a final matter to discuss regarding your father's will.

Odd. What did they have to discuss? Did her mother have to return some of the money? Nothing made sense.

She should have called Ryan and asked for help, but the lawyer said not to tell anyone. Ryan could have explained the situation to her. Beads of sweat collected on her forehead, and she wanted to drive away.

Her eyes drifted to her watch again. Thirty seconds had ticked by since she'd last checked. Bad news or not, she had to face Mr. Williams.

With her purse slung over her shoulder, she got out of the car and dropped her keys. Her key fob broke and lay in five pieces near the front tire. Her eyes closed, Erin stood still a moment and inhaled deeply. Thankfully, she didn't need the key fob to lock her doors. Stupid fob didn't work right half the time.

A shiver ran down her spine as she looked at the foreboding building. The windows above the door glared at her like piercing eyes. Were they beckoning or warning her?

Only one way to find out.

She picked up her keys along with the pieces of the fob and headed toward the brick building.

Shocking News

Erin walked into the ritzy offices of Kirkland & Williams and decided business must be pouring in. Polished wood panels, shiny hardwood floors. Even the smell of the place suggested money. She gave the receptionist her name and sat on the luxurious leather couch that probably cost more than her car.

She'd barely gotten comfortable when Mr. Williams appeared. *At least he's smiling. Maybe the news isn't all bad.*

James Williams was a short, stout man who had more hair on his face than on the top of his head. Erin noticed the glare reflecting from the chandelier and stifled a giggle. His large smile made him look like someone's sweet uncle, and his firm handshake felt like something belonging to a commander or Fortune 500 CEO.

"Hello, Mrs. uh…what is your married name?" Mr. Williams asked.

Erin's eyes turned toward the floor. "I didn't get married, Mr. Williams. We broke off the engagement."

"That's unfortunate. I'm sorry. Well, welcome back, and happy birthday. It's hard to believe it's been over a year since your father's passing. I apologize for all the mystery. I wish I could have told you more in the letter, but my instructions were very specific."

How did he know it was my birthday?

The lawyer motioned with his hand and turned toward his personal office. Erin followed him into the spacious office and sat in one of the plush chairs.

The shiny hardwood floor in Mr. Williams' office was covered by a gorgeous Oriental rug that had to cost more than all the Goodwill furniture in her house. A diploma hung on the wall near a small figurine of a bulldog wearing a red jacket. *So, he attended the University of Georgia.*

"Uh, did you say you had instructions? From who?" *Or is it whom?*

Mr. Williams sat behind his massive oak desk, which made Erin feel extremely small and vulnerable. "Yes. You see, your father gave me detailed instructions about handling his will and estate and even included the exact verbiage he wanted to be included in the letter I sent you."

"You mean that letter was from my father?" Erin shivered at the thought.

"In a way, yes. We reviewed your father's will last year after his funeral, but per his instructions, a portion of the will was not read. He wanted me to wait and share it with you on your 25th birthday. There's more—a lot more."

A fly could have flown into Erin's open mouth, and she wouldn't have known. This information was the last thing she imagined the lawyer telling her. She knew her father worked hard, but he had never made much money. They'd always struggled to buy necessities and knew extravagance only as a word in the dictionary.

Erin had to clear her throat before speaking. "I…I don't…Why am I the only one here? Why now?"

"You are the only one here because his final wishes apply only to you. I don't think he wants your mother or anyone else to know about this condition of the will."

Erin sat frozen, staring in disbelief. It seemed odd that her father would keep a secret from her mother, but stranger things had happened.

She tried to picture her father sitting in this office talking to the lawyer about a secret so private he wouldn't share it with anyone, even his wife. It was hard to imagine.

When the will had been read a year earlier, Erin hadn't been bothered about the fact her father didn't leave her anything except a small fund to pay for her wedding. *A lot of good that's going to do.*

Mr. Williams picked up a piece of paper from his desk, which brought Erin back to the present. "Miss Douglas, your father had substantial financial holdings, and no one in your family knows about them."

My father was rich? No way. "Sorry, what?"

Williams chuckled. "Your father amassed a small fortune through investments, but his key source of financial gain came from a series of decisions he made through the years that led him to become the primary owner of a pharmaceutical company located in Asheville, North Carolina."

Erin found it difficult to breathe. Her small purse fell from her lap, and she made no move to pick it up. Dumbfounded, she eyed this man who had held her father's secret for what must have been a long time.

His arms crossed on the desk, the lawyer leaned forward. "Miss Douglas, first, your father admitted to not doing a good job telling you, but he loved you and your mother very much. The thing he hated most about dying was leaving you two behind. Of course, he thought you were getting married, so he didn't think you were completely alone. I assume your breakup happened after his passing?"

Erin's gaze returned to the floor. Did she have to tell this man everything? "Actually, no. I didn't tell him."

"Hmm. Your singleness will make this a little more…complicated. Well, Miss Douglas, your father devised an unusual final idea to help you and your mother cope with his passing. His," the lawyer paused and steepled his fingers, "I'll call it *interesting*. His interesting idea is detailed in this document. Sit back, and I'll read his final wishes to you."

* * * * * *

From his office window, James Williams watched Erin stumble across the parking lot toward her car. She stopped beside her vehicle and fell against the door. One hand went to her mouth, the other across her stomach.

I think she's going to be sick.

After a moment, Erin opened the driver's side door and slumped inside. She sat motionless, her head against the steering wheel.

James stroked his beard as he considered the situation. He picked up the receiver of his phone and dialed a number. Waiting for the call to connect, he continued watching Erin.

After five rings, someone picked up.

"Bob Morrow. This is James Williams."

"Well, well, well. If it isn't the fine, upstanding lawyer from Decatur. What's up?"

"I've got a proposition for you, Bob. Well, not a proposition. More of an opportunity. I'll need some help formulating things."

"I like opportunities," Bob admitted, "especially if it has a lot of zeros. How much?"

"You've always been greedy, Bob. If you forget we talked, and if we succeed in this small venture, your payout could be around a million dollars, minus any expenses you incur, of course. How does that sound?"

Morrow whistled through his teeth. "My lips are sealed. I'm ready."

"It will take us around a year to pull off, but I'm sure for a million you could be patient."

"Job would be envious of my patience, my friend."

Williams chuckled. "Since when did you start reading the Bible? Let's meet to talk tomorrow night at Fred's. I've been wanting steak for a while."

"I suppose I'm free as long as you're paying."

* * * * *

Two hours later, tears streaming down her face, Erin pulled into a parking place at Stone Mountain Park. She had run over two orange caution cones while trying to maneuver past a string of parked cars. The little Toyota jerked to a stop, and she laid her head on the steering wheel. A sob rose from deep within her soul.

After a while, Erin looked up to see the familiar shaded area in the park. She didn't remember deciding to head west on Highway 78, but now, she stared at the spot where her family had shared a picnic on her sixth birthday.

Mr. Williams said Daddy loved me so much. Why didn't he ever tell me?

Tears flowed again.

Erin rummaged for a tissue, found a napkin, and blew her nose. Her movements seemed mechanical as she got out and walked slowly toward the huge rock where her father had hugged her so long ago. Had he hugged her other times? She couldn't remember.

What happened in my father's life to make him such a cold man?

A little girl ran past her, and Erin noticed a family had a picnic blanket spread out about twenty feet from where she stood. A woman sat on the blanket and sneaked glances at Erin.

After a moment, the woman stood and cautiously approached her. "Are you okay?"

Erin nodded. "Well, no, not really. I'm sorry. I didn't realize you were here."

Erin turned her head and saw a little girl running after the Frisbee her father had thrown toward the edge of the picnic area. Tears flowed down her cheeks again. How did she have any tears left?

"I'm sorry," Erin stammered. "My father brought me here as a little girl, and he died recently, and…"

The woman wrapped her arms around Erin's shaking shoulders. "I'm so sorry."

Erin waited for some empty comment, but the woman only hugged her tighter. The lady sniffed. *Is she crying too?* The little girl dropped the Frisbee and walked back toward the blanket.

"I'll be all right," Erin insisted as she pulled away from the kind woman. The lady's cheeks were wet.

"I'm Susan," the woman offered. "What's your name?"

"I'm Erin. I shouldn't be such a crybaby. My father died a year ago. I had to talk with his lawyer today about…something." Erin studied her feet. "It's been a hard day."

"I understand, Erin. Well, I don't understand because I still have my father. God understands, though. Do you believe God understands?"

"Do I? Well, I do. I've not thought as much about Him lately as I should have. I mean, I go to church on most Sundays, but...I don't know what I'm trying to say."

Susan reached out and rubbed Erin's arm. "It's okay. I think I can relate. I had an experience a few years ago that changed how I view religion. I don't see it as a religion anymore but a relationship."

Erin sniffed and wiped her nose. Susan picked up a napkin from the blanket and handed it to her.

"Thanks." Erin blew her nose. "Sorry. Gross, I know."

"No problem."

Erin folded the napkin and stuffed it into her pocket. "I've heard Pastor Brant talk about a relationship. I don't understand that concept very well."

Erin saw the man who had thrown the Frisbee slip in behind Susan and place his hands on her shoulders.

"This is my husband, Tom. God brought him into my life during my senior year of college. We got married after graduation, and three years later, we had this little bundle of joy. This is Amber."

"Hi." Amber giggled before pulling a strand of hair out of her mouth.

"Tom," Susan continued. "This is Erin. She was sharing about her father who passed away last year."

"I'm so sorry," Tom said with such sincerity Erin believed him. "My father died when I was young. I won't say I understand what you're going through, but I had a hard time as a kid."

Susan reached out to take Erin's hand. "You know something interesting? I read a devotional about divine appointments this morning. Meeting you here today could be a divine appointment."

"Divine appointment?"

Susan smiled and squeezed Erin's hand. "An appointment with you but made by God. It's possible He knew you'd need a hug or encouragement, so He sent us here to meet you."

Erin glanced at the carving on the side of Stone Mountain and then back at Susan. She'd never considered God caring about anything she might be going through. She knew He cared, but would He send a family to Stone Mountain Park for her?

"Thank you, Susan. I should be going. I've interrupted your picnic long enough."

"You're not interrupting us at all. You're welcome to join us if you'd like."

"Oh, no. I can't do that. I need to go home."

Tom stepped forward beside his wife. "Can we pray for you before you go?"

"Uh…sure." Erin smiled. "Prayer would be good."

They joined hands. Even Amber's miniature hand squeezed Erin's right pinky. Tom began to pray the sweetest and most thoughtful prayer. After he said amen, Susan wrote her phone number on a napkin and insisted Erin call her any time.

Stunned by the whole experience, Erin walked toward her car. Had God arranged a divine appointment for her? She'd never heard of a divine appointment, but she liked the idea. Maybe God did care about her.

What should she do now? This burden was too heavy to carry alone. Should she call Ryan? He always listened to her talk about her messed up life.

CHAPTER EIGHT

A Friend in Need

The strong smell of Chick-fil-A coffee wafted from the Styrofoam cup Erin held with both hands. Trying to decide what to do, she examined the concoction in the cup, more cream than coffee.

The empty food court should have been teeming with hungry shoppers. How did malls stay open without customers? A couple eating Chinese food at a nearby table were the only diners in sight. They talked in hushed tones, so Erin couldn't hear a word.

Steam rose from her coffee as Erin took a tiny sip. Not sweet enough. The couple seemed engrossed in conversation, and then the woman lifted a tiny baby from a stroller. The child couldn't have been more than a month old. Transfixed by the scene, Erin gawked at the young family. They looked like such a perfect little family. What would their story be in five or ten years? Would they live together happily ever after?

Erin took a sip of her coffee and pondered her current dilemma.

I've got to talk to someone about the will, and I don't have many options. There's no way I'm calling Mom. I just met Susan. I've got to call Ryan.

Reaching for her phone, Erin tried to imagine how she would convey the final message of her father's will. Within moments, she heard the unmistakable sound of a ringing phone coming through the earpiece of her iPhone.

"Well, hello, Buttercup!" Ryan oozed on the other end of the line. "I've missed you. What's going on?"

"Hey, Ryan. I've been busy. I figured you'd be out with Melissa and wouldn't answer your phone."

"Well, we're taking a breather for a week or so. You know how it is."

No, I don't know how it is. Greg and I took a breather for a lifetime.

Erin pulled the coffee cup to her lips and sipped the brew. "Well, are you busy?"

"Of course, I am. You remember what Thoreau said?"

"No, I don't remember what Thoreau said, but I would bet a thousand dollars you're about to tell me."

"Oh. Well, I won't tell you, so you owe me a thousand dollars."

"Funny. What did Thoreau say? I'm dying to know."

"'Success usually comes to those who are too busy to be looking for it.' You haven't heard that quote before?"

"Can't say I have. If you're too busy, we can talk some other time."

"Erin. Erin! Since when have I been too busy to talk to you?"

How about every day for the last two weeks? "I'm at Southlake Mall drinking coffee, so I don't want to talk too loudly." The cavernous room felt more like an echo chamber than a food court, but she may as well have been the only person on the planet. She could scream, and no one would notice.

"I'm heading to check on a rental that's not far from Southlake. If you don't mind waiting, I'll be over shortly. You can have all the time you need."

Looking like a rich real estate investor, Ryan strolled up with an iPad under his arm and two fresh cups of coffee twenty minutes later. He had investment properties, but she had no idea how many or where they were located. Well, she now knew one was close to the mall.

"Oh, Ryan. I didn't see you come in."

"I went straight for the coffee."

The smell of fresh coffee greeted her as he set a cup on the table.

"I hope it's okay," Ryan said. "I told them to make it three-fourths cream with enough sugar to make your teeth fall out."

Erin grinned. "Sounds about right."

Ryan sipped his coffee. Black and thick. "Okay, Buttercup. What's up?"

"What if I came up with some horrendous name and started calling you that all the time?"

Ryan raised an eyebrow. "Like what?"

"Maybe something like Spanky or Stinky Pete?"

"Oh, those are creative, Erin. Imagine what you could come up with if you really tried."

Erin wanted to slap the smug smirk off his face. "You make me so mad, Ryan."

"I read in a book today that no one can make you mad. You choose to be mad."

Erin flung her hands out as she started a rebuttal but knocked over her cup instead. She shrieked as coffee ran toward Ryan's iPad, but he rescued it in time. A small stack of napkins lay on the table, and she reached for one and started mopping up the flow.

"Calm down, Erin. I'm sorry. I won't call you Buttercup anymore."

Flustered, Erin plopped back down in her seat.

"I'll buy you another coffee, and we'll start over." Ryan seemed contrite. "We'll pretend like I'm walking up for the first time."

Before Erin could object, Ryan headed toward the counter. She didn't want another cup of coffee. The two cups she'd already had were more than enough, and she needed the restroom. She called out to Ryan and pointed toward the side hallway. When his eyebrow raised, she mouthed, "I'll be right back."

Ryan wore a silly smile when she returned to the table.

"Erin, glad you could join me. So, how ya been?"

She rolled her eyes and shook her head. *So much for genuine.* "You are really something, Ryan Jeffries, but I appreciate you coming over. I have a dilemma."

"Well, you came to the right place. I happen to be a professional dilemma solver. I do it all day at Gatner Enterprises."

"Okay, Dr. Dilemma Solver. This one's a doozy." Erin looked around and noticed the young couple had left with their baby. No one was anywhere close, but she leaned forward anyway. "I got a weird letter a few weeks ago from Kirkland & Williams."

"Kirkland & Williams?"

"Yes. Lawyers. They helped my father with his will." Ryan nodded, and Erin continued. "The letter told me to come to the office to see Mr. Williams on my birthday."

"On your birthday? Kind of strange, isn't—" Ryan's eyes opened wide. "Oh no! I missed your birthday."

Erin waved her hand. "Don't worry about it. I decided not to have one this year."

Ryan picked up his cup as a grin spread across his face. "Did he have a cake for you?"

"Cute. No, but he had some interesting information for me. The reading of my father's will was not complete. My dad had asked him to finalize the will with me alone on my 25th birthday."

The memory of what happened in the lawyer's office had unsettled her. She'd never felt faint like that before, but then again, she'd never heard anything like what the lawyer had read to her.

"The suspense is killing me, Erin. What did he say?"

Erin's mind snapped back to the present. "It's the craziest thing. For starters, my father didn't know Greg broke up with me. Dad died thinking I was going to marry a month later."

"So, why didn't you tell him?"

Erin swished the stirring stick around the inside of her cup. "You know how he was. I didn't want to hear him point out the obvious to me."

"The obvious?"

Erin's eyes filled with unshed tears. "That I'm a failure."

Ryan's face creased with…what? Sympathy? Anger?

A deep sigh slipped out of him. "Erin, you're not a failure."

"I didn't mean for this to be a 'Make Erin Feel Better About Herself' session. Let me tell you the rest of what Mr. Williams said." She reached for a napkin and blew her nose. "Sorry. Nothing worse than hearing a despicable girl on a crying jag."

"If you keep talking like that, I'm calling my therapist."

"You have a therapist?"

Ryan smiled as he reached for his cup. "No, but I'll find one."

Erin closed her eyes and took a deep breath. "He told me my father's will hadn't been completely read."

"Why didn't he read all of it after the funeral?"

"Looking back, I remember he and my mom talking about needing time to have everything finalized with the estate, and now I suppose I understand why. It's all final now, at least, there's nothing left to read."

"It's strange you were alone."

"I thought the same thing, but he told me my father requested I come alone. The information he was going to share was unique to me." Erin stared across the table. "Ryan, my father was rich, and no one knew it."

"Rich?"

"Yeah. He bought part ownership in a pharmaceutical company many years ago. When his partners thought the company would fold, they wanted out. He signed an agreement to pay them a small amount of money over ten years if he could become the sole owner of the company. Would you believe the company became profitable? Quite profitable."

"How much does profitable mean?"

Erin hesitated before responding. "I'm not sure the exact amount, but Mr. Williams said the company is worth millions of dollars. Like fifty-something million."

Ryan let out a quiet whistle and rubbed a hand through his hair. "So, why did your dad not tell anyone, and why didn't he want this shared with the whole family?"

Erin swallowed and dropped her head into her hands before peeking up at her silent friend. "My father said he would leave the company to me if..."

Erin deliberated before finishing. As if it would fortify her, she took a sip of the tepid coffee. *Beyond awful.* She swung her gaze back toward Ryan.

"He'd leave it to me if I would give my mother a grandchild by my twenty-sixth birthday."

Their eyes met for several seconds before Ryan started laughing. "That's the craziest thing I've ever heard."

Erin failed to see anything funny about her situation. "My dad thought if my mom had a grandchild, she would cope better with losing her husband."

"You are serious. I guess it makes sense, in a Fred Douglas kind of way."

"I don't have any siblings, so I'm the only one who can give her a grandchild. Also, he thought I was about to get married, so why not give me the challenge of producing a baby. One more thing I could fail."

"Unbelievable. Erin, I want you to quit being so down on yourself."

"I'm just speaking truth."

Ryan shook his head. "Where's this company? What's the name of it?"

"I think he said it was called *Envision* and located in Asheville, North Carolina."

Ryan pulled out his smartphone and typed some letters into the Safari search bar. Within minutes, he whistled again. "It's the real deal. I'll have to research it, but it looks like they've been profitable for years."

"That's what Mr. Williams said. He said my father left me an account of money to help me get established as the owner of the company—if I become the owner. Of course, I'm sure he expected Greg to run things because I can't even run water without screwing up."

"Erin!"

Erin looked down and considered taking another sip of coffee before deciding against it. "I wondered how he had the money to take care of my mom's needs."

Ryan's face suddenly turned devious. "So, who do you want to be the father? All you've got to do is pick someone handsome and smart. Offer him a little money, assuming it's the best time...you know, the best time of the month, and you become an instant millionaire. I'll help you start researching these guys. We could create an application that requires DNA testing, GPA, and open college records. I'll have to give it some thought."

Was he serious? Erin wanted to punch him for suggesting such a thing and would have but for the spilled coffee episode. God intended sex for married people, even though everyone she knew had different opinions. Mr. Williams also made it clear that her father included a clause in the will stating she and her husband had to be the parents.

"Ryan, sex before marriage isn't right. I won't do it. I've never had sex, and I don't intend to until I get married. I made a commitment years ago..."

"So, you and Greg didn't..."

"I keep my commitments. Obviously, he doesn't."

Ryan dropped his head and crossed his arms. "I respect your position."

"Besides, my dad included a list of stipulations at the bottom of his will. The father must be my husband."

"Interesting."

Erin huffed an exasperated breath, which made her bangs rise from her forehead. "There's no telling what my father was thinking. He had weird opinions about adoption, so who knows? I should have told him Greg left me, and none of this would be happening. Now, we'll lose the company."

Ryan cracked his knuckles and interlocked his hands behind his head. "Maybe not. We have options."

CHAPTER NINE

A Friend Indeed

Options? Erin skewered Ryan with a look that would melt an iceberg. Was he being sarcastic, dense, or, heaven forbid, sincere? *Options?* She opened her mouth to dispute this ridiculous assertion, but Ryan continued.

"Come on, Erin. Think about it. All you have to do is go to the Justice of the Peace and then get pregnant. It'll be a breeze."

"Are you out of your mind, Ryan? I'm not even dating because no one wants to go out with Erin Douglas."

"Talking about yourself in the third person won't—"

"So, what am I supposed to do? Go up to some random guy in the mall, ask for a date, and propose over ice cream? They could play the bridal march over the mall's speaker system, and we could say our vows in front of the fountain."

Ryan leaned forward on his elbows. "I'm trying to help. Getting married and having a baby in twelve months is possible. It's been done. My parents dated only a month before getting hitched."

"Aren't your parents divorced?"

"Semantics."

"It's not semantics—"

"Erin, all I'm saying is we have to find you a husband by the first of November and hope you get pregnant immediately. If we have you walking the aisle by the first of October, even better."

"Ryan, this is not some reality TV show. I can't meet some guy and marry him right away. For starters, he'll have to want to marry me. Doubtful. Also, when I say wedding vows to someone, my commitment is for life. I can't marry someone just to have a child. Even if our society is defined by throw-away marriages, mine will be permanent!"

Ryan crossed his arms again. His eyes roamed up and down for a moment, which made Erin feel uncomfortable and exposed. Trying to hide behind the table, she slid her chair forward. *What's he doing?*

"We're going to have to do some preliminary work," Ryan acknowledged as he eyed his watch.

Before she realized it, Ryan had his phone pressed against his ear. "Jenny! How in the world are you? It's been a while."

Erin eyed Ryan. *Who is Jenny, and what does she have to do with my situation?*

"Listen, Jen. I have a little favor to ask. Do you mind if I bring a friend by for you to do your magic?" Ryan paused while listening. "Sure. We'll be over in twenty." Ryan pocketed his phone and took Erin's hand. "Come on. I want you to meet a friend."

Erin pulled her hand from Ryan's. "Magic? No magic in the world could help, and I refuse to go with you anywhere until you tell me what we're doing!"

"Oh, Buttercup. Don't you trust me?"

"No! No, I don't trust you, Ryan Jeffries. You've got something up your sleeve, and I'm the one who will end up paying for it."

"This won't cost you a penny."

"I don't mean—"

"Listen, Erin. I have a friend who can help us. She has real insight, not to mention a few other fine attributes."

"Let me guess. You used to date her."

"Very perceptive."

"You've dated every female in the county between the ages of twenty and thirty."

Ryan's smile faded as Erin pulled her purse from the back of the chair and shouldered it.

"Not cool, Erin. I'll pretend you didn't say that. You're usually such a nice person."

Ryan took Erin's hand again and pulled her toward the exit.

An hour and a half later, Erin gazed slack-jawed into the small, handheld mirror. The bright blue eyes staring back at her were familiar, but nothing else about the reflection resembled the old Erin. Jenny stood behind her with a Texas-sized grin covering her face.

"So, what do you think?" Jenny cooed. "I didn't take off too much, did I?"

Erin couldn't speak. After arriving at Jenny's salon earlier, she first argued with Ryan and Jenny about having her hair cut at all. Ultimately, she told Jenny to do whatever was necessary. It couldn't hurt. After cutting her hair, Jenny insisted on applying some makeup, which Erin had never seen the point in wearing.

Not moving her eyes from the mirror, Erin heard Ryan walk into the room. When he spoke, Ryan's words came out in a reverential whisper. "Oh, Erin…you're…Jenny, take off her glasses."

Jenny nodded and removed the black plastic frames.

"Erin," Ryan continued. "You're beautiful. Why have you been hiding under all that hair for so long?"

"You have beautiful hair," Jenny interrupted, "you just needed to do a little something with it. Most women would give a year's salary to have the body and curl of your hair. I thinned it out a bit, cut some off the length, and worked with the texture. Your face is too beautiful to hide. I thought it best to let it frame your face."

"I..I, wow, uh, well," Erin stammered. "It doesn't look like me."

"It is you, Sweetheart," Jenny insisted, "and you're beautiful."

"You sure are," Ryan said under his breath.

Erin pulled the mirror back up and took in her reflection. "I don't wear makeup. I'm not sure how to…to do it."

"It's not so hard," Jenny insisted. "You're not wearing much makeup now. It's a matter of knowing how to apply it. I'll walk you through it."

After Jenny gave Erin some pointers, Erin picked up the small mirror again and backed up to a full-length mirror on the wall. Jenny had cut several inches off the back, but her hair still tapered down below her shoulders, like something out of a magazine.

"I'm afraid I'll have to come over every morning so you can make it look like this," Erin said.

Jenny smiled. "It's not hard. I used a curling iron and a brush, but your hair has a lot of natural curl. With a little practice, you'll be able to do it."

By the time Ryan and Erin pulled out of Jenny's driveway, it was 9:00. Erin's stomach growled as he turned right onto I-75.

"I can take a hint," Ryan said. "I'll stop at Zaxby's. They stay open 'til ten. I'm starving, too."

"Thanks. I mean, thanks for stopping, but also thanks for taking me to Jenny's. Not many people would have done this for me. Actually, no one but you."

"I'm your friend. We're going to create a new you. I want you to go by Walmart tomorrow for an eye exam."

"An eye exam?"

"Yeah. You need contacts. You need to show off those eyes."

"Contacts? I can't wear contacts. What's wrong with glasses?"

"Nothing's wrong with glasses, but something's wrong with *your* glasses. Why can't you wear contacts? Millions of people wear them. I suggest you buy a new pair of glasses as well as contacts. They have people, experts at putting the perfect pair of glasses with your face size and shape. Trust them and pick the frame they recommend. You'll find wearing contacts throughout the day will be a huge relief. Wouldn't you love to stop pushing your glasses back up your nose?"

"It's not so bad, but it's kind of hard to think about anything right now. If I don't eat, I'll start gnawing on the seatbelt."

Two hours later, Erin dragged into her house and frowned at Daphne as the cat rubbed against Erin's right leg. "I'm sorry I was gone so long, Sweetie." Dropping her purse onto the kitchen table, she retrieved the box of cat food from the cabinet and poured a generous portion into the bowl. "That will hold you for now."

She pulled open her top dresser drawer, selected a large T-shirt, and stumbled toward the bathroom. Erin pulled the shirt over her new hairdo and stood in front of the mirror for two full minutes before poking her cheek. Not a dream.

Girls at school had suggested she get her hair cut numerous times, but Erin had never agreed to do it. Although her hair had changed from red to auburn, it had always been a mop that fell nearly to her waist. Not anymore.

Ryan said I was beautiful. I'm not beautiful, but...well, this is an improvement.

Turning back toward the bedroom, she saw her phone lying on her dresser. The thought of reconstructing what she saw in the mirror was a bit overwhelming. *I'll take a pic and use it tomorrow to put myself back together.*

Erin didn't like selfies, but she grabbed her phone and headed back to the bathroom. Feeling like a total goofball, she smiled in the mirror, held her phone out beside her, and took the picture.

Now, to clean up that face and get to bed.

Though she turned off her light and lay in bed, turning off her brain was another matter. Thoughts of the day raced through her mind.

"I can't get married. That's the dumbest thing I've ever heard," she whispered.

Daphne leaped onto the bed and curled up beside Erin, who absentmindedly stroked her cat's clean, black fur. "Can you imagine me with a husband, Daffy girl? Insane, right? Could I find someone in the next two months who would love me and marry me? Can I have a baby by this time next year?"

The cat stared at her.

"Right. Insane."

The whole charade was beyond belief. Why had her father done this? She imagined her father coming up with this cockeyed scheme and realized it seemed perfectly normal to him. He figured she would have been married a year by the time she got the news, and getting pregnant was normal for a twenty-five-year-old woman in her second year of marriage. Twenty-five-year-old women got pregnant all the time. The problem was she didn't have a husband and had no nuptial prospects.

As she plopped her head back onto her pillow, Daphne shifted to her normal spot on the pillow beside her. "You know, Daff, if I go through with this crazy shenanigan, you'll have to find a different place to sleep. I don't think my new husband will agree to let you sleep on his pillow."

New husband? I'm losing it.

The last thing Erin heard was the soft purring coming from beside her as she tried to wrap her mind around going to bed every night with a man instead of her cat. *Ridiculous.*

CHAPTER TEN

A New Me

E rin pushed her bike inside the shed and rushed into the house to get ready for work. She rode an extra two miles without realizing the time. Hopefully, traffic wouldn't be too bad.

As the hot water rolled down her back, she couldn't quit thinking about Ryan's scheme. The idea was insane, and she'd bet money she'd be single this time next year. Still, the thought intrigued her. *What would it hurt?*

After struggling to recapture the same hair she'd seen in the mirror the night before, Erin joined the thousands of crazy people driving north on I-75 toward Atlanta. Her commute was nothing like what most of these morning zombies would be facing, but she still hated spending thirty to forty-five minutes every morning driving to Barnes & Noble. At least, she loved her job once she walked into the store.

Her schedule would change when the fall semester got underway. Though her schedule would be a bit chaotic, she looked forward to returning to school.

Her phone vibrated on the passenger seat, and when traffic stopped for the thousandth time, Erin squinted at the screen. She didn't have to read it to know it was from Ryan. Her mom didn't text, and the fact she had no other real friends in her life meant her phone remained quiet most of the time.

Her new friend, Susan, came to mind. At least she had one friend other than Ryan.

I need to remember to call her. Should I tell her what's going on? Nope. One meeting at Stone Mountain Park didn't qualify as a close friendship.

The text was indeed from Ryan. "Call when you can."

After pulling into a parking place and turning off her car, Erin picked up her phone and told it to call Ryan.

"What's up, Gorgeous."

Erin grinned before remembering she was talking to Ryan. Names meant nothing to him. "What happened to Buttercup?"

"Oh, well, Buttercup ceased to exist after one certain haircut."

"Wow. If I'd known it was that easy, I would have gotten a haircut a long time ago."

"You going to Walmart today for an eye exam?"

"Ryan, I'm just getting to work. I haven't even figured out what I'm doing yet."

"What do you mean you haven't figured out what you're doing? If it's a money issue, I'll pay for it."

"No, it's not money."

"Erin, you would have refused the haircut if you had the chance to think about it, but aren't you glad you let Jenny do her magic?"

"Well, yeah, I guess so."

"You guess so? Did you happen to notice your mirror last night when you got home? The gorgeous young woman looking back? You're a knockout."

He's kidding, isn't he? "Don't get carried away, Ryan. Knockout is a bit of an exaggeration." Erin relented. "I'll call Walmart. I have to work 'til 4:00, so I'll see if they have room for me this evening, but it seems like a longshot."

"Okay. I'm holding you to it. Let me know when you're going, and I'll meet you there."

"I can handle it, Ryan. I'm a big girl. Gotta go."

At 6:00, Erin walked into Walmart and sat down in the optical waiting area. She'd been surprised they could see her so soon.

The doctor was kind and patient with her attempt to decide which optical correction provided her the best vision. Once he determined a proper prescription, he sent her to an assistant to try on a pair of sample contact lenses.

"Hello, Erin. My name is Amanda. Have you worn contacts before?"

"Hi. Uh, no. I'm not sure I can handle putting something in my eye."

"It's not as bad as you may think."

"I guess I'm willing to try."

Amanda moved toward a table along the wall. "I've been wearing them for ten years. I've thought about having corrective surgery, but for now, I'm sticking with contacts. You'll get used to it. First, you'll need to watch a video about inserting your contacts, and then you need to wash your hands." She pulled a chair out from the table.

After watching the video and cleaning her hands at the sink, Erin was as ready as she'd ever be. At first, she struggled with trying to convince her eyelid to stay open while she inserted the lens.

The contact latched onto Erin's eye. Dabbing the tears spilling out of her eyes, she turned to gaze at the room around her in perfect focus. Unbelievable. She absentmindedly reached toward her face to adjust her glasses but then remembered.

"What do you think?" Amanda asked.

"I don't know," Erin said. "It's not as bad as I imagined."

"Well, those are a trial pair. I'm putting a couple of weeks of samples in this bag. Why don't you wear them a few days and call us once you decide if they'll work for you?" Amanda paused to review Erin's file. "I see you also want to be fitted for glasses. If you'll step back to the waiting area, Gina will be happy to help you. Matching faces with the perfect frame is her specialty."

Erin thanked Amanda before heading back toward the waiting area. The detail of the carpet caught her attention, and everything around her came into perfect focus. How was it possible to have little round pieces of plastic in her eyes and not even feel it?

Ryan smiled at her from one of the blue, vinyl chairs. He was becoming as annoying as a pebble in her shoe. Why couldn't he mind his own business?

Erin crossed her arms. "What are you doing here?"

"You didn't think I'd want to miss out on all the fun, did you? So, what do you think of contact lenses?"

"Not sure. I just tried them on for the first time. I'm not sure I can do this, Ryan. I shouldn't even be here. Nor should you."

"Yes, you need to be here, and yes, you can do this. As for me, I wanted to see how it was going. Can't I be a friend?"

A cute blonde wearing a light blue smock walked to the waiting area. "Are you Erin? I'm Gina." Once Erin nodded, Gina invited her over to a small desk where a colorful note-book lay open to a page describing frames for women with oval faces. Erin noticed Gina give Ryan the once over. Ryan also noticed and smiled at her.

Erin studied the notebook describing face types as Ryan took one of the two chairs. "I suppose I must have an oval face. I never thought about it."

"Yes, definitely oval," Gina confirmed. "Now, this suggests either square, rectangular, or round frames as being the best option. Your face shape is fine with most any frame as long as the frame isn't oversized."

Ryan grinned and elbowed Erin. "How about that? According to the experts, you've got a perfect face."

"Let's find a pair that matches your hair color," Gina continued with a little smile spreading across her face. "Your eyes are so beautiful, and they'll pop with a warm undertone like beige or brown. A light black would be okay, too, but I suggest sticking with brown."

Erin made her final decision on a frame and paid the bill. When she and Ryan passed through the exit doors of Walmart, she almost stepped in front of a passing car. Ryan jerked her arm just in time.

"Appears you do need glasses," Ryan said with a chuckle.

Erin grimaced. "Wow. Thanks. Of course, I need glasses. I've worn them all my life. This whole contact thing has me a little flustered."

"Why are you flustered? You're going to be fine."

Erin turned to look at Ryan and then let her eyes drift back down to the sidewalk. "It's...well, it's all happening too fast, Ryan. I'm not sure I can handle all this...change."

Ryan pulled Erin's chin up until their eyes met. "Yes, you can handle this, Erin Douglas. You're beautiful and fun. We're going to find you the perfect husband."

Erin rolled her eyes. "Ryan, for starters, I'm not beautiful, and there's nothing fun about me. I like to read books. I don't think guys will be standing in line to join me as I read through *Jane Eyre* or *Little Women*."

Ryan took Erin's hands. "Erin, behind those beautiful blue eyes is an exciting woman waiting to be discovered."

Erin snorted and then chided herself for sounding like a toad. If she were waiting to be discovered, it would be a long wait.

"Look," Ryan assured her. "Give me a chance. I'll show you there's more to Erin Douglas than you realize. You've got new contacts, and in a few days, you'll have an awesome new pair of glasses. Your hair is gorgeous. Underneath those floppy clothes is an amazing body."

Erin's face turned scarlet. "Ryan! I can't believe you said that. Since when have you been looking at my body?"

Ryan grinned. "I'm just saying."

"If some man wants me only for my body, I'm not interested."

"Calm down, Buttercup."

"So now, I'm Buttercup again. I suppose I'm relieved."

"You have many fine qualities, Erin. We'll work on some of the other issues."

Erin's head went down, and she noticed a penny on the sidewalk. "Like what?"

"Like looking at the ground constantly and slumping your shoulders." Ryan bumped her right shoulder. "Hold your shoulders back, Erin. Look at people in the face."

Now, he was starting to sound like her father. She looked toward her car and back to the ground. How long would she have to listen to his lecture? Ryan's hand tugged on her chin again and pulled her face up.

"Erin, I don't intend to sound like some mean guy talking bad about your posture and whatnot. I want to help. Will you let me help?"

Erin stood quietly and looked up at her friend. What if she didn't want help? She'd managed to take care of herself for twenty-five years. Who cared about getting married?

"I've got an idea," Ryan said as he rubbed his hands together. "Let's take a self-defense class together. You need a little confidence, and I saw an ad yesterday about the confidence you can gain by learning how to defend yourself. It can't hurt. Will you at least do that?"

Erin crossed her arms and noticed an ant running across the top of her right shoe. How would taking self-defense help her? She'd make a fool of herself in front of everyone.

"I'm about as clumsy as a rag doll. I can't learn how to do all that karate stuff. Why do I need to learn how to defend myself? A guy takes one look at me, and he'll hurt himself trying to escape."

Ryan stared at her and nodded. "You proved my point. You might enjoy it. Come on. It'll be a blast. I noticed a sign advertising self-defense and karate at a gym not far from where you live. Can I check into it for us?"

Erin sighed. *Uh, absolutely not. No way!* "I suppose checking won't hurt, Ryan, but I'm not saying I'll do it."

"Great. I'll check it out and let you know."

"Sure. Now, I've really got to go. Daphne's been in the house all day, and she needs to be fed."

"Okay. I'll call you tomorrow. Thanks for being such a good sport. Do you mind if I take your picture?"

"Why?"

"Because...well, because you're my friend," Ryan said as he pulled out his phone.

"No. You don't need my picture."

"Come on, Erin. We need to commemorate this moment."

Erin stared at him before finally closing her eyes. "Why are you such a pain? And why do we want to commemorate this moment?"

"Please?"

Erin huffed. "Okay. Fine."

He put his arm around her and snapped a selfie. "Perfect."

"Let me see it."

Ryan turned toward his car. "It's perfect. Goodnight, Erin."

She stared at him as he crossed the parking lot before turning and hurrying toward her car. *What's he doing?*

CHAPTER ELEVEN

A Workable Plan

J ames Williams filed some papers and wiped the dust off the desk corner. A heavy sigh escaped from his lips as he heard his assistant bid Mrs. Harrington goodbye. That lawsuit had better be finalized soon or he was going to lose his mind. Mrs. Harrington was insufferable.

He buzzed his assistant. "Angie, was Mrs. Harrington my last appointment?"

"Yes, Mr. Williams. You're done until 8:00 in the morning."

"Thank you. It's almost 5:00, so why don't you head home? I'll lock up."

"Thanks, Mr. Williams. See you tomorrow."

James reached into the top right desk drawer for Fred Douglas' file and reread it for the fourth time that day. *Ol' Fred and his millions.* The stipulations at the bottom were a bit troubling. *Husband and baby by this time next year...got to be by her husband.*

Williams eyed the file.

Married and pregnant.

The collapse of his marriage came to mind, and he crumpled the paper in his hand. Realizing he was destroying his only copy of the will, he began smoothing it. His eyes darted toward the open door of the copy room. Maybe he should make an extra copy. The original was tucked away in the larger file storage room, so he could get to it, but he'd rather not have to sign for Fred Douglas' file without cause.

If he hadn't decided to go into business with Phillip Kirkland, "Mr. Integrity," he wouldn't have to worry about signing for files. Of course, when Phillip had insisted on the practice, James hadn't thought anything about it. The rule hadn't mattered until two years ago when the need for creative alterations to a file came up in the McLoughlin case. A smile crossed his face with the thought of his home in the Dominican Republic. The McLoughlin deal had turned out to be quite lucrative.

James' soon-to-be ex-wife was another story. The island home was a secret, but she was still trying to take him to the cleaners. James thought about offering her the house at the Country Club. Any future assets could be excluded. If he could work out a deal with the Douglas girl, he'd be set for life, so losing his house wouldn't matter.

The leather chair squeaked when he put his feet on the desk and contemplated the three critical issues. Erin Douglas had to get married, get pregnant, and have a baby. Having a baby in time would be the most difficult challenge.

How could he find someone to marry the girl and then dump her? This new husband would also have to be willing to sign over everything. What were the odds someone would hand over a lucrative company and a pile of cash? Blackmail or other significant threats could be persuasive.

One more challenge would have to be worked out. The husband would need to inherit Erin's company, which means...

He'd done it before, but he'd let Bob deal with it this time. No need to get his hands dirty.

Erin Douglas would need a will, and her new husband must become the beneficiary. James could persuade her, but if not, he could easily swap some paperwork without her knowing. Wouldn't be the first time.

Williams glanced at the clock, put everything away, and packed his briefcase. The ride to Bernie's Steakhouse would take about twenty minutes, assuming traffic wasn't bad. The front cover of a magazine on his desk caught his eye. What an exquisite yacht. A smile spread across his face as he pictured himself behind the steering wheel.

After battling rush-hour traffic, Williams hurried into the restaurant and saw Bob sitting in the back booth. The smell of grilled meat reminded him he'd not eaten all day. Country music blared through the speakers spread around the restaurant, and customers laughed loudly. *Perfect.* No one would be able to overhear their conversation.

He moved toward the large man, and Bob nodded as Williams sat across from him. "Sorry I'm late, Bob. Traffic was crazy."

"No problem. Since you're paying, I came early for a drink."

James noticed a couple of empty glasses on the table. A waitress came by, and he ordered a drink and a fried onion petal appetizer. His doctor would give him grief about fried food, but he was celebrating. He could be healthy later.

"So, what's your proposition?" Bob asked.

"Remember what I said on the phone yesterday? I've resolved the payout, but you've got to help me figure out some details. I'm bringing a sweet opportunity to the table." James leaned closer to ensure the man could hear him over the music. "Your cut is a million. If you're not okay with that amount, I'll walk away and pretend we never talked."

"I assume your cut is a lot more, but yeah, no problem as long as you're paying expenses."

"We'll split the expenses."

Morrow shook his head. "I have no idea what expenses you're talking about, James. You pay, or I don't play."

The magazine cover with the yacht flashed through James's mind. Bob Morrow had always been a pain to deal with, which made James wonder if he should have called someone else. Bob was the only person he could trust to keep his mouth shut, however, and the only person who wouldn't flinch at finishing the project.

Williams fumed as the waitress returned with a drink. He watched her walk away and then lowered his voice. "I'll pay as long as you're willing to take care of the project's final phase without including me."

"So, the final phase means snuffing someone out?"

"Bob, Bob, Bob. I don't even want to talk about how you'll handle it. Is that clear? I'll only pay as long as you take care of the problem. Deal?"

"For a million?"

"For a million, paid when the whole project is complete."

Bob pretended to consider it, then agreed. "Deal. Now, what's the project?"

Williams smiled and took a sip of his drink. "For starters, we need a young man willing to play along. No need to clue him in on how this venture will end, but he does have to agree to marry the Douglas girl. The happy couple must have a baby immediately, or this deal won't work. He'll also have to sign paperwork to turn over his newly acquired assets to me at the appropriate time."

"What assets?"

"He'll inherit his wife's assets after…" James waved his hand in the air.

"I'm not sure I'm following you, Williams."

"All you need to do is find a handsome young man willing to walk the aisle and father a child. Assure him he'll be paid well and can leave the marriage once the baby is born. He'll just have to agree to give me his wife's inheritance."

"Don't you think when I mention the word 'inheritance' he'll know we're talking about k…"

"Bob, I don't even want to hear that word. I don't want to be privy to what you'll do with the girl."

"She has to be terminated, or there's no payout. I mean like de…"

"I don't want to hear about anything you'll do," James interrupted.

"Whatever," Bob muttered. The big man rubbed his chin. "I've got a guy," Morrow finally said. "He's in college right now, but he'll play along. He'll need a million, too."

James eyed Bob and shook his head. "Nope. Two hundred and not a penny more."

"You mean he's supposed to give up a year of his life for 200k?"

"Not a penny more."

"$250!"

James looked around the room before closing his eyes. Maybe he should go another route, but then again, Bob Morrow always came through for him.

"Okay," James said with a huff. "$250, but that's it."

Morrow breathed in and placed his elbows on the table. "Okay. That will work, but he'll need an advance. He ain't exactly flush with cash."

Williams sipped his drink. "Are you sure he'll cooperate?"

"Let's say I took care of someone for him in the past, and he owes me. He'll play along."

"Excellent," Williams whispered as the waitress approached their table with a plate of fried onion petals.

Once the girl set down the hors d'oeuvres and took his order, the lawyer sat back while Bob ordered enough food for three people. Williams hated the guy, but he had proven helpful in the past. The lawyer didn't think about paying the young man, so he hadn't considered an amount.

The waitress left the table, and he faced Bob again. "Tell your young friend that if he'll marry this girl, father a child, and stay with her for a year, he'll earn $250,000. I'll give him $5,000 upfront."

"He'll need more than five thousand for living expenses until the baby comes."

James crossed his arms and growled. "Ok. Another $35,000, but no more. I don't want him to hear my name or know any details. Tell him part of the deal is no questions, and he has to sign a legal document on the front end."

"I think he'll agree."

"I realize the legal document issue is a little sticky on our end, but we won't have to use it. If he decides to double-cross me, I have other friends who can deal with him. Understand?"

Bob nodded. "Completely. He'll cooperate."

"He'll also have to be convincing. I mean, he'll have to act the part."

"He's a natural, James. Don't worry."

"Okay. I'll do some additional research and figure out a way for him to meet the girl. You make sure he's ready when I need him."

Their order arrived, and James ate his meal. Hanging around Bob for too long might give him indigestion. Before Bob finished, James waved to their waitress and asked for the bill.

Morrow gulped his beer and belched. "What about dessert?"

"Too late. I'm paying, and I have to go. You're on your own."

Once home, Williams walked into his large, quiet home behind the Country Club's ninth green. He'd miss the house, but for his home in the Caribbean and his new yacht, he'd make the sacrifice.

Learning everything he could about the Douglas girl would be his focus for the next week or two. Erin Douglas. *How can I learn about this girl without paying for an investigator?*

Something his wife once said popped into his mind. "Social Media is so amazing," she said while laughing at something on her computer screen. "You can learn about anything on anyone. It's crazy what people post."

The coffee maker chimed, so he filled a mug and opened his laptop. Creating a page on social media under his real name was out of the question, but with a little effort on Google, Williams discovered how easy it would be to create a fake page. He found a photography site with pages of photographs for sale. With a few keystrokes and his credit card, several perfect images dropped into his downloads file.

An hour later, he put his hands behind his head and smiled at his new homepage. Emily Simpson smiled back. *I'm a beautiful young woman. That was too easy.* His only challenge had been working around the site's security protocol, but the internet offered helpful information on getting around the security barriers.

To send a friend request to Erin Douglas, he needed some young female friends, or rather, Emily Simpson did. Erin's page was blocked, but he'd gain valuable information once they were friends.

After a few clicks on his keyboard, James pulled up a realtor's site near Aspen, Colorado. He'd always wanted a chalet in the Rockies, a perfect contrast to the Dominican Republic.

Too bad Bob Morrow was crucial to his success, but the man would come through for him. Erin Douglas would be married and pregnant in no time.

CHAPTER TWELVE

Rules of Engagement

"Hey, Daffy girl. Did you miss me today?"

The large, black cat wrapped around Erin's legs to welcome her home. Erin smiled as she thought about the one creature in her life who cared about her. Of course, the purring feline could be selfish like everyone else.

Erin slid her hand down Daphne's furry back, and the cat leaned into Erin to maximize the experience. Whether Daphne was self-centered or not, Erin loved her.

Overcome by hunger, Erin considered popping a TV dinner into the microwave, but eating a full meal at this time of night would be a bad idea. She opened the cabinet and eyed the Cocoa Krispies she had purchased for special occasions. *Is being told by your best friend that you might have a nice-looking body under your floppy clothes considered a special occasion?*

The box of her grocery store's version of Raisin Bran also caught Erin's attention. It would be healthier. Once her mound of cereal was topped with several slices of banana, she plopped onto the couch for some mindless TV.

"You'll never believe what Ryan wants me to do, ol' girl," Erin said as if Daphne understood every word. "You'll never guess in a thousand years. He wants me to take self-defense with him. I know! Crazy, right?" The bran flakes crunched in her mouth, and she wondered why they called it *Raisin* Bran when she could count the number of raisins in the box on one hand. If she weren't such a tightwad and bought the real stuff, the cereal's name might be justified.

The television came to life, and a pretty blonde stood next to a giant football player interviewing him. Erin knew what a football was and that the two teams fought to carry the little ball across a line on the field, but that was the extent of her knowledge of the sport. The interview, however, made her think about the girl at the Walmart optometrist and Ryan sitting there with a goofy grin on his face.

Was everyone else in the world selfish? Was Ryan selfish? Why was he hounding her to cut her hair and buy contact lenses? How does he benefit from her learning how to get away from a mugger? He doesn't. He'd enjoy a good laugh watching her make a fool of herself, but he wasn't taking self-defense with her for a laugh. Maybe, there was at least one unselfish person in the world.

All his attention must be about the whole marriage thing. She stopped chewing as another possible motive came to mind. She would be out of his hair forever if she got married. Then again, he was the one who was always calling her and getting into her hair, not to mention on her nerves.

As much as Erin considered her situation, she couldn't see how Ryan would benefit from finding her a husband or making all these changes. He didn't even get a piece of the inheritance, though she'd be happy to share it with him.

If this crazy thing works out, I'll give him some money. I might even make him a partner in the company.

Erin turned off the TV, rinsed her bowl, and put it into the dishwasher. Her cat's meow got her attention, so she added water to Daphne's dish and headed to her bedroom to prepare for bed. If she were going to ride her bike ten miles in the morning before work, she had to get to sleep.

After slipping into her pajamas, she looked at herself in the mirror and thought about Ryan's floppy clothes comment.

Floppy clothes? Her clothes weren't floppy. She was just modest.

If I have to be immodest to get a man, I'll stay single. I don't want the money, and I don't need the man!

She was nothing special, but she had given herself to God the summer after seventh grade. Making that decision as a teenager at youth camp had impacted her life, and she wouldn't turn back now. Erin fluffed her pillow and stretched out in bed. That summer had changed everything for her. Her looks hadn't changed, but it comforted her to think about God loving her unconditionally.

Daphne landed on the pillow beside her and snuggled deep into it. Erin reached out and stroked her cat's soft fur. "So, my clothes are floppy, but I want a man to love me for me."

The sandpaper tongue of her cat licked her hand. "If a man won't love me for who I am inside, there's nothing else about me worth loving. Ask Greg. He didn't want to hang around."

Why would Ryan say her clothes were floppy? She'd concede they were a little oversized, but fashion had never been her focus. Buying new clothes wasn't such a bad idea, but she refused to buy something provocative.

A shiver ran down her back as the image of Ryan walking through the women's department with her flashed in her mind. *Nope! I'm shopping alone.*

Surely Ryan wouldn't bring up going with her to Belk or Walmart. There's no way he would be interested in shopping with a woman. *What does he know about clothes, and why was he thinking about my body? Okay! This line of thought is getting a little crazy. Time for sleep.*

Ryan would call her in the morning about this stupid class at the gym. Should she go through with it? It looked like the dating thing might happen, so why not learn how to defend herself? Hopefully dating and self-defense didn't go hand in hand. *Sleep, Erin.*

Erin didn't hear from Ryan the next day, but maybe that was best. He probably went out with one of those floozies he liked to date. She had worked herself up to saying yes to the self-defense idea, and now she was disappointed he hadn't called. The bag on the couch caught her attention. Buying new sweatpants had been a spur-of-the-moment decision, but at least she'd be in style.

He, for sure, won't call those sweatpants floppy. She should return them.

The plastic bag from Target lay on the couch, and she saw the book still in the bag. Her small group Bible study leader had said this book was the number two bestselling book of all time, second only to the Bible—pretty good company.

What on Earth Am I Here For?

Gripping title. Great question.

Interesting. It used to be called *The Purpose Driven Life.*

Did she have a purpose? What drove her? She'd have to think about that. Glancing at the author's name, Erin picked up the book and walked into the kitchen. "You want some tea, Rick? So, you want to know what drives me?" Shuffling back to the couch, she began to read.

Erin's cell phone ringtone broke the silence and startled her. "So, you couldn't live a day without me, could you, Ryan?" she said out loud while reaching for her phone.

"I thought I would have a whole day go by without being pestered about contact lenses, floppy clothes, or self-defense. Guess I thought wrong."

"Are you always so cheerful before bed?"

"You're right, Ryan. I'm such a grouch. You bring it out of me. Actually, I bring it out of myself. See? Case in point!"

"What are you talking about, Erin? You're not making sense."

"My point is no one will want to marry me because I'm a grouch and a failure. Face it, Ryan. I'm hopeless. You can cut my hair, buy me contacts, put me in tight clothes, and teach me kung fu, but a slug is always a slug, a mule is always a mule, and a…you get my point."

The other end of the line was silent. Erin couldn't even hear Ryan breathing. "You still there?"

"Yeah. I'm here. Erin, you're not a slug, and you're not a mule." Ryan sighed. "I'm going to make a list of rules for you."

"Rules?"

"Yep. Rules! I need to give it some thought, but first, you can no longer say critical things about yourself. Deal? You should know better than putting yourself down, Erin. You're not junk."

Her youth pastor's words came to mind from years ago: "God doesn't make junk." Ryan was right. She always cut herself down, but the things she said were true. Maybe in the future, she'd just think those words and not say them out loud. That wouldn't make them go away, but it would make Ryan happy. He was trying to help, so she may as well go along.

"Okay. Deal. I'll quit."

"Wow. That was easy. How about let's go shopping tomorrow?"

"Listen, Ryan, you crossed a line. You're not going shopping with me. If I need new clothes, I can handle shopping by myself."

"Come on, Erin. Wouldn't going shopping with me be a blast?"

"No. I have plenty of clothes, so I don't need to go shopping."

"Erin, you know I'm your friend, right? I like your clothes fine, but let me suggest you buy something for the twentieth century."

"Don't you mean the twenty-first century, Ryan?"

"Let's take this one century at a time."

Erin rolled her eyes but then smiled. "Okay, wise guy. I'll go shopping, but I'll go by myself, and about this self-defense thing," Erin sucked in a breath. "I'll do it."

"Really?" Ryan gasped. "That's...wow, Erin. I didn't expect you to agree so easily, which is a good thing. I signed us up today, and we start next Thursday night."

"Ryan! What if I didn't want to do it?"

"I knew you would, Erin. I could have canceled, but I didn't think I'd have to. This is going to be loads of fun."

"Right. I'm sure the martial arts world is waiting with bated breath."

"I've got some more news for you. Didn't you meet Matt Buffington at church once? He works with me. Remember?"

Erin remembered the singles Bible studies she'd attended. It had to have been recent if he was someone who worked with Ryan. The image of a skinny guy popped into her mind. "Yeah, I think I do. Why?"

"Because I think he wants to go out with you."

"He doesn't even know me, Ryan."

"He does now. I told him all about you, and I showed him your picture. He remembers you."

"RYAN! I should hang up and never speak to you again. The picture you took of me at Walmart has got to be the worst I've ever taken."

"Come on, Erin. Don't get bent out of shape. You're supposed to go out with guys to find a husband, and I'm helping you. He's an upstanding guy who works in our mail room."

"Ryan!"

"You'll like him, and he said he'd like to take you out. You willing to go next Saturday night?"

Erin's stomach flipped. She couldn't speak. She couldn't breathe.

"Erin? You okay?"

"Ryan. I'm not ready for this."

"Listen, it's just a date. You're not getting married next Saturday. He's a nice guy, and you'll have a great time. Some Christian group is playing in town, and he wants to buy tickets. It'll be fun."

Erin knew Atlas Rhoads was opening for Maverick City. She liked them both and had considered going to the concert, but now this…

Was it time to fish or cut bait? What does that even mean?

"Okay, Ryan. You win again. I'll go along with it. What am I supposed to do?"

"Nothing yet. He'll call you, ask you out, and you say okay."

"Don't I need to give him my number? Aren't guys supposed to ask—"

"I already gave him your number. I'll tell him you'll go. He's nervous, too, so this will be a growing experience for both of you."

"Two nervous people going out sounds more like a joke or a reality show." Erin shook her head and looked down at Daphne. "I don't feel good about this, Ryan."

"You'll be fine, Erin. Buy some new clothes, go to the concert, and have a great time. I would take you out on a dry run next week, but I have to be out of town for work Monday through Wednesday."

"Don't take your tux to the cleaners yet," Erin said.

"My tux?"

"You'll have to be my maid of honor." Erin snickered. "Or man of honor, but let's don't get ahead of ourselves."

"I'd consider being your man of honor a privilege. Oh, don't forget we've got to be at the gym on Thursday. I'll pick you up at 6:30. It lasts an hour, and then we'll get something to eat. Sound good?"

"I suppose, Ryan. Why do I let you talk me into these things?"

"Because you know I love you and will do anything to help you."

"If you say so. See you Thursday. Bring a video camera, and we can make some money."

"I thought you weren't going to cut yourself down."

"Just stating the facts."

"Thursday will be awesome. You'll see."

CHAPTER THIRTEEN

First Date

Erin viewed the room and caught another girl sizing her up. The trim brunette was probably trying to figure out what a klutz was doing in a self-defense class. Great question. Erin scanned the rest of the perfect people standing around a mat. *What am I doing here?*

The handsome young instructor introduced himself as Tim. His toned body signaled he was probably accustomed to having women fall all over him. He could have starred in one of those martial arts movies and been the envy of men and the dream of women. A girl in the back had eyes for him. She had already asked two ridiculous questions.

Tim welcomed the group promptly at 7:00 and explained the benefits of taking self-defense. He said the course had more benefits than learning to defend yourself. Ryan looked at her and winked when Tim said it would build self-confidence. Erin didn't need self-confidence. She was confident of making a complete fool out of herself.

They would meet twice weekly for four weeks, and students would receive a discount for the first three months of an advanced class if they wanted to move into additional training. Two nights a week was a significant commitment.

Tim had used her as an example of how to do the butterfly stretch. It made her feel like the cow's heart her biology teacher had dissected her junior year in high school. Everyone knew how to do the butterfly stretch, so she didn't know why the instructor made such a big deal out of her form.

At first, Erin wanted to leave, but the longer the class lasted, the more she enjoyed it. It was only the first night, but she liked learning about defending herself and was fascinated by Tim's examples of how to escape an attacker's grasp. Hopefully, she'd never have to use them, but Erin could see how this information would be helpful if someone tried to hurt her. Before the night was over, she had worked up a sweat and looked forward to coming back. She might even take Tim up on the additional instruction.

"You really got the hang of it, Erin," Tim said. "Are you sure this is your first time to take self-defense?"

"No, I mean yes." Erin stared across the room and then at the floor. Her cheeks reddened. "I've never taken self-defense, but I enjoyed being here."

"I'm glad you came."

Erin appreciated Tim's sincerity. "Tonight was a lot more enjoyable than I'd anticipated."

As Tim walked away, Ryan shoulder-bumped her. "Teacher's pet. I could've predicted it. He might be single. I could try to fix you up."

"Too late," Erin said. "I'm already going out with Matt. Remember?"

"It wouldn't hurt to have someone else in the wings, just in case."

"Ryan, you got to set a rule, so now I'm going to create one. No more than one guy at a time. Going out will be hard enough, so don't make it more challenging."

"So, what did you think of Matt? You talked on the phone. Right?"

"We didn't talk long, but he's an amiable guy. He's not as familiar with Atlas Rhoads but likes Maverick City as much as I do. I'm sure we'll have a wonderful evening."

"Amiable? Call me when you get home on Saturday and let me know how it goes. Nice sweats, by the way. I'm impressed with your taste."

Erin's cheeks began to glow. At least, the long T-shirt helped. Although the sweatpants still made her self-conscious, she decided they would be ideal for exercise and was glad she'd kept them.

* * * * *

Saturday arrived, and Erin paced around her house like a caged animal. Why had she agreed to go through with this marriage idea? Ryan was crazy, and she was a psycho. Her stomach flipped for the hundredth time as that thought of staying close to the toilet came to mind. She had to hold herself together.

Erin jumped up, ran into the bathroom, and threw up. After cleaning her face, she studied her pale reflection in the mirror. Vomiting had made her feel better, but her face was hopeless. Showering and putting on makeup would help. Wearing makeup had never been a priority for her, and she dreaded the routine. Ryan once remarked, "Every old barn needs a little red paint now and then." *Jerk.*

Once dressed, Erin sat at her kitchen table. The refrigerator hummed, and the old clock on the wall ticked, reminding her of a scary movie she'd seen as a kid. She eyed the clock—fifteen minutes to go. Her stomach began churning again.

She was excited about the concert. It was the eating out before the concert that bothered her. She'd have to puke at least twice during the meal or end up spilling her drink or dumping her plate.

The night was going to be a disaster.

The bell rang, and Erin jumped, hitting her knee against the underside of the table. She eyeballed the clock. *Five minutes early.*

Erin tiptoed to the window overlooking the porch and peeked through the blinds. Matt. She remembered him now. He finger-combed his hair with his left hand and was holding...*I can't believe he brought me a rose!* Her hand went instantly to her stomach. She noticed the rose petals shaking at the end of a long stem. *He's as nervous as I am.*

Erin reviewed what Ryan had told her. Above all, she was not to say critical things about herself, and she had to make herself look Matt in the eye. She took a deep breath and opened the door.

"Hello, Matt."

Matt's brown eyes met hers before he looked toward his feet. His hand shook so significantly that Erin thought the rose petals would fall off.

"Hey, Erin. Thanks for being willing to go to the concert with me. Here. I brought you a rose."

Erin couldn't remember getting even a daisy from a guy. "Thanks, Matt. Let me put it in a vase before we go." Her head began bowing, but she forced herself to stare at the top of his head. "Come on in a minute."

The thought of him coming into her house sent a shiver down her back. Had she left anything embarrassing lying around? Other than her robe draped over the back of the chair, everything seemed okay. The sink had dirty dishes in it, but doesn't everyone have dirty dishes sometimes?

Matt followed her into the kitchen and stood silently as Erin dug through her cabinet, trying to find something for the flower. What did people put flowers in if they didn't own a vase? Why would she have a vase? No one had ever given her a flower.

Think, Erin. Think. Mason jar. Yeah, that would work. She pulled out a Mason jar and turned on the faucet.

"This will work until I can find a vase. You are so thoughtful."

Matt looked at her again and smiled. "You're thoughtful to go out with me."

If you only knew. Not only do I want to go out with you, but evidently, I want to marry you and have a baby by August 7th. "I appreciate you asking me out. I…well, Matt, I need to be honest. I haven't dated much, so I'm kind of a flop regarding how to act." *Oh, shoot. Ryan told me not to say critical things about myself.*

"No problem, Erin. I'm not too good at it either." His eyes went toward something a little right of her left shoulder.

Erin cleared her throat. "Well, I love Atlas Rhoads and Maverick City, and I'm sure we'll have a great time. I suppose we'd better go so we won't be late." *Oh, no. That's another thing Ryan told me to avoid: taking charge. I've got to let the guy take charge.*

The traffic was light, so getting to the restaurant was easier than she'd anticipated. Picking a restaurant had been a challenge because neither wanted to decide. After discussing it for ten minutes, they agreed on two options, and Matt flipped a coin. O'Charley's. Fine with Erin. Although she felt slightly better about going out, she wouldn't be eating much.

Dinner went well, and Erin started to breathe a bit easier. Tripping over the curb while walking into the restaurant hadn't been graceful but Matt didn't notice. He had been too busy inspecting his shoes.

The concert was outstanding, except when Atlas Rhoads sang "Bride," Erin became nauseous again. The song wasn't about marriage, however. The church was the bride and Jesus was the groom. Thinking about marriage and a baby had to stop so she could enjoy going out. She remembered her dates with Greg and couldn't admit to ever enjoying going out with him. *Why in the world was I going to marry him?*

Several things about the evening were awkward, but the goodnight scene took the prize. When Matt walked her onto the front porch, he tripped on the top step and knocked her into the door.

"Oh, Erin. I'm so sorry. I'm such a klutz."

Uh, that's my line, Matt. "It's fine, Matt. Really. I trip there all the time."

A little white lie wouldn't hurt him. She was clumsy, but she'd never tripped on her steps.

Matt reached out his hand and shook Erin's like they'd settled a business deal. "Thanks for going out with me, Erin. I had a great time. Let's do it again sometime."

Erin had imagined him telling her goodnight several times, but a handshake hadn't crossed her mind. "I enjoyed the evening, too, Matt. Thanks for taking me. I'd love to go out again. I'm available any time."

Boy, do I sound desperate. I may as well have fallen to my knee and begged him to marry me.

"Okay," Matt stammered. "I'll call you sometime. Goodnight."

Matt stumbled over something on her sidewalk as Erin turned toward the door. She smiled and walked into the house to be greeted by Daphne. When she put her purse on the table, it fell over, and her phone slipped out of the side pocket. She had three missed calls from Ryan.

Really, Ryan?

He answered on the first ring. "Where have you been? I've been concerned about you."

"Hmm. So, you're my fashion consultant and relationship counselor, and now, you're my father?"

"Sorry. I started thinking horrible things."

"Like what?"

"Well, like, you could have been in an accident, or maybe Matt's not the upstanding guy I thought he was."

"Relax, Ryan. He spent the evening looking at his shoes."

"Yeah. I think he has a little self-esteem issue, but you could help him feel better about himself. How did it go?"

"We had an okay time. He's…well, polite, but I counted twenty-two self-deprecating statements."

"What an outstanding learning opportunity to see how important it is not to criticize yourself."

"The twenty-two statements came from him. I didn't count mine. I told him I'd enjoy going out again, but I don't know, Ryan. He had a hard time carrying on a conversation. I'm not the most fluid conversationalist either, so we had a lot of silence. Good thing we didn't have to talk during the concert."

"You have one date under your belt, Erin. I'm proud of you. Let me work on some things, and I'll find someone else."

"What do I do about Matt? I mean, when he calls back."

"If you want to go out with him again, do it. Otherwise, come up with some reason to be busy."

Erin hung up the phone and plopped down onto the couch. Daphne jumped into her lap, and Erin stroked the cat's back. The constant purring noise indicated ol' Daffy was happy, but Erin wasn't purring.

"Daffy, I had the craziest night. I've got to find a man with a little more confidence than me. But would a guy with more confidence want someone like me?"

CHAPTER FOURTEEN

Chip Shot

E rin didn't see Matt on Sunday, but that was no big deal. He had mentioned he went to the later service, and she attended the early one. She half expected him to call sometime on Sunday, but the only sound from her phone came when her mother called. Nosiness was one of her mom's lesser traits, so the last thing Erin wanted to do was tell her mother about going out with Matt. Telling her about the crazy part of the will was out of the question.

Crawling into bed, she thought about Matt's silence. Why would he call her? Why would anyone want a first date with her, much less a second one?

Monday evening, Erin picked up her silent phone and glanced at the screen. No doubt Matt had a horrible time Saturday night. Then again, it was Labor Day, so he may have spent it at the lake with friends. Isn't that what ordinary people do?

As she got ready for bed, her phone rang.

"Hey, Ryan. How's life at Gatner?"

"How's it going, Sunshine? If I were doing any better, I'd be twins."

"What do you mean? And, what's up with Sunshine?"

"You, my dear, are a beam from the sun, and being with you makes any guy's heart race."

"I think you need to leave poetry to Shakespeare. And it's not *race*. It's run. I make them run away. What do you want, anyway?"

"Me? I don't want anything, but I have another date lined up for you."

"What?" Erin shouted into the phone before calming herself. "Ryan! You need to talk to me before you set me up."

"Okay, Erin. This one sort of fell into my lap. I know a guy who comes to the gym all the time when I'm there, and he and I were talking. His name is Chip, by the way."

"Chip?"

"I doubt that's his real name, but he's solid. He needs a date for something his work is doing on Thursday night, and I told him you'd be happy to go."

Erin closed her eyes and counted to ten.

"Erin?"

"Ryan. Going to a concert with the mailroom guy is one thing, but going to a work party with The Rock is another story. Besides, we're supposed to go to self-defense Thursday night."

"I didn't say he was Dwayne Johnson, and it won't hurt us to miss one night. I'd say your future marriage is more important."

Ignoring the marriage comment, Erin had to think of a way to escape this situation. "I don't think I'm ready for an office party with a bunch of businesspeople. I'll be a disaster, and you know it."

"Erin, you'll be fine. Have you been doing the book on your head thing?"

"Ryan. I can't balance a book on my head. I've been trying to work on my posture, though, and I've tried to look people in the eye when I talk to them. I was very aware of that at church yesterday."

"Excellent. You'll be fine at the office party. Just be yourself."

"Hence the problem, Ryan. Myself is not a good person to be."

"Listen to me. You're beautiful, kind, nice, and caring."

"Don't all of those words mean the same thing?"

"No. They don't. You are sweet, tender, and thoughtful. You're a knockout with a beautiful smile."

"Come on! Besides, there's nothing knockout about me. I'm a disaster waiting to happen, a tsunami after an earthquake, and a mud puddle after a summer rain."

"You done?"

Erin didn't say anything. She wanted to throw the phone at the wall. Why had he set her up to go to a business party with some handsome guy she hadn't met? Ryan had gone too far. Going out with Matt had been one thing, but going to some work party with a gym jock was crossing a line. What line she didn't know, but going out with Chip crossed it.

"Erin, listen to me. Chip's a great guy. He drives a sweet car, and it seems like he's got one of those fish magnets on the lid of his trunk. Doesn't that mean he's religious or is like in the Kiwanis?"

"I don't know if I should hang up on you or let you hear me throw up in the bathroom."

"Okay, Erin. I won't set you up again without your permission, but you can do this. Please go out with Chip. You'll like him. He might be the right guy for you. Come on. The clock is ticking. You need nine months, right?"

"I'm sorry, Ryan. I can't do this whole marriage and baby thing. I'm done."

"How can you be done? You've only had one date. Go out with Chip this one time and see how it goes. I'm sure you'll have an enjoyable evening, but if I'm wrong—if it's a disaster—I'll drop everything, and you can let millions of dollars go to charity. Will that make you happy?"

Erin sat quietly as the silence was broken only by Daphne's purring. She wanted to scream or cry or both. How had she let Ryan push her into this corner?

"Okay. I'll do it. I can't say no to people, and you're taking advantage of my flaw."

"No, I'm not, Erin. I'm trying to help. I promise I won't do it again. You need to meet Chip before Thursday night. Why don't you plan to come with me to lunch tomorrow, and I'll get Chip to join us? You don't have to work tomorrow, do you?"

"No. I'm off."

"Wonderful. How about Chili's at noon?"

"This feels like another date."

"It's not. You're going to meet up with a friend. That's all. If Chip isn't free, I'll let you know by 9:00 in the morning."

"Okay, fine." Erin heard something on the other end. "Are you laughing?"

"A mud puddle after a summer rain?"

Ryan's laughter grew, and Erin couldn't help smiling. "I'll see you there tomorrow. Don't forget we've got to be at the gym tomorrow night, too," Erin shouted into the phone, which sparked more laughter from Ryan.

Erin disconnected the call, and Daphne crawled into her lap. "It wasn't that funny." She laid her head back on the couch and groaned. "What have I gotten myself into?"

Erin rode her bike fifteen miles the following morning, but her mind was far from exercise. How had she let Ryan take over her dating life? What did he know about dating? He always had a different beautiful woman on his arm whenever she saw him. Why didn't he have a trophy wife and two perfect kids by now?

She kicked her bike into high gear the last mile. Sweat poured from her forehead, and her legs screamed from the exertion, but the workout felt refreshing. Erin didn't solve any problems, but she felt better. After parking her bike in the carport, she headed inside to shower and dress for the day.

Standing in front of her closet, Erin tried to decide what she should wear to a lunch meeting where she would be introduced to her future husband and the father of her baby.

Okay, so I'm a little dramatic. There's no way I'm going to marry The Rock Junior. I'm going to meet a new friend and help him out by going with him to a business party. That's what friends do.

She propped her head against the door frame and sighed. Did all girls go through this when they started dating? Of course, most girls started dating when they were teenagers. Greg was the only person Erin had dated and dating him hadn't turned out so well.

Daphne ran out from under the bed and rubbed against Erin's bare leg. "Hey, girl. Where have you been all morning? You won't believe who I'm going to meet today. Give up? I'm meeting my future husband. Actually, I'm meeting a friendly guy who is also Ryan's friend—no big deal. We'll have lunch, and then I'm going to a business party with him. Hmmm? Well, you're right. I've never been to a business party before, and I have no idea what to do. Dump champagne all over your blouse? Gag while you try to eat sardines on a toothpick?"

Shoving clothes aside, she found a top to wear. *Slacks or jeans? It's only Chili's, for heaven's sake. Jeans.* She hung the blouse on the doorknob of the closet, closed her robe, and tightened the belt. Coffee was her greatest priority at the moment.

"Okay, Daphne. Coffee and internet and then first dates." Erin paused and looked at the cat. "You're right. This isn't a date. It's lunch with a friend and his friend."

Erin stubbed her toe on the cedar chest, hopped into the kitchen on one foot, turned on the coffee maker, and powered up her laptop. Within seconds, the beautiful, old gingerbread house popped onto her screen, the for sale sign still in place. Maybe she should drive by the house on her way to Chili's. It would help her get her mind off meeting Mr. Muscle.

The house description hadn't changed since she read it the last twenty times, and she wondered how bad a "fixer-upper" it could be. The interior pictures showed taped walls, and the floors appeared dingy. She could count the times she'd used a hammer on one hand, but she'd watched Chip and Joanna Gaines on TV.

Chip Gaines. Outstanding guy. Could her Chip be outstanding too? What was she thinking? Mr. Tough Guy wasn't *her* Chip. He was just Chip at Chili's with the perfect six-pack abs.

Beads of sweat popped on her forehead. Why was she thinking about this guy's abs?

She drank her coffee while reading from her devotional app and then slipped into her jeans and blue-striped blouse. Stopping by the fixer-upper house on the way would be a good idea. Ryan called them distressed houses.

Her heart melted as she pulled into the driveway of the cutest house, though it was in desperate need of renovation. The peeling paint and sagging front porch revealed its age. Yep, a "distressed" house, just like her life.

The front door hung ajar, so Erin slipped inside and stood still in the living room. The smell, also distressing, about made her retreat, but she had to get a closer look.

What was it Ryan once said? The worse shape the house was in, the lower the price. She could afford it, but how could she pay for repairs?

Erin walked down the hallway to the bathroom and saw straight through the floor to the ground under the house. The condition of the house worsened with every step. She could fix up the bedroom first, then the kitchen and bathroom. Then, she could move in and fix the rest of the house as she had money.

No bank would give her a loan. Besides, she didn't know anything about fixing up a disaster like this house. Looking around, Erin berated herself for considering taking on a project of this magnitude.

I need to give up this dream and stick to trying to have a baby. Oh, my. I think I am going to throw up.

Erin saw a young woman and gasped but then giggled out loud at the realization she was staring at an old mirror leaning against the wall. She stared at herself for a full minute, and her eyes landed on the reflection of her midsection. Her hands slid down to her flat stomach, and she turned sideways to view her profile.

Can I get pregnant and have a baby? Why can't I do this like normal people? I always have to make everything so complicated.

Tears spilled out of her eyes as she imagined her daddy writing out his creative idea to help her and her mother deal with his death. It was sweet in a way.

So, she was going with two friends to Chili's. One was a ripped gym rat she'd never met, who may become her future husband. The other was her ripped friend, who happened to be nuts. What could go wrong?

CHAPTER FIFTEEN

A Risk Worth Taking?

T he Chili's sign a hundred feet ahead made Erin think of the boat ride at Six Flags Over Georgia, where the little creature held up a danger sign and yelled, "Stay out of the marsh." Like the ride going straight into the dangerous swamp, Erin entered the parking lot and approached the restaurant's front door. She stood at the entrance trying to spot Ryan.

There he is, and that must be Chip. Wow. He is good-looking. Is that an earring?

Erin struggled to control her nerves and plopped down onto one of the benches near the front door. The thought of driving away and calling Ryan to tell him she'd gotten sick crossed her mind, but she happened to park right in front of the window near Ryan and Chip's table. They must not have seen her arrive, but they'd surely spot her if she tried to leave.

This is not a date, Erin. This is a… Two men in suits walked through the door. *This is a business meeting. Yeah, it's a business meeting, and we're going to talk about the business of getting married and having a baby.*

When the two men walked to a table where a woman sat, she stood and shook their hands. Their greeting looked real formal. Business-like.

Cut it out, Erin. We're going to talk about going to a business meeting. Do people do that? Have a business meeting to talk about a business meeting? Erin stood and took a deep breath.

She approached the table, and Ryan stood to hug her. "Hey, Erin. Thanks for meeting us. This is Chip Richards."

Chip reached out and nearly crushed Erin's hand. His forearm resembled a tree trunk, and his bicep could have been a small boulder covered with flesh.

"Hello, Erin. I've heard a lot about you." His eyes scanned her from head to toe like a piece of meat hanging in a Peruvian village market. Chip sat down and slid over to give Erin room to sit, but she sat down next to Ryan.

"Good to meet you, Chip." Her eyes moved toward the table, and Ryan nudged her leg. Her head jerked back up, and she looked into Caribbean blue eyes. Wow. "It's a pleasure to meet you, and thanks for inviting me to go with you to your business meeting."

"No, thank you, darlin'. You're doing me a big favor."

Darlin'? Um...

Erin cleared her throat and grabbed a menu. All the words bled together into one giant colorful mess. "So, what kind of marriage is this, Chip?" Heat rose up her neck. "I mean, what kind of meeting on Thursday evening?" *Can I crawl under the table now?*

"Oh, well, I work for a bank. We merged with another bank, making us the largest in the United States. Some of the higher-ups are coming in to celebrate the merger. They're all couples, and my wife left me last year, so I'm the fifth wheel."

Erin realized her mouth was hanging open, so she reached for her water glass and took a drink. She stared at Ryan with a *Wow, you didn't tell me this guy was divorced, and he looks at women like they're on the dessert menu, so now I'm going to kill you* smile.

Lunch ended after Erin learned about every weightlifting award Chip had won and saw pictures of his boat at Lake Lanier. Backing out of the event on Thursday wouldn't be appropriate, but after Thursday night, Chip would be a fuzzy memory, at best.

Erin finally excused herself with a bogus story about an appointment. She felt mild guilt as she remembered her small group leader calling Satan the father of lies. She had some repenting to do.

Erin's phone rang a few minutes after pulling away from the restaurant. Before she could utter a word into the device, she heard Ryan's voice coming over the Bluetooth speakers.

"I'm sorry, Erin. I didn't know he'd been married before, and I didn't realize he was so hung up on himself."

"I considered stabbing you with my butter knife," Erin said through clenched teeth. "I can't believe you put me in this situation. So much for the fish."

"The fish?"

"Yeah. The fish magnet on the back of his car. The Greek word for fish is an acrostic for *Jesus Christ, Son of God.*"

"How do you know all this stuff?"

"I just do."

"Listen, Erin. You don't have to go on Thursday. I'll tell him something came up."

"Ryan, he may be a jerk, but I told him I'd go. I refuse to be alone with him, however. You tell him I'll meet him. I don't want him to pick me up at my house. Where will this bash take place?"

"It's at the Omni Hotel downtown."

"RYAN! You mean to tell me I'm going on a date to a hotel with a muscle-bound pervert?"

"No. You're not. I'm not letting him anywhere near you."

Was Ryan trying to protect her? This big brother thing felt comforting. "Listen, Ryan. You're sweet, but you'll still have to interact with Chip at the gym. I'll help you save face by going Thursday night. I'll stay for a little while, but I'll say my mother needs me to be at her house by nine."

Erin heard silence for thirty seconds before Ryan spoke. "You're being a good sport about this, Erin."

"No problem. You never know. I could learn to be a cultured woman."

After disconnecting, Erin heard her phone buzz with an incoming text. Susan. Her mind went back to that afternoon at Stone Mountain Park.

Oh, no. I totally forgot to call her. Great, Erin. You finally make a friend, and then, you ignore her.

She pulled into a parking lot and reached for her phone to read the message. "Hey, Erin. It's Susan. You remember meeting me at Stone Mt? How have you been?"

Erin instantly pressed a couple of icons and heard the ringing sound clearly on her Bluetooth speaker. When she thought Susan's phone would go to voicemail, she heard a voice.

"Erin, so good to hear from you."

"Oh, Susan, I meant to call you several times. I'm sorry. How are you?"

"I'm doing well, sort of. I had you on my mind and hoped we could meet for coffee."

Erin sighed. "Good timing. I just sort of lied by telling a guy I had an appointment. It's a long story."

"I'm free right now if you are."

"Uh, well." Erin felt awkward. What would her new friend think about being friends with a liar?

"I've got a few hours before Amber gets home from school," Susan said. "Didn't you say you live in McDonough?"

"Yes, but right now, I'm in Morrow. I don't remember where you live."

"I may not have told you. I'm in Stockbridge, which isn't far from you. There's a Starbucks on Highway 138."

Erin agreed to meet, and a smile spread across her face as her phone went silent. When she arrived at Starbucks, Susan stood and hugged her.

"Erin, it's so good to see you. You look..." She paused and focused on Erin's hair. "I don't...You've gone through a transformation. I watched you get out of your car and didn't recognize you at first."

Erin's eyes drifted over the parking lot and landed on her little blue Toyota Corolla. "Well, I let a friend of mine talk me into going to see his..." her voice tapered off. "I'm not sure what to call her. His former flame, who happens to be a beautician."

"Well, she did an outstanding job. You are beautiful, Erin. Really. What do you want? My treat."

"Oh, Susan. I can't let you buy my coffee."

"Why not? You can buy next time, and unless you're on a diet, let's try one of those banana nut muffins. They're incredible."

Five minutes later, Erin looked across the table at her new friend, possibly her only friend, except for Ryan. Susan's honest face glowed with a genuine smile.

Erin stirred her coffee before taking a sip. "I've thought about calling you. I'm really sorry I haven't."

Susan swallowed a mouthful of muffin and shook her head. "Don't apologize. I had your number, too, and I didn't reach out until today. How have you been? You said something about a guy. Boyfriend?"

Erin about choked on her coffee. "No way. He's a friend of a friend who needs a date for a company party." Erin smiled. "Not to be pretentious, but I'm doing him a favor."

"You never know, Erin."

"No, I do know. Trust me." Erin laughed nervously and pinched off a piece of her muffin. "I met the guy today for the first time. I'll go with him Thursday night only because I told my friend I'd do it."

"That bad?"

"Worse. The man thinks he's God's gift to the world. He looks at me like I'm…well…Let's say his thoughts aren't pure."

"Oh. I see. You must owe your friend a lot."

"No, it's not like that. It's complicated. I'm not cut out for fancy dinner parties. I'll be like a fish out of water. I have nothing to wear and won't know how to act. I'm only going because I said I would and because my friend asked me to go."

"Your friend is fortunate to have you. What's her name?"

"Him. I mean, my friend is a guy. Ryan."

"Ryan? Hmm."

"He's kind of like my big brother. Well, he'd have to be more like my twin brother because we're the same age. I've known him since fifth grade."

"Have you ever dated him?"

"Oh, no. Never. He dates beautiful, hot bimbos. Sorry. I'm not his type. However, I am his type when it comes to helping a charity case find a boyfriend." Erin changed the subject. "How are Tom and Amber?"

"Couldn't be better. Tom got a promotion at work, and Amber has been preparing to play piano at church."

"Amber plays the piano? Wonderful."

"Yeah," Susan beamed. "Would you like to come tomorrow night and hear her play?"

"I'd love to, Susan. I live a very boring life. All I do is work and go home to care for my cat."

Erin and Susan visited for a while before Susan had to leave to pick up Amber from school. Erin almost told Susan about the will several times but couldn't bring herself to admit she was so desperate.

Susan stood and took Erin's hands. "Erin, I have a black evening dress you could borrow for Thursday night. We're about the same size."

Erin studied a crack in the floor and pulled her hair behind her ear. "Oh, uh, I couldn't impose."

"You're not. I brought it up. I'm sure it'll fit. It has spaghetti straps, but I wore a white wrap the few times I've worn it. You can borrow the wrap, too."

"You're so sweet, Susan. Thanks. I would have to go shopping, and I don't want to spend the money on something I may never wear again."

"I'll bring it and the sweater tomorrow night. Seven o'clock at First Baptist Church in Stockbridge."

"I can't wait. I'll arrive a little early if I can. I'm so glad I got to see you today, Susan."

Erin hugged her friend again and almost skipped to her car. Her phone revealed she had enough time to get home, change into sweats, and make it to the gym. This would be a stellar day, after all, and going with Susan and her family tomorrow to hear Amber play the piano would be the cherry on top.

CHAPTER SIXTEEN

On the Town

E rin strained to see the top of the Omni Hotel from the sidewalk. It made her feel small. Insignificant. How much would it cost to rent a suite on the twenty-fourth floor that could host a business party? Tugging on the top of the black party dress she'd borrowed from Susan, she found it to be as secure as it had been three minutes earlier. She pulled Susan's wrap around her tighter and imagined snugging it up to her neck.

The service the night before with Susan and her family had been excellent. Amber played the piano well, and Susan had been excited about loaning Erin the dress. Erin would wear it proudly and attend the party for her friend's sake.

Her new black shoes were already scuffed. She'd spent so much money on shoes for an event she didn't want to attend.

The polite doorman at the Omni Hotel greeted Erin, and she turned in circles in the lobby, taking in the plush surroundings. Finding the glass elevator was easy, and she squeezed into the tight space with eight other people. The maximum weight allowed crossed her mind as she began mentally adding up her guess of each person's weight. She felt more like a cow being herded to slaughter than a young woman attending a fancy party. An image of Katniss Everdeen from *The Hunger Games* riding up the elevator of doom came to mind.

Erin stepped off the crowded elevator and saw Chip wearing a tuxedo. Several other men stood around him, laughing at something he'd said.

As Erin approached the group, she recognized her father's lawyer beside Chip. Why would James Williams be attending this event? The bank must be a client.

Chip turned and saw her. "Oh, my." Chip managed to sustain two tiny words over thirty seconds. A suggestive grin spread over his face as he slowly scanned her from head to toe. So, this was what a prize heifer at a cattle auction experienced.

His gaze didn't stop on her face. The thought of her little black purse colliding with his nose flashed through her mind, but she opted to pull her sweater tighter instead.

"Hello, Chip. I hope I'm not late. I'm not used to this Atlanta traffic."

He slid his arm around her waist and pulled her close. "You're right on time, darlin'. You should have let me pick you up."

Erin felt both violated and humiliated. The image of an octopus wrapping its tentacles around its prey raced through her mind. Her gaze dropped, and she inspected the colors woven together in the carpet. How could someone create such a design?

Chip's right hand squeezed her waist.

"Um, well, I have to go by my mother's house on the way home, so I figured I'd better drive."

"I'm sorry to hear you've got to leave. I have a room down the hall, and I thought—"

"My mother's been through a lot," Erin interrupted as she stepped away from his reach. "I'm afraid she's quite dependent on me these days."

"My, my, Chip," an older man bellowed. "Where did you find such a beauty? And she agreed to come with you?"

Are all these men so rude and arrogant? Erin's eyes drifted to her shoes, and she imagined them stuffed into the old man's mouth.

"Gordon, I want you to meet my friend, Erin Douglas. Erin, this is Gordon Smithers."

Erin managed some semblance of a smile. "Pleased to meet you, Mr. Smithers."

"Please, Erin, call me Gordon."

"And this is Burt Jenkins and James Williams. James is one of the attorneys for the bank. Burt's an old friend"

Erin kept the fake smile in place. "Hello, Mr. Williams. A pleasure to see you again."

"Oh!" Chip gaped. "You know one another?"

"I handled some business for her father before he passed," James explained.

The crowd began moving toward the open door of the suite, which saved Erin from other pointless drivel. Erin recognized a Louis Vuitton purse she'd gawked at online a few weeks ago. The cost of the shoes in the room would put a significant dent in the national debt.

Erin fingered her Target costume jewelry while taking in the beautiful jewels adorning some women in the group. One woman's necklace was probably twice the value of her little house.

What am I doing here?

Erin gasped as she entered the suite. A crystal chandelier hung in a large room that caused little diamond reflections to dance around on the walls. Tables covered with fancy cuisine divided the room in half, and Erin's stomach reminded her it had been a while since she had eaten. Yet, when her eyes landed on a plate of snails, she lost her appetite. *Disgusting.*

She wanted to turn and head back to the elevator, but Chip's arm slipped around hers, imprisoning her. Erin checked her watch and was relieved she'd only have to endure this place for two more hours—two long tortuous hours.

While moving food around her plate, she marveled at the pointless conversations. Chip mentioned two body-building awards he'd won and bragged about three business deals he'd closed in the last two months. He idolized the sound of his own voice, and Chip Richards was his favorite topic.

Erin froze when Chip's hand settled on her knee. Her mind raced in a dozen directions before devising two possible scenarios: *stab him with a fork or bolt for the restroom.* She opted for the restroom.

The evening dragged on, and Erin shook enough hands and endured enough stares to last her a lifetime. However, the bank president was friendly, and he and his wife, Madelyn, were down to earth. Their authenticity surprised Erin. They were rich, but she could imagine chatting about a good book with Madelyn. She shouldn't lump all rich people into the same category.

At 8:35, Erin leaned toward Chip and told him she needed to leave. Getting out of this hotel and away from Chip's straying eyes and roaming hands couldn't happen fast enough. He tried to discourage her, but she stood and told the small group she had to leave to check on her mother.

"Oh, Erin," one of Chip's co-workers said, as if Chip had paid the man to plead his case, "you should stay. The evening is young."

"Sorry. My father recently died, and I have to help my mother." It had been a year since her father's passing. Did a

year qualify as *recently*? Sure. Grief didn't pay attention to cal-
endars.

Hurrying toward the door, she sensed Chip behind her.
Once at the elevator, she pressed the call button, and Chip
reached for her arm and stepped closer. His body heat and
musk cologne assailed her.

"Erin, are you sure you have to go?"

Erin faked another smile. "Sorry, Chip."

His deceitful blue eyes raked over her, causing her to feel
sullied, and his offensive breath smacked her. "I hoped you
might stay, and we could go to my room for a drink."

Erin dropped all pretense of a smile. "Do you fish, Chip?"

"I'm sorry?"

"Do you fish?"

"Do I...?"

"Do you fish?"

"Uh, I have before, but I can't say it's my favorite pas-
time." He grinned. "I have a few other things I'm better at."

Erin heard the elevator ding as it arrived, and the door
slide open across her back. "I once read where an old Scottish
politician said, 'The charm of fishing is that it is the pursuit of
what is elusive but attainable.'"

"Interesting, but I'm not sure what you mean."

"I'm not attainable, Chip, so throw your line in another
pond. Goodnight."

As the doors closed, Erin ignored Chip's strange, confused expression. She hoped that would be the last time she
ever saw the creep. "I can't believe a John Buchan quote came
to my mind—weird," Erin said to an empty elevator. *I've got to
get a life, but if it has to include the likes of Chip and his buddies, I'll
stick with my bookstore.*

Erin hurried across the lobby of the Omni Hotel. She couldn't get to her car and out of Atlanta fast enough. Someone grabbed her hand, and without thinking, Erin whirled and slapped the person across his cheek.

Erin gasped. "Ryan? I'm so sorry. I thought you were Chip. Wh…What are you doing here?"

Ryan stood stunned and rubbed his jaw. "Apparently, getting the fire slapped out of me."

Erin reached out as if her touch could somehow remove the sting of her slap, and the people around them gawked. Ryan pulled her toward the exit as Erin repeatedly apologized.

"It's okay, Erin. We know no one will hurt you without paying a dear price. Self-defense is already paying off," Ryan joked. "Let's go for coffee."

He led her out of the hotel and across the street to a small, crowded cafe.

Ryan pulled out Erin's chair. "You hold our table, and I'll get coffee."

"What I'd like is something to eat. I'm starving."

"Erin, you just left a dinner party, and you're starving?"

"They don't serve edible food at shindigs like that."

Ryan sat and waved for a menu. Once he ordered coffee and Erin ordered a sandwich, a brownie, and soda, he propped his elbows on the table. "So, what happened?"

Erin gave him a play-by-play, including her John Buchan quote, which Ryan found hilarious. She smiled and then laughed until she cried.

As the laughter subsided, Erin found her voice and returned to her earlier question.

"Why are you here, Ryan? I mean, why are you downtown?"

"Why?" Ryan smiled and shook his head. "I'm here to make sure you're okay. You had to go out with that creep because of me. I planned to give you another thirty minutes, and I was coming up."

Erin's eyes began to water. No one had ever cared enough to rescue her from anything. That was the sweetest thing he'd ever done.

Erin walked into her home at 11:00 and she collapsed onto the couch. The night ended up being okay. El Creepo had been kept at bay, and she had a lovely time with Ryan. The food at the café was excellent.

When she opened her laptop, her social media page welcomed her. One of the girls at church had gotten engaged and posted photos. Erin couldn't help being curious, even though she wasn't a fan of social media. No one cared about her life. She scrolled through half a dozen pictures of the happy couple.

If Greg hadn't run off with Julie, Erin would be married by now. If her wedding pictures were posted online, would she be as happy as this girl? *Doubtful. Good thing I'm still single. I think God saved me from disaster.*

Erin checked the time on her phone—midnight. *I have to go to sleep. Five o'clock comes early.* Staying up so late had not been such a good idea.

CHAPTER SEVENTEEN

Taking Shape

J ames Williams watched Chip return to the banquet room alone. The young, muscle-bound man didn't appear happy. *Dropped like a hot potato. That's a relief. This night was making me nervous.*

He wouldn't have recognized Erin Douglas if he'd passed her in the lobby. The change was remarkable. Even when Chip had introduced them, he still wouldn't have known she was *the* Erin Douglas, except she knew him. What a stunning transformation. The girl was beautiful, which would make his plan easier. Taking a few covert pictures of Erin had been simple. No single young man would hesitate to snatch up this girl.

Williams watched Chip head toward the men's room, and he excused himself. Upon entering the restroom, he looked around to ensure they were alone.

"So, how do you know Erin?" James asked as he reached for a paper towel.

"I don't really know her. Let's just say she's a friend of a friend."

"I'm assuming she left?"

"Yeah. Had to take care of her mother, but no big deal. Not my type."

"She's a beautiful girl. What type is she?"

"What do you mean, James?" Chip grinned. "You asking if she likes old lawyers?"

Williams smiled. "I'm afraid I'm out of the market. I have a young nephew, however."

"Well, I don't think she's dating anyone. Her best friend is a friend of mine. Ryan Jeffries. Works for Gatner Enterprises. Seems like a platonic relationship."

"I suppose it doesn't matter," James concluded.

"I can tell you your nephew's best bet would be to meet her at church. She goes a lot."

"Really? Where does she attend?"

"I think it's South something. Southfork? Southside?" Chip shook his head but then remembered. "Southpoint. Yeah, that's it. She invited me to come, but I'm not into religion."

Williams eyed Chip. The boy was lying through his teeth. Erin Douglas didn't want the blowhard to go anywhere with her.

"My nephew attends church, so I may mention her to him." *Too bad I don't have a nephew. It would make this financial endeavor easier.*

As Williams left the men's room, he began working on a plan to exit the party. Sorting through this new information was now his greatest priority. Maybe he should send out some friend requests under his assumed identity. The trick would be to find some young women at Southpoint Church. Having friends from Southpoint might lead Erin to accept his friend request once he sent it.

Like taking candy from a baby. Williams found the bank president and said his goodbyes.

Already thinking ahead, he left the party. How many young women from Erin's church would accept a friend request from Emily, and would the beautiful Erin Douglas take the bait? Emily could be new to Southpoint. Some pictures he'd chosen for his assumed identity might need to be updated. If Emily was a Christian girl, she wouldn't dress like a floozie.

Once Williams was home and online, he deleted the beach shots from his fake page and added a few others. The royalty-free photo sites were perfect. After finding Southpoint's page, he pressed the "Like" button, and added some pictures of the church to his page. Then, he scrolled through a list of young women who attended Southpoint. *Okay, girls. Let's be friends.*

The throwaway phone lay on the desk, so he snatched it up and called Bob. This man being his accomplice made him cringe. What were the odds a degenerate would answer a call from a strange number? He didn't.

Williams texted, "It's me. I've got a new phone."

Within seconds, his phone buzzed.

"Thanks for calling me back."

"Yeah, well, sorry I didn't answer. Thought you were a bill collector. Those crazy people call all hours of the night."

"How are things going with your boy?"

"No problem. He's on board. He's asked for an advance on the money. He's got to move to Georgia."

"I said I'd give him $40,000, but he hasn't even moved here yet."

"Yeah, well, he'll have to find a place to live down here, and he'll need a job."

"A job?" Williams wondered aloud.

"The kid's not rich, James. Would he be willing to marry a girl, get her pregnant, and then knock her off if he had money?"

"Guess not, but I told you I didn't want to hear anything about your plans to finish the project."

"The advance?"

Williams sighed. Working with Bob and his young associate was going to become a problem. "Okay. $5,000."

"Ten will work for now."

The lawyer huffed but agreed. "Bob, I have some news. You'll never believe who I ran into at the Omni Hotel."

"The King of England."

"The girl," Williams said, ignoring Bob's sarcasm. "Erin Douglas. She's changed. I mean, really changed. I took a few pictures of her. I'll send them. Listen. I also found out she attends Southpoint Church on Highway 42."

"That a fact?"

"I suggest you convince your boy to go to church. It could be a great point of contact."

"Good idea, Counselor. I'll work on it. A little religion sure wouldn't hurt him."

"We don't want him to have too much church. At least, not yet. Let him finish this job before he finds religion."

"Yeah." Bob laughed. "Church is a sweet place to meet women. I used to do it."

"I don't want to hear about your perverted methods of picking up women."

Bob cursed and whooped as if William's comment was the funniest thing he'd ever heard. "When I was a kid, James. What do you take me for?"

Williams ignored the question. "I'm trying to connect with the girl online. Keep me informed about your progress, and I'll pass along any information I learn."

He hung up and checked his laptop. A big grin spread across his face when he saw that two girls had already accepted his friend request. *Yep. Candy from a baby.*

* * * * *

Erin slipped into the break room at 11:00 the next day. A red velvet cake sat on the table. What was the occasion? She had almost finished her ham sandwich when Tyler Matthews plopped down into the chair across from her. His curly blond hair flopped into his eyes, but he ignored it.

She'd met Tyler not long after starting at Barnes & Noble, but the two hadn't had many opportunities to talk. Their shifts overlapped, and they rarely shared breaks.

Erin's gaze fell on the copy of *The Silent Governess* in her bag, and she wondered if it would be rude to read. When she looked up, Tyler was staring at her. *Do I have mayonnaise on my face or something?*

"Hey, Erin. How's it going?"

Other than going out with Creep of the Year, I'm good. "Fine. How about you?"

"Same stuff, different day," Tyler monotoned. "My life's pretty boring. Want some cake? My aunt sent it from Alabama."

"I wondered where it came from. What's the occasion?"

Tyler's head dropped. "It's my birthday."

"Oh, wow. Happy birthday, Tyler. How old?"

"Twenty-three, I mean twenty-four. You'd think by now I'd have a real job instead of working at a bookstore."

Erin frowned. "I like working here. Why don't you?"

"Oh, I like it okay. Sorry. I'm just not in the best mood."

"It's cool. I don't like birthdays, either. You doing anything special? I mean, for your birthday?"

"Nah. I might watch the Braves game, but I don't have any plans. Like I said—boring life."

"It can't be more boring than mine. All I do is read, care for my cat, and check on my mom," Erin admitted. "Well, I ride my bike in the mornings and go to church on Sundays."

"Sounds busy. I sit around the house most of the time."

"You should do something fun for your birthday. Why don't we go to the laser show at Stone Mountain? We could walk around the park before the show. You'll enjoy it."

"I've never been," Tyler said. "What's it like?"

Erin described the huge mountain of stone that had turned into one of the most visited parks in Georgia. The museum stuff was okay, but the highlights were the trail to the top and the laser show that's offered every night during the summer.

Trips to the park were among the few things her family had done together. Then, her brother was killed, and all the family fun died with him. Erin said she'd gone by herself several times over the last few years.

"I always go early and hike to the top," Erin said. "Then, I return to the grassy area, spread out a blanket, have a picnic, and read a book until dark when the show starts. They shoot lasers up onto the rock face and play music. It's cool."

"Sounds interesting. Sure. Why not? I ought to do something other than listen to my neighbors yell at each other. I get off at 3:00. What about you?"

Erin wadded up her napkin and threw away her trash. "Not 'til 5:00. I'm fine with going straight from here, except I don't have any clothes for the hike to the top."

A bag in the car containing her new sweatpants flashed through her mind—tight sweatpants. "Oh well, I doubt we'll have time for the hike, anyway."

"Okay, well, I'll pick you up here at 5:00."

Erin put her lunch bag back into her locker. "I'd better get back to work. Maybe I can have cake on our picnic."

Stunned at what had just happened, Erin returned to the sales floor. She had gone to the breakroom with the sole objective of eating her sandwich and reading. Instead, she ran her mouth to some guy she didn't know and suggested a trip to Stone Mountain.

It's not like she was asking a guy out. She was just being kind to a lonely guy on his birthday.

Right?

CHAPTER EIGHTEEN

Stone Mountain High

E rin watched a red Ford F-150 pull to the curb in front of Barnes & Noble at 5:00. A familiar mop of curly, blond hair bobbed up and down inside. After shelving two final books, she headed to the locker room and hung her smock in a locker. She clocked out, wished Mr. Winslow a good night, and walked out to meet Tyler. Free at last, like a helium balloon let go by a child, and she was heading to Stone Mountain. Erin loved that place. It reminded her of happier times.

To her surprise, Tyler stood beside the passenger door, holding it open. No one opened a door for her except Ryan. Chivalry wasn't dead.

"Thanks, Tyler."

Erin took in the spotless truck that smelled like leather and men's cologne. Did he clean his truck for their outing, or did he always keep it clean? Tyler climbed in behind the steering wheel and started the engine. The sounds of the radio blasting through the speakers. *I can't believe he listens to Christian radio.* Tyler reached for the off button.

"I love Lauren Daigle," Erin said. "'Look Up Child' is one of my favorite songs."

Tyler turned down the volume a little and returned his hand to the steering wheel as they listened to the song's conclusion. He reached over and turned the volume down a little.

"I like her, too, but I've got to admit I'm kind of new to Christian music."

"Who's your favorite?"

"I like For King & Country and Maverick City."

Erin buckled her seatbelt as Tyler pulled out of the parking lot. The cake container sat on the back seat, and thoughts of food came to mind. In the past, Stone Mountain meant family picnics, back when she had a normal family. *Normal was a long time ago.*

"Since it's your birthday, why don't you pull into a KFC closer to the park, and I'll treat? We can take it into the park with us, but we'll have to make do without a picnic blanket."

"I've got a blanket in the back. Not exactly clean, but better than the ground.

"That'll work."

I can't let you pay, Erin. You were thoughtful enough to suggest going out. I should buy."

Were they going out or just hanging out? What would Ryan say?

"I insist, Tyler. For your birthday."

They drove around Interstate 285, and Erin cracked up when Tyler shared a funny story about trying to ride a pig on his grandfather's ranch in Texas. His grandfather's plan to expand his livestock to include pigs proved ill-fated. What would it be like growing up on a three-hundred-acre ranch? Tyler was a real cowboy.

"So, why did you leave Texas?"

"It's a long, boring story. Let's say I left for a change of scenery."

Erin thought about the scenery of her life. Doesn't everyone have baggage? Maybe she needed a change of scenery, too.

When they stopped at KFC, Erin thought she would have to fight Tyler over paying for the meal. He agreed to let her pay on the condition she let him take her out on a real date when he could pay. When he said *real date*, chills ran down Erin's back. No need to get too worked up. He'd never want to go out again after a night with an ole brown bagger. Besides, it wasn't an actual date.

Tyler guided the truck through the entrance to the park, paid the fee, and drove toward the main parking area. "After I got off work, I read about the park online. I like the idea of climbing to the top, if you do. I mean, we could probably make the hike before the show starts. What do you think?"

"I'd love to, Tyler. I'm not exactly dressed for climbing, but who cares? Let's do it."

Erin had climbed the mountain so many times that she could do it with her eyes closed. Her favorite thing was climbing early in the morning and watching the sunrise. Darkness had been her close companion so often that gloom was normal and regret her default. The brilliant first colors that fled the piercing rays of the morning sun offered a subtle reminder that light was an option and hope a possibility.

Erin's mother must have shared this love of dawn because she often took pictures of sunrises. She and her mother had even climbed Stone Mountain one Easter morning with a church group for a sunrise worship service.

When Tyler came to an intersection, she pointed straight ahead. "Follow this road to the right, and the trail to the top is a couple of miles or so."

Tyler pulled into a parking place, and they hurried around a building and across the train tracks to the hiking trail. Too bad she didn't have a pair of shorts, but jeans would do. She told Tyler about how her family always came to the park when she was a little girl, and she had climbed this mountain a hundred times. Again, memories resurfaced, most of them pleasant.

Once the trail steepened, Erin noticed Tyler had no trouble keeping pace. No doubt he worked out. Erin couldn't believe it when he told her he enjoyed cycling.

"I love to ride, too," Erin said. "I try to ride every day."

"Have you ever raced?"

"Oh, no, just for fun. Have you raced?"

"Yes. I raced in Hiawassee, Georgia, two weekends ago. I didn't come close to winning, but I enjoyed it."

"I can't see myself riding in a race. I wouldn't have a chance."

"I don't ride to win," Tyler said. "It's just a real accomplishment to finish, and the atmosphere around races is like a carnival. The camaraderie between cyclists is encouraging."

"Sounds a little scary."

Tyler smiled and shook his head. "Not scary, fun. I'll tell you when I'm going to race again, and you can enter, too."

"I'll think about it, but don't count me in yet."

The view from the top was spectacular as usual. The impressive Atlanta skyline always captured Erin's attention, but the more prominent mountains to the north drew her focus. The significant difference in air quality to the north caused her to want to pack her bags and move to North Georgia.

After getting water bottles from the visitor's center, Erin led Tyler to a fence along the cliff's edge. They talked about the carvings in the stone below them, and Erin pointed to a flat, green spot below where they'd be sitting for the laser show.

When Erin got to her favorite spot, she stopped and pointed. "See the heart carved in the stone? My parents did it."

"Yeah, I see it."

"I suppose it's tacky to carve on the stone, even illegal. They came here on dates a lot and made it a ritual after getting married. My dad once told me he retraced the heart with a rock every time they came here, and it eventually made a little carving in the stone."

"Cool. Your parents still married?"

Erin frowned. "My father died last year. He and my mom had been married almost thirty years."

"I'm sorry, Erin. How's your mom doing?"

"She's okay, but it's been a hard year. What about your parents?"

Tyler laughed, but Erin knew his laughter wasn't from humor. "I don't have any parents. My mom left when I was seven, and I haven't heard from her since. I prefer to think I don't have a father, either. I spent most of my childhood on my grandparents' ranch, and I've been on my own a long time."

"That can't be easy."

"Nah, it's fine." Tyler changed the subject. "So, how often do you come up here now?"

"I used to come a lot, but this is my first time climbing the mountain since before my father died." Not wanting to reveal more, Erin checked the time on her phone and suggested they head back down. "We want to be ready when the laser show starts."

The chicken was cold by the time they stretched out the blanket on the grass, but the food was okay. Hiking had been exhilarating, and they had just enough time to finish their picnic before the lights dimmed and the crowd hushed.

Multi-colored beams of light shot through the air to create drawings on the face of the stone. Erin had seen it so many times that she knew all the songs and could see the laser drawings in her mind before they formed on the side of the carvings. The show offered a few new songs, but most were familiar from previous shows. It didn't matter. She could come here every night and never tire of it.

Erin looked toward Tyler out of the corner of her eye and thought he sat closer than he'd been at first. Did she imagine it, or could she feel his body heat? *Imagining it.*

His hand brushed her arm as he readjusted on their blanket. It almost felt like a shock of electricity.

It was an accident, Erin. He's not making a move.

Tyler was impressed with the laser show. Elvis' version of "Battle Hymn of the Republic" was Erin's favorite, and she relished the part where the laser traced the images of the carvings and somehow made the soldiers ride off the mountain.

After the show, Tyler picked up the trash left over from their picnic. "This will be a memorable birthday, Erin. Thanks so much."

"You're welcome. I had a wonderful time, though the traffic getting out of here is going to be a challenge."

Once they got back to Barnes & Noble, Tyler parked beside Erin's Toyota and rushed around the truck to open the door for Erin to climb out.

"Thanks for the evening, Tyler. I really enjoyed it."

"I did, too, Erin. I'm afraid I don't go out much, and tonight was fun. I meant what I said earlier."

Erin's mind replayed the conversations of the evening, and she couldn't imagine what he was talking about. It must have shown on her face because Tyler grinned and shook his head.

"You've already forgotten. Wow. I don't make good impressions with beautiful women. I said I would take you out on a proper date."

It was as if the world had stopped turning, and everything froze. Erin barely heard his last sentence. *Did he say I'm beautiful?*

"So, yes or no?" Tyler crossed his arms.

"Uh, well…"

"Okay. Let me make this real proper. Will you go to dinner with me tomorrow? I'd enjoy spending more time with you."

Erin reached for a strand of hair blowing in the night breeze and stopped before pulling it toward her mouth. "Sure. I'd enjoy going out with you."

"Awesome. I can pick you up at 6:00. Would that be okay? Are you all right with me picking you up at your house? Some girls…"

"That'll be fine," Erin interrupted. "I'll send you my address. Oh, wait. I don't have your phone number."

Tyler reached for his phone. "You give me your number, and I'll call you right now from my phone."

Forty minutes later, Erin pulled into her driveway, sat in the car, and gazed into the starlit sky. The stars twinkled more, and the moon had to be brighter than ever. A guy had asked her out and had been so sweet about it.

The whole night had been enjoyable, and the only awkward part was the goodbye in the Barnes & Noble parking lot. They'd both stood at the back of his truck for a bit before moving toward her car. He opened her door. What were they supposed to do? Shake hands? The closest he came to anything intimate was touching her hand as she was about to get in her car.

Ryan's going to flip. I'm going on a date and didn't need his help. Could Tyler be the guy?

CHAPTER NINETEEN

The Real Thing

E rin handed change to a customer and checked her watch—again. It wasn't even noon, and she was going on a date in about six hours. Saying yes last night had seemed like such an easy thing, but as another wave of nausea hit, Erin doubted her decision.

I was way too impulsive. I shouldn't have agreed to go out.

She thought about her meeting with the lawyer and took a deep breath. *I cannot allow myself to think about marrying Tyler and having a baby. Going to Stone Mountain was just an enjoyable outing with a friend, and this is dinner with the same guy—no big deal.*

"So, like, are you going to ring me up, or what?"

Erin focused on the girl with green hair standing in front of her. "Oh, excuse me. I'm sorry." She took the book from the girl's hand and scanned it. Mr. Winslow approached the checkout desk, so it must be time for her break. Thank the Lord! A little time for regrouping would help.

As the afternoon crawled by, she convinced herself that going out with Tyler had nothing to do with getting married or having a baby. Ryan wasn't involved in this outing, so she was going out with a guy to have an enjoyable evening. The only problem was she'd never gone out with a guy as just a friend and didn't know what to do. Her dates with Greg had been far from fun.

Quitting time came, and the drive home took forever. Why were so many people driving south down I-75 on a

Saturday afternoon? *Maybe they all have dates, too. Would they need as much time to do their hair?*

After an eternity, Erin parked in her driveway and jumped out of the car. She pulled the house key from her pocket and dropped it between the cracks of the front porch boards. *Crap! Crap! Crap! Okay, breathe, Erin.*

Erin stepped into the flower bed near the door and reached for a small, fake rock. When she slid open the little trap door, nothing fell out.

"Where's the key?" The last time she'd used it, she must have taken it into the house. After racing from window to window, she finally discovered the bathroom window cracked open.

Erin eyed her neighbor's house and turned her attention back to the small bathroom window. The space beneath the window was more of a taunting leer than an opportunity for entrance. She'd have to be a gymnast to reach it.

She stacked several concrete blocks from her neighbor's yard and reached for the window. As she started pulling toward the open window, the blocks toppled, and she crashed onto the ground. Lying on her back, she noticed a nest covered with wasps above the window.

Can my day get any worse? It began to drizzle rain, and Erin stared into the sky. "Why now?"

Pulling the blocks back into place, Erin ensured their stability. The nest buzzed with activity above her head, but at least the pests were several feet higher than the window. "Okay, guys. You mind your own business, and I'll mind mine."

Once on top of the blocks, the windowsill was about chin high. Reaching up with both hands, she pushed open the window and heaved half her body inside. She grabbed hold of the top of the toilet, wiggled through, and screamed. "It stung me on my...Aaahh! That's two!" Erin jerked the rest of her body through and tumbled onto the floor. The little demons flew around just outside the window, so she scrambled to her feet and slammed the window shut.

Her phone buzzed, and Erin struggled to free it from her pocket.

"Hello." She glanced at the caller I.D. "Mr. Rakestraw." She listened for a minute. "Yes, sir. I dropped my key in the crack of the front porch and had to crawl through the window. Thanks for checking on me."

Erin couldn't help but smile, thinking about her elderly next-door neighbor calling to ensure she was okay. Now, she needed a quick exit strategy, or she'd be on the phone all night.

"Mr. Rakestraw, thanks so much for calling me, but I have an appointment. If I don't hurry, I'll be late. Thanks again for calling." She hung up while he was saying something about his Begonias. *Well, it can't be helped. I'll stop in and see him later.*

Erin's backside throbbed. *What do you do for a pair of wasp stings back there? I won't be able to sit.*

An hour later, as Erin attempted to put on mascara, the doorbell rang. Her hand froze in midair as she grimaced into the mirror.

I think I'm going to faint. After taking several deep breaths, she leaned in toward the mirror to inspect her handiwork. It would have to do. Hoping to meet Tyler's approval, she hurried to the front door.

Ryan suddenly popped into her head, and she could imagine exactly what he would say: "Buttercup, don't be worried; be confident. Your date should be honored to have the privilege of spending the evening with you. Now, put a smile on your face and open the door."

She reached for the doorknob and pulled the door open.

"Hey, Erin. You look...I don't know. Different? No, great. How's it going?"

Other than going out with Creep of the Year, I'm good. Wait. I look great? "Fine. How about you? No one ever said things like that except Ryan, who was blowing smoke. Of course, there was Chip. The memory of her night at the Omni Hotel was one experience she'd like to forget. Whatever that creep had said to her that night meant absolutely nothing.

When she was in elementary school, the other kids laughed at her and called her names. She had been called Carrot and Matchstick. One bully had called her Flame, and all the kids around her howled. Thankfully, her hair wasn't flaming red anymore.

"Hey, Tyler. Sorry to keep you waiting." *I may look great, but my rear end is frozen from sitting on an ice pack.*

Tyler held the front door open for her. "You didn't keep me waiting. Where do you want to go eat?"

Erin felt like a deer caught in headlights. "Uh, well, I don't care. I'm good with anything."

Tyler grinned. "I had a feeling you'd say that. Do you like LongHorn?"

"I love LongHorn." *I did eat there. Once. Four years ago.*

Mr. Rakestraw stood at his mailbox as Tyler pulled out of the driveway. The old man waved, and Erin wondered if he'd think she was a liar.

Going out with a guy was sort of like an appointment.

"How was your day?" Tyler asked.

Erin tucked a lock of hair behind her ear. "Boring," she lied again. The "father of lies" scripture came to mind. *No more lying, Erin.*

Once seated at the restaurant, Tyler insisted Erin try one of LongHorn's famous steaks. She'd never eaten a steak at a restaurant. Once the waitress came to the table, she suggested he go first. The smaller version of what Tyler wanted would work fine for her, so she ordered it.

"So, tell me about Erin Douglas," Tyler said as he reached for the knife to cut off a piece of bread.

Erin's smile disappeared. "Not much to tell. I've lived a boring life in a boring town for twenty-five boring years."

"Not true. Everyone's life is an exciting adventure that has either started or is about to begin. What's your adventure, Erin?"

Erin thought about it. *Let's see, getting dumped by my fiancé a month before my wedding, burying my father when he was way too young to die…Yeah, super exciting.*

"Well," she said as she twisted a strand of hair with her right hand. Ryan would tell her to quit playing with her hair. "Um, well," she repeated, dropping her hair back onto her shoulder, "I started back to school."

"Sounds like an exciting adventure to me. It took a lot of nerve to go back to college. What are you studying?"

"English literature. One day, I want to teach high school literature."

"I'm impressed. I suppose studying English lit and working at Barnes & Noble could go hand in hand. What about your family? You said your father died last year?"

"Yeah. Cancer. It was me, my mom, and my dad. I did have a little brother, but he died years ago."

"Oh, Erin. I'm sorry."

"Yeah. Well, it shouldn't have happened." Erin straightened her silverware. "It was my fault, at least, my father thought so. I should have taken my brother with me to Steak 'n Shake, but I didn't."

Erin couldn't believe she had opened up to Tyler. She'd never told anyone her brother's death was her fault. Not even Ryan. She felt exposed and vulnerable. *Tone it down, Erin.*

"Erin, no matter what anyone said, your brother's death was not your fault."

"I don't like talking about it. My father brought it up enough to last a lifetime."

"I don't like talking about my father, either."

"I didn't exactly say that," Erin defended herself. The less she talked about her pitiful family the better.

"You didn't have to. I can read between the lines."

Although Tyler was hesitant to talk about his father, Erin prodded him. He finally told her his painful story, though she was sure he had omitted many details. His father sounded like a piece of work. It's a wonder the man hadn't been arrested.

"My grandfather was okay, however. I lived with him 'til I was sixteen."

"Sixteen? You left home at sixteen?"

"Yeah. I had to leave Texas. I met a girl at the restaurant where I worked, and she moved to Georgia. I decided to follow her, but she didn't want anything to do with me once I got here."

The more Tyler talked the more Erin became absorbed in his story. It made her feel sad. Sad for him, but also for her. Guilt consumed her for the bad things she'd thought about her father through the years. Unlike Tyler, she had a father and a mother.

Tyler was such a sweet guy, and he'd been through a lot. From what he told her, his father was an alcoholic, and his grandfather was stern and didn't have much time for little boys.

He told her about enrolling in a GED program in Georgia so he had the equivalent of a high school diploma. Once, he enrolled in the community college but just took a few classes.

Erin checked her watch. How had two-and-a-half hours passed by so quickly?

They left the restaurant and drove to a nearby park, where they followed a walking path for more than a mile, talking about anything and everything. Somehow, talking to Tyler was so easy. She even admitted to once being engaged. Though the subject of her near marriage should have been off-limits, she told him anyway. The Erin Douglas history lesson didn't seem to faze him.

Once back in her driveway, Erin had a sudden thought. "Oh, shoot."

"What's wrong?" Tyler asked as he turned off the truck.

"Oh, it's nothing, really."

Tyler raised an eyebrow. "Erin, when I bring a lovely girl home at the end of an otherwise pleasant evening, and she suddenly blurts out 'Oh, shoot,' I've got to believe something's wrong."

Erin laughed. "Well, it's a long story, but I remembered I don't have a key to my house. I can get in. I just—"

"Do you have to crawl through a window?"

"Yeah. It's not a big deal." *Except I got double-tapped on the backside by wasps when I did it earlier.*

"I'll crawl through the window for you. I insist."

Erin protested, but he refused to listen. How could she stop him from taking a header into the bathroom?

Tyler exited the truck and opened her door. "Which window did you crawl through? Is it still unlocked?"

Erin shook her head again and wanted to crawl under a bush. She told him she'd seen a wasp nest above the bathroom window but didn't tell him she'd been stung.

"Nighttime is the best time to get rid of wasps," Tyler said. "I'll just need a stick."

En route to the backyard, he broke off part of a tree branch. He suggested she stand behind a tree while he knocked the wasp nest onto the ground and stomped on it.

Once Tyler climbed through the bathroom window, Erin cringed with thoughts of him walking through her house. Had she left clothes on the floor? Would Daphne be nice? She hurried around to the front of the house.

Tyler opened the front door, and Erin stepped inside.

"Thanks so much, Tyler. This whole night has been wonderful."

Tyler took her hands and gazed into her eyes. Her heart skipped a beat.

"I've had a great time. I hope we can do it again."

"Me, too," Erin said, fighting the urge to look down.

He grinned and turned to his truck. "See you tomorrow."

Forty-five minutes later, Erin lay in bed. Going out with Tyler had been so much fun. He had been a Christian for a year and attended church each Sunday. On top of that, he had agreed to go with her to Southpoint the following day.

Her phone buzzed, and she groaned. Her screen revealed she'd missed two phone calls from Ryan. She opened the text and rolled her eyes. "If you don't call me in the next five minutes, I'm coming over."

CHAPTER TWENTY

A Proper Date

E rin recalled her first date with Greg two years earlier. Ryan had hovered over her like a mother hen.

When Greg took her home, they sat in the car for an hour with fogged-up windows and numerous missed phone calls and texts. Erin had no idea; her phone was on silent.

Ryan's pounding fist had about given her a heart attack. No matter what she said, she couldn't convince Ryan that Greg's defrost was broken, and they were just talking.

While not at all funny then, the memory now made Erin smile.

Her smile turned to a frown when Julie Harwood's plump red lips and flawless skin came to mind. Erin hadn't heard anything about Greg and Julie since her relationship with Greg ended, and she wondered if they'd gotten married.

So, Ryan, the dating police, will be coming over if I don't call him? Reaching for her glasses and phone, she called Ryan and heard only one ring before his clipped voice sounded on the other end.

"Why are you ignoring me?"

"I'm trying to find a husband and have a baby if you don't mind."

"You're what?"

Erin shut her eyes and felt she might explode. Throwing off the covers, she swung her feet to the floor and stubbed her big toe on the nightstand.

Pain shot through her foot, and she sucked in air while leaning over to grab the bedside table. Her hand knocked a glass of water, spilling it all over the table and onto the floor.

"RYAN!"

"Calm down, Erin. What are you doing?"

"What *am* I doing, or what *was* I doing?" Erin yelled into the phone and focused on her bleeding toe. "I was lying in my bed trying to go to sleep. Now, I'm watching water spill over my nightstand and soak the carpet while blood gushes from my toe. What should I be doing this time of night?"

Erin retrieved a washcloth and towel. After throwing the towel on the wet carpet, she wrapped her toe with the rag and applied pressure. Her heart pounded. She'd never yelled at Ryan in the past.

"Ryan?"

Ryan answered. "I was worried about you, Erin. You always answer your phone."

Erin rubbed her eyes and ran her hand through her hair. She sucked in air through her clinched teeth and said, "I'm sorry, Ryan. I…I stubbed my toe and lost my temper."

"Wow!" Ryan laughed. "I'm impressed. You've had one self-defense class and already found your hidden aggressive side."

"Funny. Did you call me to harass me?"

"No, like I said, I got worried when I couldn't reach you. Is your toe really bleeding? Where have you been?"

Erin took a deep breath and berated herself for being the world's worst friend.

"Erin?"

"I've been on a date, and yes, my toe is bleeding."

"You've been where?"

"I know. Shocker, right? Freckle-face Matchstick got a date all on her own, without anyone's help. I'm stunned myself."

"Erin, you don't have freckles anymore…"

Erin found a Band-Aid in the drawer of her nightstand and put it on her wounded toe. "I should have gotten your permission, let you make all the arrangements, or, at least, had Tyler go through your interview process, but I kind of forgot about those details."

"Okay, Erin…"

"A good-looking, single guy wanting to go out with someone like me is the mystery of the century. Ranks up there with what happened to Amelia Earhart, but it happened."

Erin sucked in a breath and checked the screen to see if they'd been disconnected. "Ryan?"

"I'll call back tomorrow after you've had time to sleep off your attitude," Ryan said. "Goodnight, Erin."

Silence. "Ryan? You there?" Erin looked at the screen of her phone. "Ryan?"

Tossing her phone to the other side of the bed, Erin startled her cat that had somehow slept through the ordeal. Reaching over the bedside table, she turned out the lamp beside her bed and fell back on her pillow.

Why did I get so angry at him? He's only trying to help, and he cares about me.

She reached for her phone and pressed Ryan's number, which was still displayed on the screen. Ryan's phone rang a couple of times and stopped. "Ryan?"

"What?"

"I'm sorry. I'm a jerk and an ungrateful friend in desperate need of psychotherapy. Please forgive me."

Erin heard a heavy breath on the other end. "Erin, I could say so many things regarding our last conversation, but let's start with, how was your night?"

Erin grinned as she imagined Ryan trying to rein in his emotions. "My night was enjoyable. I didn't tell you about it because it wasn't a date. Technically, it was a date, but not really. We, you know, went to dinner. I took him to Stone Mountain last night for his birthday, and he was paying me back, so tonight was just payback, sort of."

"Either it was a date, or it wasn't. Stone Mountain?"

"Well, I suggested to Tyler, a guy from work, that we go there for his birthday last night. Then, he said he wanted to take me on a proper date."

"A proper date? He didn't think taking you to Stone Mountain was a proper date?"

"Not really. I suggested it because he didn't plan to celebrate. He's a lonely guy who needs a friend. I thought I'd be a friend."

"What did you do tonight?"

"We went to LongHorn and then took a walk in the park. It was lovely."

Erin stopped and took a deep breath. "Ryan?"

"Sorry, Erin, I'm speechless and proud of you."

Your new, favorite line. Am I supposed to glow now that you're proud of me? Heat radiated from her face. Was she glowing?

"Thanks. We had a pleasant evening, and we're meeting at church in the morning."

"Sounds like you're off to a perfect start, Erin. I had been working on someone else, but I'll give it a break and see how this thing with Tom goes."

"Tyler."

"Yeah, Tyler. Sorry to have disturbed your beauty sleep. Talk soon."

Erin placed her phone on the nightstand and nestled under the covers. Having a friend like Ryan was a real blessing. If not for him, she wouldn't have anyone except her mother, and her mom didn't count. Ryan had been bossy and overprotective since middle school, but he was still her best friend.

Middle school was the worst. As an awkward, red-headed kid, she couldn't combine two meaningful sentences when boys were around. Then, of course, there were the bullies. Christopher Nichols came to mind. He always had it out for her and thrived on cutting her down.

One day, in the lunchroom, he strutted over to where Erin sat—alone as usual.

"So, what are you doing Friday night, Flame?" Christopher's smug eyes leered at her.

The middle school dance was on Friday night, and everyone was going, everyone except her. She struggled to think of an excuse for not attending the dance but ended up staring at the white, whipped goo that was supposed to be mashed potatoes.

"She's going to the dance, Bozo," Ryan said as he dropped his tray onto the table beside Erin.

Since Ryan had gained popularity as the middle school football team quarterback, he ate with the cool kids. Now and then, though, he left the popular table to join her.

Erin looked up to see the *Yeah, Right* expression on Christopher's face. A hush had fallen over the lunchroom as her schoolmates tried to digest this late-breaking news about Flame Douglas.

Ryan took Erin's hand. "She's going to the dance with me. What are YOU doing Friday night, Loser?"

Reports about what happened spread like wildfire. The consensus was that Erin was a charity case, and Ryan was like a protective brother. Erin ended up getting a stomach bug on Friday morning and couldn't attend the dance.

A lot had changed since middle school, but Ryan was still around and was as protective as usual. Erin reached for her phone again and set the alarm to ring early. Riding her bike in the mornings was more than a ritual. It had become a passion, so she couldn't skip it. Tomorrow would be…memorable? She had never met a guy for church except for Ryan.

Tyler was a different kind of guy. He'd hesitated to tell his story but eventually opened up. He'd described his life, being dumped by a girlfriend a few years ago, and his anger toward his family.

One day while fishing at Lake Lanier, Tyler made a new friend, who happened to be a minister. Tyler told Erin about the significant difference his friend had made in his life. He may still have some unresolved issues with his father, but she didn't think he was angry anymore.

I'd like to meet that pastor who befriended him.

Erin reached over and rubbed her sleeping cat. Daphne had it made. She didn't have a thing to worry about.

God will supply all your needs according to His riches. "Whoa! Where did that come from?" Erin asked out loud. Daphne raised her head and regarded Erin before closing her eyes again.

"Sorry, Girl," Erin whispered.

Weird. Like God put a Bible verse in my mind?

Compared to many people, she had it made. God had provided for her every step of the way. He'd even had His hand in her doomed relationship with Greg. *Greg was bad for me. God knows what He's doing.*

Erin closed her eyes. She didn't need to worry about marriage, babies, or anything else. God was in control.

God will supply my needs according to His riches.

CHAPTER TWENTY-ONE

Identity Theft

The worship band wrapped up the last song before the message, and Erin sat and thought about the lyrics, "We will overcome." What did the guy who wrote them have to overcome? Erin had a long list, starting with herself. Ryan had told her a million times, "You are your own worst enemy, Buttercup." He was right.

Ryan had dropped the Buttercup moniker, but the rest of the statement was true. How could she not be hard on herself when she was always doing stupid things? Erin wiped a tear running down her cheek and hoped Tyler wouldn't notice.

Pastor Brant began his message about identity theft, and she wondered where he was going with this idea. Identity theft was a big deal these days. She remembered hearing millions were at risk when a credit reporting company was hacked. Was someone trying to steal her identity?

"We have an enemy far greater than whoever might hack into the credit card company or department store records," the pastor said. "Our spiritual enemy works hard to keep us from realizing our true identity in Christ."

He began to teach from the book of Psalms, which was one of Erin's favorite books in the Bible. The verse he mentioned, however, wasn't familiar. "Keep me as the apple of your eye; hide me in the shadow of your wings."

The apple of God's eye?

By the end of the service, Erin felt sure the preacher had been watching her life for years and wrote that sermon for her. She felt raw. Exposed. But also loved and valued. How God could know everything about her and still cherish her was beyond her comprehension.

Pastor Brant had insisted she was not only cherished but protected. The Psalmist used the imagery of being sheltered under a wing to describe the believers' security.

After the message, Tyler slid his pen into his pocket, and Erin noticed his note page was covered with words. He'd been touched by the sermon as well. She considered their potential conversation about the service and decided she preferred to process the message alone.

Tyler leaned over as the worship team sang the final song and asked her to lunch. *Oh, brother. I knew he was going to do that. I'd rather be alone, but I can't say no. What would he think?*

Erin squeezed through the crowd at the front counter of the restaurant and followed Tyler to a table. Pulling the top off the little tub of red beans and rice, Erin eyed Tyler as he readied his meal. Her stomach growled.

Tyler grinned. "Looks like we got here just in time. So, what did you think of the sermon?"

Why did he have to bring up the sermon? She would have been more comfortable talking about their unhealthy meal or the Brave's losing streak—like she knew anything about base-ball.

"Uh, well…"

"I'll tell you what I thought. I thought he had been reading a journal I've been writing all my life."

"You keep a journal?"

Tyler chuckled. "No, but if I did, I would write things in it like the preacher was talking about this morning."

"Like what, Tyler?"

"Like I have a chip on my shoulder, for one thing. My anger toward my father has made me a bitter person."

Erin was stunned at Tyler's transparency. "You don't seem bitter to me."

"Oh, I am. I've hidden it around you so far but give me time. I'm sure it'll surface. God didn't make me bitter, and I should love others."

"It's hard to love others when you're angry with them," Erin agreed. "You should try to put yourself in the other person's shoes. Maybe you could see things from their perspective."

"Sounds easy, but..."

"Who makes you the angriest? Let me guess—your father."

"You got it. I've never told anyone this because I'm ashamed, but I hate my father. I'm bothered about it because I know that love for God and hate for others can't live in the same heart. I'm not sure what to do about it."

"I used to struggle with bad feelings for my father. Maybe, I shouldn't say *used to*. Even though he's dead, I still do sometimes. Prayer has helped me a lot. A couple of years ago, I started praying for my father. Hate and prayer can't live in the same heart either. I discovered I'd have to make a choice: quit hating my father or stop praying for him. I didn't stop praying."

Tyler shook his head. "I don't want to pray for my father. I know that sounds bad."

"I understand. Why don't you start by praying about your father? God already knows what you think, so you may as well be honest with Him. Over time, prayers *about* your father will turn into prayers *for* your father."

Tyler sat quietly for a bit and then nodded his head. "Pray about my father instead of for my father? I can do that. How did you get to be so smart about spiritual things? You should become a counselor."

Erin's face glowed. She wasn't smart about spiritual things and had struggled with her own nightmare of heartache and sorrow. Counseling was the last thing she should pursue, but she had learned valuable life lessons from her circumstances. Before her father passed away, she had spent a whole year praying about him before asking God to help him cope with whatever issues had turned him into a critical person.

"I couldn't be a counselor," Erin insisted. "I've got my own issues. The fact is that sermon was for me, too. Even though I prayed for my father for a while before he died, I still battled negative feelings about him." She jabbed at a few vegetables in her Styrofoam bowl. "My problem is a little different than yours. You rebelled against the words of your father. I've accepted my father's words as true, though they were hurtful. I always feel like such a disappointment."

Tyler grinned over his drink. "Now, Erin Douglas, remember what the preacher said. Sounds like someone's trying to steal your identity. Pastor…what's his name?"

"Brant."

"Pastor Brant said, 'God makes you a winner, not a loser.'"

Erin nodded. "Remember, I said he was preaching to me, too. I've been viewed my whole life as the world's greatest underachiever. Being the dumbest and ugliest kid in school didn't help. I could never do anything right in my father's eyes."

"You're not ugly, Erin. I think you're…"

"Refresh your drink, ma'am?"

Erin saw the employee standing next to their table, and she knew the girl had said something to her, but she couldn't turn her attention away. *I'm what, Tyler? You think I'm…*

"Ma'am, would you like more to drink?"

"Uh," Erin hesitated, "sure."

"So, what do you have going on the rest of the day?" Tyler asked.

I don't want to talk about the rest of my day. I want to know what you were about to say before that girl interrupted you.

"I've planned an exciting day of washing clothes and cleaning my house," Erin said. "I have to work the next five days, so I figured I'd finish all my chores before the crazy week starts. I also have small group. You want to come? To small group? I don't think you want to help me wash clothes."

"I'm pretty adept at the laundromat if you like pink underwear."

Pink underwear? Her eyes dropped to her food, and heat crawled up the back of her neck. He'd seen her clothes on the bathroom floor the previous day.

"I somehow managed to wash a new red shirt once," Tyler continued, "and everything came out with a nice shade of pink. I had to throw away most of it. Pink isn't bad, but I have limits."

Erin laughed and relaxed. She had to quit being so uptight. "So, small group? Do you want to go?"

"Oh, well, sure. I like hanging out with you."

"You do? I mean, well, I—I mean, I'm not really…"

"Erin, don't let the thief steal your identity. You're awesome, smart, and beautiful. And you're not hung up on yourself. I'm so glad you suggested we go to Stone Mountain on Friday."

Erin melted. "Me, too."

Erin floated into her house a while later. The music in her head drowned out Daphne's insistent meowing and begging for food. Erin fell back onto the soft recliner, and Daphne jumped onto her lap.

"I'm awesome, smart, and beautiful, Daphne. He's lying or blind, but I've waited my whole life to hear those words. Ryan says stuff like that, but he doesn't count."

Daphne meowed and inched up Erin for a neck snuggle. Leaning her chair back, Erin closed her eyes and wrapped her arms around her fuzzy best friend.

"So, someone may have considered me smart, but beauty hasn't been attainable except in my wildest dreams." The familiar wet sandpaper of Daphne's tongue on her neck made Erin giggle. "Quit licking me. Okay, earth to Erin. Wash clothes, or you'll be late for small group."

Two hours later, the dryer dinged. Erin pulled the fresh-smelling mound out of the machine and dumped it onto the couch. She hated folding clothes. Grabbing her phone, she said Ryan's name and moments later heard his familiar voice.

"Hey, gorgeous. How was church with a new man?"

Erin didn't like to think about church with a man. Worshipping had a more important purpose. Having a new male friend with her in church, however, had been a refreshing bonus.

"The service was really inspiring, Ryan. You should've come."

"I went across town. Going to your church with your new boyfriend would have been a little awkward."

Erin rolled her eyes. "He's not my boyfriend, Ryan. Next thing you know, you'll have us married and pregnant."

"That's the objective, though, right?"

"An instant family can happen on reality TV, but it won't work for me. This marriage and baby thing is more than I can do or want to do. I want to take time to get to know Tyler. If he's right, God will show us if and when we should marry."

"I hear what you're saying, Buttercup, but your father's offer doesn't make time an option."

"So, I'm Buttercup again?"

"Oh, sorry. Force of habit."

"Ryan, my life and future are far more important than a pharmaceutical company and a pile of cash."

"Of course, my dear, but a multi-million-dollar company and a ton of cash could make the unknown future more tolerable. Just test the waters, but let your test be quick. If he's right, I'll help him pop the question."

"Ryan, please stay out of this. Please don't mess up a good thing. He's going with me to small group, so let's take this one step at a time."

"Step one: go to church. Step two: go to small group. Step three: meet with the preacher for a few vows. And step four: buy a pregnancy test."

"Ryan, you have a way of making something sacred sound like something dirty."

"Calling it as I see it, and I don't want you to miss out on the pot at the end of the rainbow. I've never thought of sex as sacred."

"Well, it is. God invented it and even wrote a book about it in the Bible. You shouldn't degrade something so holy. I'd rather you not talk about it at all. Let's see where things go, and I'll decide whether I'll hurry the process based on our relationship, so don't start the celebration yet. From my perspective, I'm going to be a poor single woman a year from now."

"A lot can happen in a short period. Think of *The Little Mermaid*."

"*The Little Mermaid?*"

"The Disney movie."

"I know what it is. I'm surprised you do."

"I have a niece, remember?"

"Oh, yeah, I forgot."

"Well, Ariel made it all happen in a weekend. You've got skills, too, my love. Just put 'em to use."

Erin snorted as she dug through the pile for a matching sock. "I'll start looking for my dinglehopper."

"Was a dinglehopper the pipe?"

"Sounds like you may need to watch *The Little Mermaid* again. It was a fork she used as a brush. Ryan, I need to put up my clean clothes and go to group. I don't need or want to discuss skills you think I have. Next time, we'll talk about your love life."

"Oh, my dear, that's a subject so vast it would take us hours. Your love life is much more interesting."

"I'll keep that in mind, but I think we should consider this challenge of finding me a husband hopeless. Let's drop it."

"I'm not dropping anything except the garter Tyler shoots toward me on your wedding day."

"Goodbye, Ryan. Go watch *The Little Mermaid*."

Erin closed her phone and eyed her open laptop beside the couch. She logged into her social media account and saw a friend request. *Emily Simpson? Haven't met her.*

Erin clicked on the request and scanned Emily's page. Emily lived in McDonough but was new to town. Chelsey invited this girl to group, and she's friends with Amy, too. Erin should accept her request. Why not? Making a new friend wasn't a bad idea.

CHAPTER TWENTY-TWO

Coaching

The gym smelled like a mixture of sweat, plastic, and perfume. Erin stuffed her purse into one of the lockers and scanned the rubber exercise mat. She had dreaded her first session, but now, she enjoyed these classes. *I've got this.*

Ryan was already beginning his stretching routine when Erin stepped onto the mat. He was more focused, however, on the cute blonde beside him. Erin sat a safe distance away but tuned into Ryan's conversation to see if he scored for the weekend.

The stiffness in her legs slowly began to dissipate with a butterfly stretch, and Erin winced when Ryan began to talk about his position at Gatner. *Ryan, don't talk about yourself. Note to self: talk to Ryan about his arrogance.*

The girl twisted and turned almost entirely away from him. *Doesn't he get it?*

"Good evening," Tim said from the front of the room. "I hope you've had a relaxing weekend and are ready for our third session."

The instructor's eyes roved over the group and paused as he met Erin's gaze.

"Some of you missed Thursday night," he continued. "You'll find a video of the second class online. Catch me before you leave, and I'll give you the password."

Ryan gave Erin a curt nod before glancing at the blonde. Erin wanted to throw something at him. *Stop trying to play with the Barbie doll and focus on why we're here.*

"While you're all stretching and warming up," Tim continued, "I want to review three important safety tips. These tips come from one of our core values: Common sense before self-defense. Turn to your partner and tell her, or him, the first thing that comes to mind when you hear our first core value."

Ryan leaned toward the blonde, but the beauty moved from him toward another girl. Erin scooted toward her friend.

"Wow, crash and burn," Erin whispered with a wry grin. "I wanted to watch you in action. I'm amazed your skills aren't as proficient as I anticipated."

"My skills, dear, are acute. I'm just getting warmed up."

Erin jabbed him in the ribs. "If you say so, but you may need to hear my opinion first. My opinion is tied to our course values. Common sense says you don't always think of yourself. If you try to pick up a woman while making yourself the focus, she'll use a little self-defense on you, like run away."

"Cute, Erin."

"I'll take cute. That's certainly an improvement."

The instructor stepped back in front of the group. "I hope you had a meaningful discussion. Here are the three rules. First, always remain aware of your surroundings. You can avoid bad situations by staying aware of what's happening around you. Remember, the object of self-defense is safety, not engagement."

Erin eyeballed a muscle-bound guy across the gym. His biceps flexed as he crossed his arms. He didn't appear to want to avoid a bad situation.

"Second," Tim said, "always stay in well-lit areas. Doesn't matter if you're a man or a woman. Don't set yourself up to be mugged. Finally, don't put yourself in any situation you don't want to be in."

Erin leaned toward Ryan and whispered, "Does that mean going out with a guy so he can become the father of my baby?"

"It's easy to let someone talk you into doing something or going somewhere because you don't want to be a killjoy," Tim continued. "If you're uncomfortable going to someone's car or following him somewhere, don't. Listen to your inner voice. Your inner voice may become your best friend."

Ryan whispered, "Your inner voice is not speaking very clearly, so you should listen to mine."

"Let's gather in a circle," Tim said. "I want to show you another important move."

The group gathered around their instructor, and Erin noticed only two men had signed up. The rest were women.

"Imagine someone comes up behind you and grabs you in a bear hug," Tim said. "Erin, do you mind assisting me?"

The blood drained from Erin's face. Why did he have to call on her? Ryan's hand pushed on her back.

"Can you wrap your arms around me like you're the bad guy?" Tim asked as Erin made it to the center of the circle.

Wrapping her arms around Tim's firm body, she heard a girl whisper to someone else in the group, "I'm happy to volunteer next time."

"Okay, Erin," Tim instructed, "hold me tight like you're trying to hurt me."

Erin squeezed his body with all her strength and felt his muscles tighten.

"Your first goal is to inflict pain so you can break his grasp and escape."

"What if you don't want to escape?" one girl asked, and the group snickered.

Tim ignored her and continued, "Take a deep breath so your chest expands. Next, you'll do several things in quick succession. Drop your chin and blow out air while, at the same time, move downward. I'll demonstrate it. Hold me tight, Erin."

Erin squeezed harder and felt his muscular chest expand. Before she could think about it, Tim had dropped down through her arms and held her right arm.

"Grab your assailant's arm near the wrist and give him a swift kick to the groin. You could go all the way around and push your palm into his elbow, but a groin kick is more effective. Once you kick the guy, run. Now, pair up and try this move. Thanks, Erin."

Erin left the center of the circle and rejoined Ryan. Before she could say anything, Ryan wrapped her in a firm hold from behind. His warm body was hard from regular workouts. He smelled good.

Before he could say anything, Erin dropped straight down. She slipped from his grasp, grabbed his wrist, and turned his arm. As her foot traveled toward its destination, Erin watched Ryan's eyes bulge with fear.

She stopped before making contact.

"Impressive, Erin," Tim called from across the room.

Ryan rubbed his shoulder. "Uh…you're a fast learner."

"Did I hurt you?" Erin allowed a flicker of a smile.

"I'm fine. Now, you grab me."

Erin wrapped her arms around Ryan, but he was a bit taller than Tim, so it felt like her arms were around his abdomen instead of his chest. This wasn't going to be as easy for Ryan. Within seconds, however, he was out of her grasp and had pulled her into his arms.

"You're supposed to kick me, dummy, not hug me."

"But you're adorable. I can't even pretend to kick you."

"Okay, guys," Tim called above the noise in the room, "I want to show you more ways to get away from an assailant, and you need to learn about the Superman Pluck."

Two hours later, Erin stepped out of the shower and wrapped a towel around her wet hair. The faint sound of her phone buzzing in the bedroom drifted through the open door. Only Ryan would call this late.

While wiping water from her eyes, she found her phone and pulled it to her ear. "Hey, Ryan."

"Erin? It's Tyler. Hope I'm not calling too late."

"Tyler?" Erin fumbled the phone before pulling it back to her ear. "No, it's never too late."

I can't believe I said that. Am I a pitiful high school girl begging for a date? No, just a lonely single woman begging for a husband.

"I've called a few times, so I figured you were still at the gym."

Erin checked her phone and saw the missed calls. *Shoot. How did I miss three calls?* "Yeah, well, Ryan and I stopped for coffee on our way home. I told you about Ryan, didn't I?"

"Yeah. Best friend, right?"

My only friend, except now maybe you're number two. Well, there is Susan. "Yeah. I had to give him a few pointers on picking up women." *Idiot. What is wrong with you?*

Tyler laughed on the other end, and Erin wondered if his laugh was from more relief than humor. *It is funny to think of me giving anyone advice about anything.*

"How was your first day of class yesterday? Didn't you start back to school?"

"Oh, yes. I did. It was brutal. A Monday-only, four-hour class. I hope I can handle it."

"You'll handle it fine, I'm sure."

Erin sat on the edge of her bed. "We'll see. I figured it would help me keep my full-time hours at work."

"I looked at the schedule today and saw we both work the same shift tomorrow. Would you like to catch a movie after work and grab something to eat?"

Is he asking me out again? "Uh, well, sure. I mean, I need to check my full schedule first. Let's see, I have to feed the cat and clean the bathroom, but I think we could squeeze in a movie and dinner."

"Perfect. I bet your cat won't mind waiting for his meal. Or is it her?"

"He is. I mean, she is." Erin inhaled and exhaled. "My cat's a she. Daphne."

Tyler chuckled. "Okay, sweet. How about tomorrow night?"

"Yeah. Thanks. I'm looking forward to it."

"Well, you and Daphne get some rest. I'll see you in the morning."

Erin headed to the kitchen and heated some water for tea. Before her call from Tyler, she'd been sleepy, but now, she might be awake all night. Tim had recommended the video from the previous session. Since sleep didn't seem to be in her near future, she might as well go ahead and watch it.

Erin added milk to her tea. She'd once watched a British television show, and they all used milk in their tea. As the hot, creamy liquid touched her lips, she closed her eyes and savored the flavor. "Bloody good."

She tied her robe tighter, headed for her favorite spot on the couch, and booted up her computer. Trying self-defense moves alone would be counter-productive, but watching the video would at least be informative.

According to her mother, Erin was a biter as a kid. When she was in elementary school, she'd punched a few people, including the bully in the boy's bathroom who was trying to beat up Ryan. Something changed in middle school, however. She'd become an introvert. Sneaking into empty schoolrooms to eat lunch alone became more common than going to the cafeteria.

Erin paused the video because she had no idea what she'd watched. *Why did I turn into a recluse in middle school?* Bullies picked on her, and kids made fun of her, but one event stuck out as significant.

She had been walking down the hallway near her parents' bedroom, and their door had been left ajar. Her name came drifting through the crack, so she paused to listen.

"I don't know how Erin ended up being such a loser, Francine," her father's gruff voice reverberated in the hollowness of her heart. "We've given her every opportunity, but she wouldn't recognize an opportunity if it slapped her in the face."

"Fred, don't be so hard on her. She'll grow out of this stage."

"If I'm not hard on her, she'll never grow into anything except obscurity."

With tears running down her face, Erin had managed to slip quietly down the hall.

Now, thirteen years later, the words pierced her as if they'd been spoken today. She reached up to wipe away fresh tears.

Loser? Why didn't he love me? Was I really so contemptable when I was twelve years old? Maybe Daddy was the one with the problem and not me.

Pastor Brant's Sunday sermon came to mind. He said God always saw her as a ten, not a one. "The enemy wants to destroy your sense of worth, but God thought you were so valuable He sent His Son to die for your sins." The pastor's voice was so clear it was as if he stood beside her in the living room.

Erin closed her eyes and repeated the first part of one of the few Bible verses she knew. "For God so loved the world that He gave!" She closed her eyes and prayed, "The enemy wants to destroy me because he is a thief. You must really love me since you sent your Son to die for me. Please help me do like Pastor Brant said Sunday and claim my identity in Jesus." She leaned back on the couch as fresh tears trickled down her cheeks.

Two hours later, Erin awoke with a start. It took her a moment to realize she'd fallen asleep. The computer remained in her lap, and Daphne lay in a ball on a pillow beside her. The cat opened a sleepy eye. "Daff, looks like we both fell asleep. Let's go to bed. I've got a date tomorrow."

Slipping beneath the sheets, Erin closed her eyes and tried falling back asleep. Thoughts of her time with Tyler made sleep impossible. For the first time, she imagined spending the rest of her life with him. He said he had bitterness issues, but she couldn't see them. He was intelligent, kind, and gentle. On top of that, he was a believer, and it didn't hurt that he was handsome in a Texas cowboy kind of way. Brilliant, even. She might fulfill her father's final wishes after all.

Would she be a good mother? A sense of dread and fear began to stir within her. She didn't know how to be a mother.

Erin had to turn off her brain. Motherhood was her last concern at the moment. A few other things still needed to happen first.

She rolled over and stroked Daphne's black fur. What would it be like to be Mrs. Tyler Matthews?

CHAPTER TWENTY-THREE

Ragamuffin

Wednesdays at Barnes & Noble were usually quiet days, but this one proved beyond crazy. The store manager had worked with the city council to promote literacy and wanted to sponsor a book festival and offer significant discounts. The festival didn't start until Friday, but several employees worked overtime to prepare.

Shoppers filed into the store all day while employees prepared for the weekend. Erin spent most of the day unpacking shipments of extra books and sorting the new merchandise.

Though Erin and Tyler had little interaction throughout the day, everything seemed fine at first. As the day progressed, he became more preoccupied. By late afternoon, his mind was somewhere else. Was he having second thoughts about going out?

A couple of hours before their shift ended, Tyler entered the large storage room where Erin sorted books. "Erin, Mr. Winslow asked if you could help me unload the truck."

"Sure."

"The boss is impressed with your progress sorting these books."

"I can't say it's been my favorite day working here, but I'm excited about the festival. It may be a little crazy, but it should be exciting."

Tyler still appeared distracted. He wouldn't hold Erin's gaze, and she knew something was wrong.

"Are you okay, Tyler? You're not yourself."

"I'm fine."

Liar.

"I have a few things on my mind. Come on. Let's unload the truck."

Tyler handed Erin a box from the crate, which she placed onto the hand truck. Erin blushed when his knuckles grazed hers, but Tyler wasn't fazed.

"You still good with going out?" Erin asked.

Tyler let go of the hand truck and turned to Erin. "Of course. It will be the highlight of my day."

Am I reading him wrong? Erin had no idea what was going on, but the smile he gave her made her whole body tingle. "I must look like a sight, but since we're working late, I don't think I'll have time to go home and clean up."

"You're a sight, all right, Erin Douglas, but not a bad sight. Consider what movie you want to see, and we can discuss it over dinner."

Erin watched him push the books toward the sorting area. She had clean clothes in her gym bag in the car, so she could change into a fresh top.

I'm a sight but not a bad one?

Once off work, Tyler led Erin across the parking lot and opened the passenger door of his truck. He helped her climb onto the front seat. Trucks seemed to sit higher off the road than in the past. Her father had driven a truck, but his was fifteen years old and closer to the ground. Erin had a hunch that bigger trucks tapped into the typical male macho image. Men were so hard to understand.

Tyler slid behind the steering wheel. "I know of an Italian restaurant not far from here."

"Perfect. I like Italian."

"Did you decide on a movie? I pulled up a list of current movies from the Regal Cinemas."

Erin liked that Tyler had chosen the restaurant and had already considered the movie. She didn't need a wishy-washy husband who couldn't make up his mind. *Husband? So weird.*

Tyler handed her his iPhone, and she scrolled through the movie options. Two interesting movie trailers jumped off the screen. *God Bless the Broken Road* seemed the best option, though she also wanted to see *Incredibles 2.*

I should watch a cartoon alone in case he thinks it's immature. Then there's also the Rich Mullins rerun I want to see.

"How about *Ragamuffin*? It's a movie about Rich Mullins. My youth group used to sing his song, 'Awesome God,' when I was growing up. He wrote a lot of Christian music in the 80s and 90s, but I don't know much about him except that he was killed in a car accident. Have you seen it?"

"Nope. I'm unfamiliar with him, but 'Awesome God' is an amazing song. *Ragamuffin* sounds good."

Erin cried numerous times during the movie. The scenes with Rich Mullins' father made her think of her father. Hiding her tears was difficult, and she saw a tear or two on Tyler's cheek as well.

At the end of the movie, Erin felt spent and sad. God had used Mullins to write incredible music, but he also struggled with his demons. She felt convicted to deal with her issues to avoid spending her life struggling.

Erin prayed before she and Tyler left their seats: *I don't want my past to determine my future. I surrender it to you, God, and ask you to heal my brokenness.*

As they headed out of the theater, Erin zoned out. She needed to get home to process her feelings.

Tyler's voice brought Erin out of her reverie. "It's late, but would you like to go for coffee? I need to talk about something, and you're my only friend."

"Sure." While happy to be considered a friend, Erin worried about Tyler. This issue must have been what had him in a funk all day.

Tyler slipped his hand into hers and pulled her through the mass of people. *Is he holding my hand or just helping me through this crowd?*

His statement reverberated in her mind. *You're the only friend I have.* Two damaged souls pushed together by the currents of life. Was it only a brief connection, or would it be something permanent that would last the rest of their lives?

When they got to the coffee shop, the place was filled with people even though it was a bit late. They sat across from one another with hot, steaming cups on the table in front of them. Something significant was about to happen. Tyler had not dropped her hand after leaving the crowded theater.

"Erin, I do not doubt God brought you into my life at a critical time. The very fact you picked *Ragamuffin* was providential."

Erin felt stunned and humbled to think God was somehow using her. As she gave Tyler her full attention, his eyes held unshed tears.

"I've told you about my relationship with my father," he said. "That movie could have been about me, at least, the part about his father-son relationship. I needed to see it."

"I thought the same thing about myself," Erin admitted. "I kept seeing a little girl in those scenes, and the girl was me."

"Well, it goes even deeper for me now," Tyler said. "Earlier today, you asked if I was okay. I'm not, so I suppose I lied when I told you I was fine. I checked my messages a little bit ago and had one from a man who said he was my father's pastor."

"Your father's pastor?"

Tyler nodded. "Yeah. For starters, I doubted my father had a pastor. I almost didn't return the call." Tyler pulled his cup to his lips.

Erin thought back to Tyler's behavior change earlier in the day. This phone call explained it. "So, you called him back?" Erin prompted.

"Yes, I called him back. He's from a small nondenominational church in the town where my father lives. He said my father had been attending services for a couple of years and had become a Christian."

"That's wonderful, Tyler. I'm surprised your dad hasn't reached out to you."

Tyler inspected his coffee cup for a long moment before replying. "He has, Erin. The thing is, I've gotten calls from my father through the years, but I always ignore them. I delete his voicemails without listening to them."

"I see," Erin said, her eyes glued to his. "Well, I understand why you wouldn't want to talk to him. He hurt you."

"The pastor told me my father is dying of cancer. He thought I would want to know and suggested I come to see my dad and consider taking care of him."

Erin's heart sank. Besides Ryan, Tyler was the first guy she'd felt so comfortable with. Now, it sounded like he was leaving. However, caring for his father was right, and moving toward reconciliation would honor the Lord, but...

"The problem is," Tyler continued, "I don't want to move back and take care of him. I can't wipe away all the years of hurt after one phone call." Tyler threw up his hands in frustration. "Part of me is angry he became a Christian. I always wanted him to burn in hell."

Erin closed her eyes. She'd had the same desire for her father.

Tyler took a deep breath. "It's horrible, but..."

To her surprise, Erin reached across the table and grasped Tyler's hand. "Don't be ashamed of those feelings, Tyler. They're not right, but they came out of your struggle. It's what you do with those feelings now that matters. The fact you admitted them to me is huge."

"I'm not sure I can forgive my father. I'm afraid time and hurt have made me so bitter toward him."

Erin thought of her struggles with her father and understood. She'd worked through similar feelings and still battled some issues. Now, however, her father was dead. Making things right with him was impossible.

"Tyler, I once heard a guy on a podcast say bitterness is like acid in the heart. It will only destroy you. He said God loves you so much that He wants you to forgive others. While it might help someone else if you forgive them, it first helps you."

Tyler closed his eyes before turning his coffee cup in his hand. "I don't think I'll ever feel right toward my father."

"It's not really about feelings. I've also heard that forgiveness is first a choice of the will before it becomes a choice of the heart. I've experienced this personally, Tyler. I'm not saying I've got it all figured out. I still struggle with some residual stuff, but when I decided to forgive my father, my feelings for him started to change. I think you'll find the same thing to be true."

Tyler smiled. "I've got a lot to think about and some decisions to make." He squeezed her hand and released it. "I suppose I better take you home, Erin, but thanks for being my friend and willing to speak the truth."

CHAPTER TWENTY-FOUR

Divine Appointment

Erin went to work on Thursday, expecting a hectic day. Not only did she have to work an entire shift, but she also had to start two online courses when she got off, which meant she'd have to miss her self-defense class.

School stressed her out, and she had never taken online courses. Taking a one-day-a-week class that met for four hours might lead to the end of her sanity. This semester would be a real test. *I'm going to graduate in May if it kills me.*

When she arrived at work, the place was already hopping. Though the store hadn't opened yet, employees scurried around like ants in a disturbed anthill. Tyler didn't come in until 1:00. Erin figured they wouldn't have much time to talk, but she wanted to know if he'd made any decisions concerning his father.

Tyler walked through the door a few minutes before 1:00 and came straight to her cash register where she rang up a customer. Dark circles cradled his eyes. Although it was cute, Erin wanted to reach over and smooth down some of that wild hair sticking up.

Erin read the customer's credit card before handing her the bag of books. "Thank you, Mrs. Davidson."

Tyler leaned toward Erin. "Today will be crazy, but can we talk during my break? Don't you get off at 5:00?"

"Yes, 5:00. I have an online class tonight, and I'm supposed to log in for an introduction video at 7:00."

"If I take my break at 5:00, could you hang around a minute? We could go over to Arby's. I'll treat."

"Sure, Tyler. Are you okay?"

Tyler shrugged. "I suppose. I didn't sleep at all last night."

"Yeah, my powers of perception are amazing."

Tyler smiled. "Wow. I didn't know I'd been dating a superhero."

Another customer walked up to the counter, and three more got in line with stacks of books. Tyler rushed off as Erin greeted the next customer.

Four hours later, Erin dipped a curly fry into ketchup as she watched Tyler walk toward the soda fountain. She hadn't eaten much, and Tyler didn't seem to be too eager to talk about whatever was on his mind. *Good news or bad news?* The latter seemed more likely.

Memories of the night her mother revealed her father had stage 4 colon cancer flooded her mind. Her mom had insisted they'd fight it and win. Erin realized now it had been hopeless, and her mom was presenting false bravado. In the end, they lost.

Erin's fragile world had started collapsing around her.

She would forever struggle with why her father hadn't sought to get his spiritual life in order before his death. Erin invited her father to church many times, but he hadn't been interested. When a person knew he was dying, preparing to meet God should be first on his mind.

Pastor Brant visited him several times in the hospital, and the pastor told Erin they had a healthy conversation about spiritual things. *Did Daddy become a Christian before he died? I hope so.* If she knew he was a Christian, his death would be negative and positive, but Erin would have peace.

Tyler arrived back at the table. The floor moved with his bouncing knee, and he couldn't quit fidgeting with the napkins. The food on his plate sat untouched. Nervous or uncomfortable? Lost.

"Erin, I'm not sure how to start. Returning to Texas is the last thing I want to do, but I feel like not going back would be the most selfish thing in the world."

Erin struggled to keep the look on her face warm and supportive. The last thing Tyler needed was to see her disappointment with the idea of him leaving. Somehow, her advice had to remain neutral so whatever he decided would be his decision.

"I struggled with it for a long time last night," Tyler continued, "and I thought a lot about what you said."

Erin wrinkled her brow. "Um, well, we said a lot of things last night, Tyler. What specifically are you talking about?"

"The part about bitterness being like acid in your heart. Or, in this case, in my heart. I've become bitter, especially toward my dad. The thing is, I don't have a right to be unforgiving. Since God forgave me, how can I not forgive others? Even my father?"

Erin felt a strange sensation come over her as she thought about helping someone make a crucial spiritual discovery. A small group lesson on willingness to be used in ministry to others flashed through her memory. Did God use her?

"You convinced me last night that I don't have to feel forgiveness before I grant it." Tyler grew silent a moment and watched a kid struggling to get a refill of soda.

Tears spilled from his eyes as he looked up at Erin. "My unforgiving spirit is not only hurting me, but it's also hurting God. I've asked Him to forgive me and to help me forgive my dad."

"Oh, Tyler." Erin took hold of his hand. "I can't think of a better place to start."

"Right, well, I first had to confess this to God before the next step."

Erin knew the answer to her question before asking it, but she asked anyway. "What next step?"

"Other than forgiving my father, He wants me to go back to Texas. If Jesus could leave heaven and come to Earth for me, shouldn't I be willing to leave Georgia and go to Texas for Him?"

Erin bit her lower lip. *I can't start crying. I've got to be supportive.*

"Tyler…Wow. I'm overwhelmed. I mean, I'll miss you, but I think this chapter in your life will have a happy ending."

"I started praying for my father this morning—like you said. I began praying *about* my dad, and before I knew it, I was asking God to help him deal with his hurts and disappointments."

"That's so good, Tyler. Sounds like your heart is already changing for your father."

Tyler nodded. "I think it is. I'm not all the way there by any means, but it's as if I'm gaining a new understanding of my father. I'm seeing some of his struggles and problems and why he became a calloused man, but," Tyler held up his index finger to make his point, "he's a Christian now, so God is making him a new man."

Joy and sorrow filled Erin's heart, and nothing could stop the flow of tears down her cheeks.

"Erin, you've been such an awesome friend through this whole experience. I believe God brought me to Georgia to meet you, so I could mend my relationship with my dad before it was too late."

Tyler checked the clock on his phone. "Oh, no. I didn't realize so much time had passed. I have to get back. I plan to tell Mr. Winslow I need to return home to be with my father as soon as possible."

Erin used her napkin to wipe away the tears. How could God use her in something so much bigger than herself?

"I hope you'll stay in touch, Tyler. I'm eager to hear how things go with your father. Also, let me know what Mr. Winslow says."

"I sure will. I'm sorry I have to run, but I don't want to be late. I'll call you later."

Erin watched Tyler hurry out the door and hop into his truck. Her half-eaten sandwich lay on the plate, and she didn't feel she could finish it. Tyler was her friend, and the thought of God using her to do anything was stunning. Did God have her in mind when Tyler left Texas years ago to come to Georgia? What was it Susan had called it? Divine Appointment. Mind-boggling.

She wrapped up her sandwich and asked for a bag from the girl behind the counter. The rest of her meal would go down better after completing her online introduction. A thousand miles wouldn't keep her from being Tyler's friend, but those miles would keep them from being more than friends.

Thirty minutes later, she pulled into her driveway and hurried through the kitchen door. Staring through the kitchen into the living room, she felt like the house was as empty as her heart.

When she walked into her bedroom to retrieve her computer, the letter from her father's lawyer caught her eye. For some reason, she'd kept it on the top of her dresser. Maybe she should toss it into the trash and forget this whole crazy idea. Erin wouldn't find a husband and have a baby by her next birthday. Three weeks had passed, and she was starting over again. The whole thing was ridiculous, and she planned to tell Ryan she was out of the running for nuptials.

A phone call to Ryan would have to wait, however. Preparing for British Lit was her current priority. After putting water on for tea, she situated her computer at the kitchen table. She also laid out the remaining portion of her Arby's sandwich in case her stomach started growling during class.

Daphne ran over to make her familiar leg wrap move. "I suppose that's one advantage of going to school online, Daffy. I can eat, and no one will care."

As she booted up her computer, her phone buzzed with a message from Ryan. "What's up, Gorgeous? I haven't heard from you in a while. Have you and Todd gotten married yet?"

Erin rolled her eyes and picked up her phone. "His name is Tyler, and no, we're not married. I'm about to start my online class. I'll call you later."

Her phone buzzed again. "Don't you worry your pretty little face. I've still got a few things up my sleeve."

Don't worry? I'm only talking about a husband and a child here, not to mention the rest of my life. Sure, no need to worry.

Erin logged into her school account and clicked the link. She'd have to shelve thoughts of Tyler and Ryan so she could focus on British poetry. The countdown to the beginning of her class neared zero, so she poured water over her teabag and sat in front of her screen.

CHAPTER TWENTY-FIVE

The Great Bear Hug Escape

"How's the new owner of Envision Pharmaceuticals feeling?"

"Hey, Ryan," Erin said with a yawn, pressing the phone to her ear with her shoulder as she reached for her robe. "I'm sorry I forgot to call you." Erin noticed the clock on the bedside table and saw it was almost 11:00. "Hold on a second."

She laid the phone down and grabbed a dry towel from the counter in the bathroom. After doing her best to dry her wet hair, she wrapped another dry towel around it and returned to her phone.

"Sorry. I just got out of the shower."

"No problem. Bathing always clears the mind."

Erin caught a drop of water with the edge of the towel. "Funny. I've never thought about a shower as clearing my mind."

"How was your Intro to British Lit?"

"It was okay. We had a video. There will be a lot of reading and papers."

"You like to read, and you're handy at writing, too. I'd say you're right in your element."

Erin smiled. Reading had been her passion for years, and the whole writing thing was growing on her.

"So, what happened with Tyler? I thought he would have proposed by now, or at least you would have proposed to him."

"Not going to happen. For starters, I don't think women should do the proposing. I think I talked him into moving back home to Texas to care for his father."

"You did what?"

Erin spent the next ten minutes giving Ryan a brief version of recent events. It was hard to believe it had only been a few days since she had coffee with him after Tuesday's self-defense class.

"How was Kung Fu Panda tonight?" Erin asked. "Did you tell Tim I was sorry I had to miss?"

"Kung Fu Panda? Cute. I told him. He's planning a makeup session on Saturday morning at eight because so many people had to skip. Can you go?"

Erin reviewed her calendar app to see when she had to work this weekend. "I think I can fit it in. I have to be at work by 11:00, so I'll cut it close. What did y'all do?"

"I don't know," Ryan admitted. "When he told me he'd offer a makeup, I decided to skip to go with you."

"You did? Let me guess. You don't think I'll go, so you have to go with me to make sure?"

"I've got a lot invested in you, Buttercup. I've got to prepare you for the next MMA championship fight."

"MMA?"

"Yeah. Mixed Martial Arts."

"Oh. I don't think you need to worry about my fighting skills. I'm doing good to accomplish the Superman Tuck or whatever you call it."

Ryan laughed. "Superman Pluck. I figured I'd rather go when you go. I feel a little weird in there with all those women."

"So, I'm not a woman?"

"Oh, no. You are definitely a woman." Ryan emphasized each syllable of definitely.

What does that mean?

"You're my best friend, Erin. I'd rather go when you go."

Heat climbed up her neck, and she realized a smile had spread across her face. "Thanks, Ryan. You made my night. I had trouble admitting it was best for Tyler to move back to Texas, so talking to you is like a breath of spring air."

"Hmm. A breath of spring air? You need some coffee and counseling?"

Erin could hear his smile. "Coffee and counseling do sound tempting. I'm standing in my robe with wet hair, however. I think I'll have to take a rain check."

"A rain check it will be. I've been working on some things and may have a new option."

"A new option for what?" Erin sat down on the edge of her bed.

"For a husband!" Ryan blurted out. "What else."

"Ryan. I'm done. I can't take marriage so lightly. I won't."

"Haven't you heard of love at first sight? It could happen. I'm just a facilitator."

"It's not going to happen with me. I think I'm done."

"Oh, Buttercup. Don't be a quitter. Why don't you have a restful night's sleep, and we'll talk about it later. I still need to work on a few things."

Erin took a deep breath. "Buttercup again? Really?"

"Slipped out. Sorry. I'll see you Saturday. How about showering at the gym afterward, and we can grab a quick coffee and croissant before you go to work?"

"Sure. I'd like that."

On Saturday morning, Erin woke up in a good mood. She turned on her playlist to provide background music while she tidied up a few things. She played with Daphne and hummed a tune by Maverick City as she got ready to go to the gym. Starting the day with a self-defense class was a good idea.

Erin pulled into a parking place and noticed Ryan sitting in his car texting someone. *Probably his latest fling.* Her mood dimmed slightly but then rebounded as she moved toward his car. Her phone buzzed. *Oh, not his fling. Just me.*

He hadn't noticed her standing there, so she yanked open his door. "Of course, I don't want to miss the Bear Hug Escape."

Ryan jerked his head around, face ashen, and turned his bug-eyed expression on her. Erin smirked.

He tossed his phone onto the seat beside him. "Not funny, Douglas."

"What, no Buttercup?"

"Erin, you scared the—"

Erin turned and started walking toward the building. "Sounds like an amusing way to spend my Saturday morning."

Erin heard the car door close, and Ryan appeared at her side. He wasn't winded at all, though he must have had to hurry to catch up to her.

"Why would I want to escape a bear hug?" Ryan asked. "That sounds like an enjoyable experience."

"It depends upon the identity of the bear."

Erin grilled Ryan about his latest fling, but he hadn't gone out in a week. Shocking. *He must be losing his touch after being turned down by the blonde the other night.*

Tim thanked the group of eleven people for coming. "Tuesday night, we discussed escaping an unwanted bear hug. If a bad guy wraps his arms around you from behind, you may struggle to get away. Let's start with a refresher on how to deal with this kind of attacker."

Erin scanned the group and noted Ryan was the only guy besides Tim. What if a bad guy accosted a strong man like Ryan from behind?

"Surprise is always your ally," Tim continued. He looked at Ryan. "You mind helping me with this move?"

"Sure," Ryan said.

"Remember to fill your lungs with air, drop your chin, and blow the air out while slipping out of his grasp."

Ryan left Erin's side and strode toward the front of the group like a resident black belt. Tim told Ryan to get behind him and wrap his arms around him like a bear hug. As soon as Ryan's arms were in place, the instructor dropped straight down out of Ryan's grasp, grabbed his arm, and twisted it as he stepped back.

"At this point," Tim said as Ryan grimaced, "you could break the bad guy's elbow, which would help you escape. You might prefer to kick him in the groin. Does anyone remember the three strike positions?"

"Knee, elbow, and palms," Erin offered.

"Good, Erin. Obviously, in this position, your palm is your only option. You pull the hand outward and hit the elbow with your palm. I think Ryan would rather me not demonstrate."

The small group laughed as Ryan rejoined Erin. He didn't appear to like being the subject of the instructor's demonstration.

"Now, team up and practice," Tim instructed. "And don't break any elbows."

Ryan wrapped his arms around Erin from behind and held her tightly. His hard chest pressed against her back, and his biceps bulged against her arms as he joined his hands in front of her. Had she been hugged like this before by Ryan? Of course, this wasn't really a hug. Though he'd hugged her when her father passed, Ryan had not been a hugger through the years.

"Okay, Grasshopper," Ryan breathed into her ear. "Slip out of my grasp."

His arms tightened even more as if he was making sure there was no way of escape. Erin took in a deep breath, allowing her chest to expand. Before exhaling, she stomped on his right foot and slid out of his grasp. Her hand slipped off his sweaty arm as she tried to grab his wrist.

Erin wiped her hand on her pants. "Gross."

"Why did you stomp my foot?" Ryan asked as he hopped around. "I don't remember that being in this move."

"I had to do something. You were squeezing me to death."

Tim called from across the gym. "Good job, Erin. Ryan's right. I didn't think about stomping on the bad guy's foot, but anything you can do to get him off balance will work."

"Suck up!" Ryan said under his breath. "I bet you brought the teacher an apple, too."

"It's in my gym bag." Erin shot back as she got behind Ryan.

She pressed against his back and wrapped her arms around his muscular body and pulled back. "Disgusting. Your shirt is like a wet dishrag."

"A little sweat never hurt anyone. You're just looking for an excuse to get out of getting your due."

"Getting my due?" Erin furrowed her eyebrows.

"Yeah. You don't want to give me a chance to get you back."

"Right. So, I stomped your foot, but your sweaty body is as slick as a greased pig."

Erin wrapped her arms about Ryan's strong chest. The expanse of his back was like a brick wall. He was several inches taller and had an unfair advantage, but she rested her cheek against his back and waited to feel his chest expand. He stood still.

"What are you doing?" Erin whispered.

His chest came out, and before she knew it, he was out of her grasp with her wrist in his hand. Pain shot up her arm.

"You're hurting me, Ryan."

He let go of her wrist. "Sorry. Didn't mean to hurt you."

Erin rubbed her wrist. "Well, your move works pretty well."

Tim returned to the front of the group. "Now, let's talk about the most effective targets on an assailant."

When class ended, Erin headed to the locker room to shower and dress for work before joining Ryan in his car. He suggested Einstein's for a bagel and coffee. Erin tuned into the music playing when they sat down at a table.

"Notice that song?" She motioned up to the speaker.

The chorus to Phil Collins' hit from the '80s began, "You can't hurry love, no, you just have to wait..."

"It's my new theme song, Ryan."

"Yeah, but that song was originally sung by the Supremes. So, you should think about the words to 'Stop! In the Name of Love' instead, which is all about love at first sight."

"No, it's not. What does it say?" Erin reached for her phone to Google the lyrics.

"Never mind the lyrics. Love at first sight happens all the time, and you have time for love not to be at first sight. What are we down to? A little less than twelve months?" Ryan made a grand gesture with his hands. "Plenty of time."

Erin put her hand onto Ryan's as she had done with Tyler. "Ryan, aside from the occasional excruciating arm twist, you're sweet. I appreciate your concern. You've helped me discover a side of myself I didn't know existed. I'm still evolving, but I don't think I can go through with any of this marriage thing. I would have to find someone and marry him in the next month. I can't do it."

Ryan's large hand wrapped around Erin's. "You have almost three months, but who's counting?"

"I am."

"Erin, you've been amazing. I'm so proud of you. I knew a beautiful, confident woman was hiding under all that..." He paused a moment.

"All that, what?"

"I'm not sure."

"Come on. You started the sentence, so finish it."

"Um, all that...insecurity."

"You were going to say something else."

Ryan shook his head. "Doesn't matter. You're amazing. Please don't give up yet. Think about it. We'll talk again tomorrow. How about I meet you for church? My church won't miss me if I don't show up."

"I'd love for you to come with me. Why did you start going across town?"

"Remember Brianna? She used to go to Journey, so I started going with her. It's a solid place, but I like yours, too."

"Fine, but I don't think this is a good idea—the marriage and baby thing, but you going to church with me is a phenomenal idea."

"Okay. I'll see you tomorrow morning. You need to get to work."

CHAPTER TWENTY-SIX

All Things New

E rin took her purse from the locker and headed out the front door. What a day! Every muscle ached, and her rubbery legs seemed unstable. Her back felt like a doormat that had seen a lot of foot traffic. She remembered seeing a pregnant lady holding her back earlier and wondered if the poor woman's back hurt this bad.

Work had been enjoyable, and Mr. Winslow said the store set a new sales record. So, the hard work was worth it, but the emotional and physical toll was significant. She considered resting on the bench outside the front door before hiking toward her car.

Erin looked across the parking lot and gasped when she saw a man leaning against the hood of her Toyota. Before retreating to the safety of the store, she recognized Tyler's red truck three parking spaces over. Tyler! She had wanted to talk to him, but different schedules had gotten in the way.

Tyler stood up as Erin approached her car. "Hey. I was wondering if Mr. Winslow was going to work you late."

Erin unlocked the car with her remote and opened the driver's door. "Sorry. I've got to sit down. I'm about to drop." She plopped onto the driver's seat with her feet still on the pavement.

"It was quite a day," Tyler admitted.

Erin sighed. "You can say that again."

"It was quite—"

Erin shook her head. "You're a comedian now?"

They both laughed, and a few moments passed before Tyler spoke.

"So, I told you I talked with Mr. Winslow about leaving. Before I clocked out today, he called me into his office and asked if I wanted to leave immediately."

"What did you say?" Erin whispered before realizing how dramatic she sounded. When he hesitated, she cleared her throat. "Tyler?"

"I told him I had expected to have to work my two-week notice but hoped to leave for Texas as soon as possible. He said a friend's nephew needed a job, so I could go ahead and leave if I wanted, or I could work a two-week notice."

"Oh. Well—"

"I thought about it for a second," Tyler interrupted, "then decided to go ahead and leave. Mr. Winslow even gave me $100 to help me get home."

Erin had seen the softer side of the Barnes & Noble manager several times but giving money to Tyler seemed out of character. He was a good man deep down.

Tyler looked down before looking back into Erin's eyes. "I think I'll head west tomorrow. I don't have much to pack. I can be on the road by 10:00."

"Wow." Erin felt like the wave of a feather could blow her over. "I didn't expect it to be so soon."

"Me neither," Tyler admitted, "but I need to get there as soon as possible. I've considered calling my father, but I don't know. Maybe I'll just show up."

Erin realized her mouth hung open, so she closed it. Tyler was so confident about the path he should take. Good for him, but he would be leaving Georgia. She had two friends, and one of them would be halfway across the country.

"I should go." Tyler reached for Erin's hands and pulled her back to her feet. "I hung around so I could tell you good-bye. I don't know when I'll be back in Georgia."

Erin felt tears beginning to fill her eyes. *Why am I teary-eyed? It's not like we're a couple.* Her lip quivered so she bit it, hoping to staunch the flow. She opened her mouth to speak and swallowed a sob.

"Tyler," she finally whispered. "I'm glad you're going back because it's the right thing. Will you stay in touch?"

"Sure. I'll text you and try to get on Facebook more often." Tyler squeezed Erin's hands and peered deep into her eyes. "I would never have done the right thing without your help. I'm grateful."

"I didn't do anything you wouldn't have done for me. I'm glad our paths crossed."

Tyler pulled Erin toward him and wrapped his arms around her. Silent tears began to flow as she pressed her cheek against his chest. He held her a moment and pulled back. A tear ran down his cheek.

"I've only had one real friend in my life," Tyler said, "and I'm glad it's been you."

"Me too. I'll be praying for you and your dad, Tyler."

"Thanks. I wish you the best, Erin."

Leaning toward Erin, he brushed a light kiss on her wet cheek. Without another word, Tyler climbed into the cab of his truck and drove away. Erin watched his truck turn right out of the parking lot and disappear. Her world was crumbling.

Nothing seemed real. She dropped into her car seat and leaned her head against the steering wheel. Tears flowed freely down her cheeks, and she began to weep. Had she been falling

in love with Tyler? No. It was too soon, but it wasn't fair that
he had to leave.

for a second before sliding into her car and starting it.

Conflicting thoughts pulled on her mind, and her heart
didn't know how to process what had happened. A full night's
sleep would help.

Erin took almost an hour to drive home, shower off the
day's stress, and collapse into bed. Still processing, she felt
both happy and sad about Tyler and about her life.

Her friend Susan popped into her mind. So, she may have
three friends. Erin considered telling her everything about her
father's will. Susan was wise and might be able to offer helpful
counsel. Of course, there was always Ryan, but sharing her
most debilitating struggles with a female friend felt right.

Before sleeping, Erin reached for her cell phone and
typed, "I assume you won't see this message 'til tomorrow,
but would you like to meet for coffee sometime soon? I'm free
Monday morning."

She laid her phone onto her nightstand and closed her
eyes. When was the last time she felt so tired? Before drifting
off, she prayed for Tyler and his father and thanked God for
the privilege of being used by Him to help her friend.

Daphne purred on the pillow beside her, and Erin reached
over to stroke her furry friend. A smile crossed her tired face.
Counting Daphne, she had four friends.

Tyler had found his way.

Now, I need to find mine.

The following morning, Erin slipped into the back row of
the church auditorium before the service started. The praise
band would be in the back, preparing to begin the service, but
in the meantime, Erin half-listened to recorded music played

over the sound system. Though excited about being at church, thoughts of Tyler heading west had subdued her spirit.

She'd only known Tyler briefly, but minutes had been like months. He'd become a true friend, and he could have been more. Of course, Texas wasn't on the other side of the world. A long-distance relationship could work. Some people did it all the time.

Tyler's final words confused her: "I wish you the best." It didn't sound like he wanted to maintain a long-distance relationship. Wishing someone the best was more like saying, "Have a good life."

Was this the answer to whether she should pursue something more intimate with Tyler? Erin chided herself for arriving early to prepare for worship but thinking about a guy instead.

As she reached for her Bible, her phone buzzed. *I've got to remember to turn off my phone.* The text was from Ryan. *Shoot. I forgot he was coming today.*

"GM Gorgeous. Did you stand me up? I'm waiting in the lobby."

Erin smiled and shook her head as she hurried to meet him. *At least I'm Gorgeous again.* Ryan's elbow rested on a counter while he sipped from a cup of coffee.

"Sorry, my brain was turned off."

"No problem. I thought I was going to have to bail. My boss called and wants me to fly to Chicago for several meetings, but I don't have to leave until after church."

"Chicago? I remember you flying up there before."

Ryan sipped his coffee. "I used to have to go there a lot for work, but I haven't been lately."

What was it like to have such an important position that your company flew you around the country for meetings? Glamorous.

"You've got meetings on Sunday?"

"Well, tomorrow is a company picnic, and my boss wants me to fly up today so I can attend. We need another department in our corner, and he figures a picnic will provide the perfect backdrop for casual, off-the-record conversations. I'll have more meetings all day Tuesday."

"Monday is a strange day for a picnic."

"Agreed, but the Chicago division won some award for production, and the picnic is their payback. They're not shutting down for the day, however."

"Well, I'm glad you could come to church. Do you want to grab lunch afterward? Do you have time?"

"Doubt it. I packed this morning so I could go straight to the airport."

"Oh."

Ryan held open the door for Erin, and she guided him back to her seat as the auditorium began to fill up. Moments later, the band came out on stage, and the service began. The worship leader welcomed everyone and invited them to consider God's incredible greatness.

Erin loved music and wished she could play an instrument or sing. Although she enjoyed singing, only God wanted to hear her. In a service weeks earlier, a little boy in front of her gawked at her as she started singing.

I wasn't singing for him anyway.

The band wrapped up their song, and with soft keyboard accompaniment, the worship leader started telling the story of the prodigal son. The son had taken his inheritance early and blown it. Erin knew the story, but the leader said prodigal meant extravagant or reckless. He said the parable of the prodigal son was a story about a prodigal father who loved with extravagance. Interesting.

"God's love is like the prodigal father," the worship leader continued. "He loves you with reckless abandon. It's an extravagant love that keeps on loving and giving."

God loved her. She had no doubt He had been with her through the difficult days after her father's death. The One who knew her best loved her unconditionally, but she struggled with loving herself. Was God offended by her struggle?

"His love started long before the cross," the worship leader continued. "The Bible says God loved you before you were born. He knew you in your mother's womb and designed plans for your life."

Several other instrumentalists started to play, and the music grew in intensity. She looked at Ryan. His eyes were wet.

The worship leader's excitement grew. "The prophet Zechariah even said God sings over you. He's crazy about you. His love for you is extravagant and reckless."

He began to sing a song Erin had heard many times. She'd not considered the meaning of the lyrics, but now thoughts about the reckless love of God burned deep inside her.

After the service, Ryan walked Erin to her car and seemed to be struggling inside. The talkative, jovial Ryan was now quiet.

He rested on her little blue car and slipped his hands into his pockets. "The service was incredible. I've not been moved like that in a long time."

When the band sang "All Things New" at the end, she saw tears running down Ryan's cheeks. Erin wanted to talk with him about his feelings but did not mention it.

"I love Pastor Brant," Erin said. "Each sermon he preaches is like he's talking to me. This whole Identity Theft series has my name written all over it."

Ryan studied her. "When he said something about God making everything new, I thought about you."

"Me?"

"Yeah. I've watched you become a new person, Erin. And I don't just mean a haircut."

Erin's cheeks burned as she inspected her shoes. She'd made many changes. Was God changing her on the inside?

"Erin, I want to be a new person, too. I've got a lot of ugly stuff in my past."

Erin couldn't hold back her own tears. Ryan had gone to church his whole life, but a new life meant more than just empty religion.

"I think God wants you to be a new person, too, Ryan."

"I suppose it's best I'm about to board an airplane because I've got a lot to process. Want to hear something funny? Well, not funny, but significant?"

"What?"

"After I thought of God making things new in my life, Sarah Hardwick popped into my head."

"Who?"

"Sarah Hardwick. You don't know her, but I mistreated her the last time I was in Chicago. I need to find her and apologize."

"Sounds like a good start, Ryan, but doing good things won't make you right with God."

"I know. It's a relationship. I understand what that means for the first time, and I want it. I've been a real jerk for a long time, Erin. If God takes jerks, then I'm all in."

Erin could tell Ryan meant what he was saying, and without thinking, she threw her arms around her friend. She didn't want to agree with him about the jerk part, but the synopsis of his past was accurate. Thankfully, God was in the changing business. How different she felt now than when she entered the church earlier.

Maybe God was changing them both.

CHAPTER TWENTY-SEVEN

Old Wounds

Ryan stepped off the plane at O'Hare International Airport and headed toward the car rental booths. His assistant had reminded him to take a shuttle to the multi-modal facility. What a name. How did a multi-modal facility differ from every other car rental location in the country? Probably not much.

While flying from Atlanta, he contemplated his upcoming meetings and one particular encounter he hoped to arrange. Sarah Hardwick worked for Gatner when he was here last. Through checking the company's directory, Ryan learned she was still there. She was a beautiful girl desperate for a husband, and Ryan played her like a violin. He dropped his head and closed his eyes. He would somehow make things right.

Why didn't I call her back after the incident?

A shiver went up Ryan's spine as he thought about what he'd done. All things were new, but what did a guy do about the stupid things he did in the past?

Sarah's favorite restaurant two years ago had been Shaw's Crab House, and she used to eat there every Sunday night. His stomach growled at the thought. He might as well get something to eat. Odds were he wouldn't see her, but he'd be able to enjoy a memorable meal.

The hostess took him to a booth near the window where he scanned the menu. Nothing had changed much from the last time he and Sarah had come here. He couldn't remember what he ordered then but decided on the red snapper, iced tea, and coffee. As he sipped his coffee, a couple sitting on the other side of the restaurant caught his attention. He regarded the girl and gaped. The woman's profile revealed she was indeed his beautiful friend—ex-friend.

He craned his head to see them, but it looked like she was crying. The guy was holding her hands, and…*And what? Is he consoling her? Whatever is going on is intense.*

Ryan had envisioned talking to Sarah tonight and asking for her forgiveness, but it wouldn't happen now. Was the guy breaking her heart? How many times could a woman's heart be broken?

Sarah and the man rose and headed toward the door, but Sarah broke off and went for the restroom. When she came out, she looked right through Ryan and gave no indication she recognized him, Ryan Jeffries, the jerk. The guy reached for her hand, and they headed outside.

Ryan could see them in front of a car in the parking lot. It was her car. He remembered. She was crying again, and the guy pulled her into a tight embrace.

Their long, intimate kiss caused Ryan to turn his head. Was the guy her husband? Boyfriend? Who knew? A lot of time had passed. When Ryan looked out the window, Sarah's car pulled out of the parking lot.

Oh, well. Ryan's confession would have to wait until Tuesday.

* * * * *

Erin finished up her early morning bike ride and got ready for work. The ride had done nothing for her feelings. She was upset with Tyler for leaving, though it was right. Mr. Winslow asked her to work overtime today to help the new guy adjust. Why had she agreed to help? She didn't want to help anyone do anything.

As was her Monday morning practice, Erin stopped by her mother's house for breakfast on the way to work. Her mom had started leaving the house more. She took Erin up on her suggestion to volunteer at the hospital and even said she might attend church with her.

"So, what did you do with the old lighthouse painting?" her mother asked.

A smile spread across Erin's face as she sipped from her coffee mug. "I hung it in my living room. I love that old picture."

"You used to stare at the thing when you were a little girl. What's the attraction?"

"Not sure. Maybe I envy the guy standing in the doorway. Calm and relaxed while the whole world crashes around him."

Erin talked about the boring events of her life but opted not to go into specifics. She did not need her mother to start prying into her personal life. After a second coffee, she kissed her mother goodbye and headed to work.

The reality was that nothing in Erin's life was boring, thanks to her father's will. One day soon, she'd have to tell her mother about the will and her crazy attempt to find a husband but now wasn't the time. She chewed her nail and tried to imagine breaking the news to her mother. On second thought, she didn't have to say anything because it looked like nothing would ever happen.

"Good morning, Mr. Winslow," Erin called out as she entered the empty bookstore. The quiet store enveloped her, and she felt peace or comfort in the presence of all her friends.

She snorted out loud. *I'm a piece of work. All my friends are old, dead authors or live ones I'll never meet.*

When she didn't hear a reply from her boss, Erin figured he was back in his office. After relocking the front door, she headed toward her locker where she stowed her purse and lunch bag. He usually started his day in his small office in the back room.

Mr. Winslow sat behind his desk, studying a spreadsheet on his computer. "Good morning, Erin. Hope you've recovered from the weekend."

"It was hectic," Erin admitted, "and I'll need more than a Sunday off to recover. I'm sure you were busy here, but thanks for letting me be in church yesterday."

He smiled. "We were busy, but I told you from the beginning I would let you have Sundays off unless it couldn't be avoided. Everything worked out fine yesterday. I should have asked Tyler to wait until today to leave. I could have used him yesterday."

"That thought crossed my mind."

"Well, I could tell he believed getting back to his father as quickly as possible was important. I decided to work the floor myself."

Her boss had a tender side. Amazing. He had done Tyler's work, so her friend could leave. Deep down, the older man was sweet, but now, he rose a few notches in her estimation.

"We have a new employee coming in today, Erin. I sent you a message yesterday about him and about working with him a little before you leave this afternoon."

"Yes, sir, I saw your message. I think I replied, or at least, I meant to."

"I don't want to let him check out anyone for now. We'll use him for stocking and see how he does with customer service." The boss grinned at her. "I'm counting on you to whip him into shape. He's supposed to start today at noon."

"Happy to help."

At eleven forty-five, a broad-shouldered guy who looked like he had stepped out of a sports magazine walked into the store. His short-sleeve shirt stretched across his chest and strained at his biceps.

"Hello." The young man smiled down at Erin. "I'm Cody Wilson, and I'm looking for Mr. Alfred Winslow."

Erin checked the time display on the cash register and figured this was the new guy. Looking more like a movie star than a book stocker, he turned the heads of a few of the women in the store. Hopefully, he was the new stocker. They didn't need a movie star.

* * * * *

On Tuesday morning, Ryan sat in the lobby of the Chicago offices of Gatner Enterprises. The day before had been exhausting. His boss owed him for taking half the day Monday and spending it with people he didn't know. Overall, the company picnic had been productive, and the higher-ups would be pleased with the team he was building for future projects.

The day before him was important, though exhausting. He had many critical meetings, but his most significant encounter was unscheduled.

A beautiful blonde walked through the front doors. He hurried toward the elevator bank to intercept Sarah Hardwick. He'd been waiting for his planned impromptu meeting for an hour. *Showtime.*

"Sarah. It's been a while."

Sarah's head turned, and Ryan watched the color drain from her face. Her lips twisted into a sneer. "Hello, Ryan," she said, unable—or unwilling— to hide her disgust.

The speech Ryan had rehearsed all morning vanished. He stood before Sarah, unable to speak or move. Recovering his voice, he said, "I know you hate me, and with good reason. I shouldn't have left without talking to you, and I never…Well, there are many things I shouldn't have done. I was a self-centered jerk who deserved to be hated."

"I have to get to my office before I'm late."

Ryan walked beside her and pressed the elevator call button when they arrived at a row of four elevators. "Sarah, I don't warrant your friendship or forgiveness, but I'm sorry, and…" He looked at the floor and sucked in a deep breath. "I'm hoping you'll forgive me."

Sarah turned her beautiful green eyes toward him, and her lips tightened like she was trying to bite back what she really wanted to say. He felt even worse and wondered about the wisdom of this encounter.

Sarah stared at the floor as the elevator door opened. "I'm surprised, Ryan. I suppose you think you can apologize, and everything will be like old times?"

"No. Honestly, I don't. Two years ago, I was a selfish idiot who didn't know how to treat a woman. I don't deserve your forgiveness, and I won't blame you if you hate me for the rest of your life."

The elevator door closed behind her as Sarah stood frozen in place. She crossed her arms and stared up at him. "I should forgive you." She hesitated. "I'll think about it."

"I suppose that's a start. I'm here 'til tomorrow afternoon." Ryan noticed the engagement ring on her finger. "A lot's happened in these two years, but I hope you'll forgive me and allow me to show you I can be a friend. Can we meet for lunch?"

"I don't think going out is a good idea, Ryan. I'm engaged."

Ryan nodded. "Yeah, I saw your ring. Congratulations. I want to try to mend our friendship, but with no expectations."

Sarah still looked suspicious but relented. "I guess lunch won't hurt. I'm free at noon as long as we eat downstairs in the cafeteria."

"The cafeteria sounds perfect," Ryan agreed. "I'll meet you here in the lobby. And thanks for not ignoring me and running away."

The elevator door opened again, and Ryan said he'd see her in a few hours. He returned to the lobby and grabbed his computer bag and briefcase. Somehow, the load on his shoulders had lifted a bit.

Sarah carried some deep pain. How many other women had Ryan hurt over the last few years? A fresh wave of regret washed over him.

He had been selfish. He used women and dropped them whenever it became too intense. Selfishness had led to loneliness.

Since he had decided yesterday to seek a different path, he would need to consider what God wanted him to do.

The thought of creating a list of women he should apologize to was possible. Coming clean might take a while but apologizing to Sarah had been the right thing to do. Uncomfortable but necessary. Maybe she'd forgive him one day and allow a friendship.

Whatever came next, he knew making things right would always be a priority.

CHAPTER TWENTY-EIGHT

Starting Over

E rin pedaled up a hill, determined to maintain her speed until she crested the top. The sun peeked over the horizon, making the storm during the night a distant memory. The morning air smelled clean as the Creator had washed the Earth during the night. She stopped at the bottom of the next hill and stared at the cows spread across an open field.

A man tossed out hay, and the herd shuffled around his pickup truck. *The farmer lives on a little slice of heaven and doesn't realize it.*

Too bad she didn't have more time to linger, but Mr. Winslow asked her to spend the first half of the day watching over Cody and the second half running the cash register. The day would be slow, and showing the new guy how to do inventory on a shipment shouldn't take long.

While leaning her bike against the wall of her carport, Erin's phone buzzed with an incoming text. After frantically digging through her fanny pack, she saw a message from Susan. Why hadn't Susan replied to her text on Saturday night?

"I'm so sorry I didn't reply sooner. I left my phone at my mother's house on Saturday and just returned to pick it up. Still up for meeting this week?"

So, that explained Susan's silence. Erin laughed. Losing a phone was as common to her as brushing her teeth.

Erin thumbed her reply. "Hey. No problem. I have to work every day this week except tomorrow and Sunday. You available tomorrow?"

"Tomorrow's perfect. How about breakfast at Steak 'n Shake on Broad Street in Stockbridge at 9:00?"

Erin smiled as she thought about meeting with her new friend and replied, "I'd love to!"

Could she tell Susan about her dilemma? Susan would freak out over the whole get-a-husband scheme. Erin decided to tell her about Ryan's idea but would say she didn't plan to follow through with it.

As she entered the house, her fat cat ran to her legs and began the figure eight food dance. "Okay, fatso. I need to put you on the treadmill."

Erin reached down and scratched behind her cat's ears. Daphne closed her eyes and purred. The cat lived for this, and well, eating.

Realizing she was under a time crunch, Erin hurried through her shower, and when she reached down to turn off the water, the bathtub faucet handle broke off in her hand. Water continued to run down her back, but it was now cold. Although she pushed in the knob so the water would come out of the spout, it wouldn't turn off.

She jumped out of the tub and stood staring at gallons of water pouring down the drain. What could she do? The sink had a shut-off valve, but bathtubs didn't have any valves, at least not that she knew about. She remembered helping her dad once with a plumbing project and had an idea.

After quickly drying off and throwing on her clothes, Erin ran to her father's old bag of tools her mother had given her. She riffled through the tools and pictured her father digging through the tool bag once, looking for a pair of pliers. She wrapped her hand around the channel locks.

Now, she had to find the lid of the water meter. After searching around the front yard, she finally discovered the metal lid half buried under pine straw.

She scraped the pine straw off to the side and removed the metal lid, only to discover the valve was covered with dirt. Kneeling on the ground, she began digging the dirt out of the meter box and found the valve. Grabbing the channel locks, she squeezed the brass piece sticking up from the pipe and twisted. Nothing happened. *What did you expect to happen, stupid? The water is running inside, not outside.*

Erin rushed back into the house and discovered all the water had been shut off. *I learned something valuable from my father, after all. I wonder if he'd be proud of me.*

Getting her hair and makeup just right was no easy task, and then she realized she had forgotten to give Daphne water before turning it off at the meter. Reaching inside the refrigerator, Erin pulled out a cold water bottle and poured it into the cat's bowl. Daphne stuck her nose in it and pulled away. "You're so spoiled. It will warm up soon."

Erin snatched her purse from the kitchen table and rushed out the door. *If traffic is bad, I'm going to be late for work.*

* * * * *

When the elevator door opened to the second floor, Ryan saw Sarah standing at the door as if she were waiting on him. He'd already decided she wouldn't show and was almost shocked. She stepped into the elevator and pressed the button.

Sarah's eyes drifted to the floor of the elevator. "The cafeteria is in the basement."

Her floral scented perfume reminded him of happier times. She'd been willing to move to Georgia, and they could've been married if he hadn't been such a jerk.

He once told her he loved her. Tears had spilled out of her eyes, and she'd melted into him. Real love was not his true motivation.

His declaration had worked. He never considered his words might mean commitment, marriage, and children. Ryan closed his eyes. The fact that she stood with him alone in an elevator spoke about *her* character. Maybe, she'd rub off on him.

"I'm paying," Ryan offered as he pointed to the food line in the cafeteria. "I'll meet you at the cashier."

Sarah didn't resist. He owed her a lot more than just the cost of a meal. Buying her lunch for the rest of her life wouldn't erase the pain he'd caused.

Ryan arranged his silverware and picked up a French fry. Sarah's blonde hair was pulled back with curly strands dropping down the sides of her face. More than one man had looked at her as they sat there. Probably jealous. If they only knew. He took a bite of the fry but didn't have an appetite.

Sarah stole glances while she appeared to gather her thoughts. Maybe coming to see her was a bad idea. Ryan could have emailed or called.

Finally, she broke the ice. "I had a life-changing experience last year."

Ryan opened his mouth, but nothing came out. Shame washed over him as he recalled sending her money for an abortion. How had he let things spiral so out of control? A stab of pain hit again with the realization that his selfishness had changed her life in the worst way imaginable two years ago. What could have happened last year?

"I had a hard time dealing with my guilt, Ryan. After you disappeared, and I lost the baby, I didn't want to live anymore. A friend invited me to attend a support group in her church. My past collided with my present, and I knew I desperately needed forgiveness for what I had done. I couldn't live with myself."

Ryan sat stunned as the weight of his sin and failure crashed down upon him. He had urged her to have the abortion, and after sending her a few thousand dollars, he hadn't given her or the baby another thought. How could he have treated life so casually? What kind of man would insist a woman have an abortion and then let her go through such a crisis alone?

A tear rolled down Sarah's cheek. "I had a rough year of counseling and personal struggle, but I can honestly say I found forgiveness and hope for the first time in my whole life."

Neither had eaten anything on their plates, and Ryan had just made Sarah's day even more challenging. "Sarah, I can't find the words to communicate my sorrow and regret. Please, please forgive me for all I've done to you. I don't deserve your forgiveness, but I hope you'll consider it."

Ryan felt such regret. How could he forgive himself? He thought of all the pep talks he'd given Erin and realized those talks may have been for himself. Don't let your past define your future, Buttercup. Every day is a new day.

"I've thought about you all morning," Sarah said. "I did a lot of soul-searching last year and committed my life to Jesus. I realized this morning I had to forgive you. Since God forgave me for what I'd done, how could I not forgive you?" She smiled across the table through wet eyes. "It may take a while to like you, but I forgive you."

Had Ryan heard her correctly? Forgive? He had a faint memory of Jesus telling someone he should forgive seventy times seven. That was a lot of forgiving, but this issue was huge.

"You do?"

"Yeah. I do. If you'd come a year ago, I would have...Well, I don't know what I would have done, but I'm confident we wouldn't be sitting here."

Ryan smiled, and relief coursed through him. His soul felt washed. Sarah's forgiveness was like a gift of grace. "Your forgiveness is an amazing place to start. I hope you'll one day like me again. Sarah, I made an important decision this past Sunday, too. I've attended church all my life, but I realized God wants more from me than religious rituals. He wants a relationship, and I want it, too. I think that's one reason your forgiveness means so much."

Her wet cheeks reminded him of seeing her at the restaurant Sunday night.

Sarah dabbed her face with a napkin. "God's grace has become so real to me this past year, and His forgiveness is complete. I've been praying for you, Ryan."

Thoughts of how many times he'd heard the words "God's grace" over the last few days flashed through Ryan's mind. "I don't know what to say, Sarah. Thank you. I'm so grateful for how God has worked in your life despite me."

Sarah glanced away. In the awkward silence, Ryan reached for his sandwich and took a bite.

"Sarah, I must confess I saw you at the Crab House Sunday night. I wanted to say hello, but I saw you were with someone, and you were, well, you were crying."

Sarah nodded. "He's my fiancé. We met at a singles event at my church. He's in the Army Reserves and got called up at the last minute."

"Oh, I'm sorry. Congratulations on your engagement. Sounds like a lot of exciting things are happening in your life. Where is your fiancé going?"

"Afghanistan. I'm so worried about him. He won't be able to contact me regularly, and our wedding is supposed to be next summer."

"Wow. The timing sounds awful, but it sounds like you've got a good man. I mean, he goes to church and all, right?"

"Well, yes." Sarah sighed. "Church is more a social event for him, not an overflow of his faith. I'm so concerned something may happen to him in Afghanistan, and I'm not sure where he stands with God." She dabbed at her eyes. "I'm embarrassed you saw me in such a mess the other night, but I've been feeling anxious."

"Understandable. Don't feel weird about crying or feeling anxious." Ryan took a deep breath. "Sarah, prayer hasn't been a big part of my life, but it will be in the future. I'll pray for him and you."

* * * * *

Erin bolted into the store at precisely 9:30. She preferred to arrive at least ten minutes early, but today, being on time would have to suffice. Her father always said if she was on time, she was late, and if she was ten minutes early, she was on time. Breezing past Cody, she clocked in at the cash register.

"Sorry I'm late, Cody," Erin said, turning to him at the information desk. "Hope you haven't been waiting for long."

"Not long. I got here a few minutes ago."

Cody's eyes focused on her knees. Erin looked down and thought she would pass out.

"Oh, no! I can't believe I didn't realize I had dirt on my pants." Erin wanted to crawl into a hole.

"What happened?"

"I had the worst morning. The knob broke off in my bathtub. I'm such a klutz at some things. I watched more than a few gallons of water go down the drain until it dawned on me to turn the water off at the street."

"Did you notice if water was coming out where the handle broke off? Was it running down inside your wall?"

Erin froze. The possibility of water running down inside her wall had never crossed her mind.

"No," she said, plopping onto a stool. "I didn't notice. All I thought about was somehow getting the water turned off."

"I used to work for a plumber. You want me to come by after work and check it out for you?"

Erin considered him and realized she was chewing on her fingernail. She dropped her hand to her side. "I couldn't ask you to do that, Cody."

"You didn't. I volunteered." He flashed a dimpled smile.

"You're sweet to offer. I should call my landlord or a plumber."

"If you had called a plumber back where I used to live, I may have been one of the guys sent to your house. Why don't I look at it for you? If it's a big deal, we can call your landlord. It's probably an easy fix, though."

Erin started to protest again when Cody held up his hand. "Listen, Erin, I'm all about scoring points, and if repairing your plumbing gets me points with Mr. Winslow, I'm all for it."

Erin smiled and processed his offer. "Well, I'm not sure how much pull I have with Mr. Winslow, but I suppose it's okay if you promise not to look at my dirty house."

"Scouts honor," he said, raising his right hand and holding up three fingers. "What time do you get off?"

"I work until 6:00 but attend a class at 7:00."

"What kind of class?"

Erin smiled. "Uh, a fitness class."

"Cool. Why don't I meet you somewhere afterward and follow you to your house? I can borrow some of my uncle's tools and stop at Home Depot to pick up a valve and knob for your bathtub."

"Wow, Cody. That's such an inconvenience to you. I feel like I'm putting you out."

"Nonsense. I'm the one who volunteered."

Erin dug through her purse. "Okay. I hate to take advantage of a new friendship, but I guess I'm kind of desperate. Here's twenty dollars. Is it enough to cover the materials you'll need?"

"Twenty should work," Cody said. "Any idea what the name brand is on the faucet?"

Erin squeezed her eyes shut and visualized her bathtub. "Mmm...Delta, I think. Is Delta a name brand?"

"Sure is." Cody pulled out his phone, found the Home Depot website, and showed Erin the screen. "Look familiar?"

"That's it."

"Awesome. I'll buy a replacement valve."

"Thanks so much, Cody. Let's meet here at about 8:15."

Chapter Twenty-nine

Problem Solved

When Erin didn't have customers at the cash register, she thought about the wisdom of letting a strange guy come over to fix her bathtub. Cody wasn't exactly strange, but she'd just met him. *Should I be grateful or embarrassed? Both?* She tried to remember if her home was presentable, but the morning had been crazy.

Ryan had always told her she was a clean freak, but dirty laundry on the bathroom floor wasn't too weird, at least not when someone was in a hurry to get to work. *How can I convince Cody to let me go into the house first to ensure the coast is clear?*

Erin worked until 6:30 and then hurried to the gym a few miles away. She took a picture of the front of the gym and sent it to Ryan. "Hey, Slacker. I'm holding up my end of the deal."

A minute later, her phone buzzed. "Some people have to work for a living."

Erin smiled. Her fingers flew across the face of her phone. "Some people will do anything to avoid exercise." She pocketed her phone and rushed into the locker room to change clothes.

A little after 8:00, Erin waved to Cody as he sat in a white SUV near the front of Barnes & Noble, and he pulled out behind her.

Entering through the front door and going straight into the bathroom was not an option. What if she'd left dirty clothes on the floor?

Once she and Cody stood near the front door of her house, Erin paused as she was about to put her key in the door. "Uh, Cody, my, uh, cat may not respond well to you at first. Let me go in and pick her up before you come in."

"Sure. No problem."

Rushing into the bathroom, Erin scooped up yesterday's dirty clothes and tossed them into the hamper. *I've got to quit being such a slob.*

She carried her cat to the front door. "Sorry, Cody. This is Daphne. Once she knows you're a friend, she won't freak."

Cody reached out and stroked the cat. "Hello, Daphne. Can I be your friend?"

Her new best friend? What did that mean?

Erin sat Daphne down and the cat scampered back into the bedroom. "Do you want me to turn the water on at the road?"

"Take me to your bathroom first, and then you can turn it on, count to five, and turn it off again."

Erin guided him through the living room and down the hall to her bedroom. She snagged the pliers lying on her dresser. Her dad would have been proud. He probably thought every girl should keep a pair of these handy.

"Bathroom's in there," Erin said, pointing to the open bathroom door.

Once outside, she lifted the lid off the meter box, turned on the water, and counted to five. After twisting the valve again, she hurried back into the house.

"You're in luck," Cody said. "You completely closed the valve with the knob before it broke. Don't think any water leaked into your wall." He held up the plastic Home Depot bag. "I got this earlier today. I'll have the broken valve replaced in no time."

Once Cody had everything put back together, Erin tested the new knob. "Works great. I don't know how to thank you, Cody."

"Glad I could help."

Erin's stomach growled, and she realized the time. "Have you eaten dinner? I can fix something. It's the least I can do."

"I didn't have a chance to eat, so yeah, I'd enjoy something to eat, not to mention the company."

He wanted her company? Really?

Erin thought for a second. "Spaghetti?"

While they ate, Cody told her story after story about what it was like growing up in Wisconsin. Erin couldn't imagine so much snow and cold temperatures. The South was the place for her. When she asked why he'd moved to Georgia, he told her he got around to using some of his military scholarships to go to college, and Georgia Tech was the best choice for his major.

"Wow. So, you got into Tech. You must be very smart."

"I'm not in yet, but my GPA and test scores should open some doors. Tech's got a respectable program for an engineering degree, and I expect to start next semester. I came down to settle into a job before starting school."

"Where are you living?"

"I've got an uncle who lives on the east side of Atlanta, so he's letting me live with him. He and Mr. Winslow are friends, which is how I got the job at Barnes & Noble."

Erin told Cody some about her life growing up and her former job at Regis. For such a tough-looking guy, he seemed sensitive and asked a lot of questions.

At 10:30, Cody said he had to leave. He'd promised to work for his uncle the following day, and his morning would start early. Erin couldn't believe it had gotten so late.

"I don't remember ever enjoying a plumbing job like I did this one," Cody said with a grin. "I mean, spaghetti and the works."

Erin's face warmed. Was he flirting with her? "Well, it might be better than messing with someone's septic tank."

Cody laughed. "Yep, better than a septic tank. Do you want to do something sometime?"

"Like...go out, I mean hang out?" Erin's heart began to pound in her chest.

"Sure, like go bowling or something?"

Erin frowned as she tried to imagine herself with a bowling ball. "I've never been bowling."

"It's a piece of cake. I'll teach you. How about tomorrow night? We could grab a bite and bowl a few games."

"I don't know. I'd probably hurt someone or put a hole in the floor with the ball."

Cody grinned. "I said I'll teach you, and I'm a really good teacher. We'd have a lot of fun."

You'd have a lot of fun laughing at me. "I'll give it a try."

Cody agreed to pick up Erin Wednesday evening at 5:00. She stood at the door watching him drive away, unsure of what had happened. Was she going out with him on a date? No, they were just new friends hanging out. First, Tyler, now Cody. What would Ryan say?

Cody's brake lights lit up at the end of her road before he disappeared.

Erin eyed Daphne. "Just friends. That's all. Friends with a tall, muscular, handsome guy. Doing me a huge favor, eating in my house late at night, going bowling, but friends."

On Wednesday morning, Erin hurried into Steak 'n Shake at 9:00 and saw Susan at a corner booth.

Susan stood and welcomed her with a hug. "I'm so glad you could come."

"How's your week going?"

"Oh, honey. I feel more like a taxicab driver than a mother. I can't imagine how insane my life would be if I had more than one child."

"Do you want more than one?" Erin couldn't imagine having one child, much less two or three.

"We hope to have at least one more."

A middle-aged waitress handed them menus. "You both want coffee?"

The women nodded. When the waitress returned with steaming coffee, Erin and Susan gave her their food order.

Susan began telling Erin about the crazy weekend at her parents' house, including Friday night swimming at Lake Lanier and breakfast with her childhood friend. Her daughter, Amber, had stepped on a rusty nail, and they went to the urgent care.

"She'll be fine. You know kids. Nothing stops them. I want to hear about your date last week."

Date last week? Oh, my word. So much has happened in a week.

"Thanks for loaning me your dress. I have it in the car. The night, though, was one I'd rather not repeat."

Erin told her friend about the Omni Hotel incident. She tried to convey the beauty of the dining room while revealing her total disgust with Chip. Susan especially liked how Erin described handling the brute.

"You were amazing, Erin. I bet he'll think twice before taking advantage of another woman."

"I hope so, but I kind of doubt it. He's so arrogant he probably brushed it off by the time he returned to the ballroom."

"Do you have any other prospects?" Susan asked as she grinned across the top of her coffee cup. "I suppose I'm prying a little."

Erin thought over the last couple of weeks. If someone had told her a month earlier she'd go out with three guys, she wouldn't have believed it.

"Not really, but I am going out with a new friend from work. He just moved to town. I had a plumbing issue, and he came over to fix it. He seems like he could use a friend."

Was she trying to be a friend or trying to get a husband?

"What's he like?"

Erin laughed. "Would you believe it if I told you he's tall, dark, and handsome?"

Susan grinned. "Sounds promising."

The waitress arrived with a tray of pancakes, eggs, sausage, and grits. Erin and Susan talked about Susan's family, work at Barnes & Noble, and life as a college student while they ate.

Erin finally wiped her mouth, sat her fork down, and took a deep breath. "Susan, for a while, I've wanted to talk about something that will make me sound crazy. But I need help or advice. I may need a shrink."

Susan smiled. "You don't need to apologize, and I doubt you need a psychiatrist. What's on your mind?"

"Before I tell you the most unbelievable story, you must know I was engaged before my father died. I was supposed to get married a month after he passed, but about a week before he died, my fiancé left."

"Oh, Erin."

"Well, it was for the better. I don't regret it now. At first, it was like the end of the world, though, and I never told my father. I didn't have the nerve to tell him."

Susan reached across the table and placed her hand on Erin's.

"I didn't care to hear my father's comments about my ability to keep a man," Erin admitted.

Susan squeezed Erin's hand, and Erin felt the warmth of friendship. The moment felt surreal. She hadn't experienced this kind of friendship with another woman her whole life.

"I'm so sorry, Erin. One thing about every father, and every person, for that matter, we're all broken. Your father was a product of this world, past relationships, choices, and sin...all of it. Like the rest of us. It's hard to overcome some patterns so ingrained in our minds. It probably started in his life when he was only a kid."

Erin's head and shoulders drooped as overwhelming sorrow took hold. Though she'd spilled enough tears over her father and vowed not to shed another drop, she felt powerless to stop them.

"I'm not excusing anything he may have done," Susan continued, "but I've found it helps me if I can somehow separate actions from the actor."

Erin sniffed and reached for a napkin. "Separate actions from the actor?"

"Let's say your father was abused as a child and grew up to be an abuser. While he was responsible for his choices, an element of his behavior was greatly influenced by outside forces. For one thing, those outside forces were evil and bent on his destruction. Other contributing factors may have included parents or other people in his life when he was young."

"I don't know much about my dad's past, and I never met any of his family."

"Interesting. Please don't think I'm laying the blame on anyone's doorstep. We have enough of that going on in our world. At the same time, when someone hurts you, it helps if you understand that at least some of the source of those actions may have come from places and circumstances beyond the person's control."

Erin remembered finding an old photo album of her father's when he was a boy. She'd turned through the pages seeing faces of people she'd never met but to whom she was somehow connected. When she had asked her mother about it, her mother took the album and told Erin not to bring it up again. She said painful memories were best buried.

"I can forgive others a lot easier if I can somehow separate the actions from the person," Susan concluded. "It helps me to be able to pray the Lord's Prayer and mean it."

Erin tried to quote the Lord's Prayer in her mind. "I'm not following."

"Do you remember the part that says, 'forgive us our trespasses as we forgive those who trespass against us'?"

"Sure. Makes sense. I guess we're asking God to forgive us the same way we forgive others. If we don't forgive…"

"Right," Susan interrupted. "We don't earn forgiveness by forgiving others, but God's grace should affect how we treat others."

"Makes sense," Erin repeated. "Whatever the reason, I did my best to stay away from my father after Greg left. I never did anything right in my dad's eyes, and I'm sure he would have said losing my fiancé was my fault."

"You know it wasn't your fault."

"I know," Erin murmured. "Now, I'm glad Greg left me. My life would have been a disaster if we'd married."

The alarm on Susan's phone began to ring, and she reached to silence it. "Oh, goodness. I didn't realize it had gotten so late. I have to be at Amber's school at 11:00. She's giving a speech, and parents are invited to hear the students."

"Sure, sure, go. And I've got breakfast," Erin insisted. "Remember last time? You said I could pay next time, which is today."

Susan gave Erin a quick half-hug. "Thanks, Erin. We'll catch up soon."

Erin watched Susan rush from the restaurant. Did she feel sorrow or relief?

I didn't tell her about Dad's will. Probably for the best.

Chapter Thirty

Striking Out

Early Wednesday morning, Ryan sat in his hotel room reviewing notes from the previous day. His meetings had been productive, but his company's production problem still loomed large. He had to figure out this issue, or Gatner would continue to drop in sales and lose ground in the stock market.

Ryan studied his notes about the previous years and noticed a loss and reduction pattern. This problem has lasted a while. Why hadn't anyone addressed this issue?

He found the phone number for the production plant and made an appointment to see the manager.

"Is there anything I need to do to help Mr. Miller prepare for the meeting?" the plant manager's assistant asked over the phone.

"Can you pull the profile report for the last three years of production?"

"Sure. We'll see you at 10:30."

Ryan had hoped to return home by early afternoon. Now, he'd be pushing it to make it home by his usual bedtime. He spoke his assistant's name into his phone.

"Hey, Ryan." Her voice sounded clear even from 700 miles away.

"Good morning, Lori. Just checking in. I told you I'd be back by this afternoon, but I've found something I need to discuss with Joe Miller in production."

"Okay. Mr. Caruthers said to give him an update as soon as possible. He's nervous about something."

Ryan thought about his boss and wasn't surprised to hear he was nervous. He should be. His job might be riding on whether Ryan solved this problem for the company. Working for Gatner for almost twenty years didn't mean Steve Caruthers' job was secure. No job was safe in this market.

"Okay," Ryan said. "I'll give Steve a call. There's also a chance I'll have to fly to Dallas. It all depends on how things go with Miller."

Ryan called his boss and gave him a report of his meetings from the day before, including some patterns he noticed in the production reports. While he couldn't promise a solution to the company's production problems, he could help discover the source of the problem.

"Glad to hear it," Steve said. "I'll anticipate a full report by Friday."

Ryan hung up and reached for another stack of papers while looking at his phone to check the time. He had a little time before he met with Miller. Something was missing in this report, but he couldn't put his finger on it.

If he didn't figure out the problem, his employment at Gatner might also be in jeopardy.

* * * * *

Erin plopped onto her couch and opened YouTube on her laptop. Several videos popped up after typing "learn how to bowl" in the search bar. Erin was about to put the *You Can Learn Anything By Watching YouTube* theory to the test.

"Learn how to bowl like a professional." Bowling like a professional would be an amazing accomplishment, but there's no chance she'd be a pro by tonight. Erin scrolled down and found another promising option: "Basic Bowling Techniques Part 1."

She knew the general idea behind bowling but had never tried the sport. All you had to do was throw a ball down a lane and hit the pins. Erin remembered a bowling trip with the youth group years ago. Bowling wasn't so simple.

All her friends had thrown the ball into the gutter, and every time, the other students shouted "gutter ball" in unison. Erin had known her ball would be gutter bound each time, so she opted not to try.

The YouTube video made the process look simple. She'd have to remember a forty-five-degree angle, pendulum swing, and twist her wrist.

Well, okay. I watched a video. I've got this.

Erin watched another short video, a little kid's version of bowling. A little girl walked to the line, put the ball between her feet, and shoved it down the lane with both hands. Cute, but Erin imagined herself using the two-handed approach, not so cute.

Cleaning house consumed the rest of the day. What would it be like to be so rich you could pay someone to do the cleaning? At least it provided plenty of time for thinking, and Erin's thoughts drifted toward Ryan.

Why did Ryan need to apologize to that girl? He'd never divulged what he'd done, nor was it any of her business.

Three days had passed since Ryan told her he wanted some changes in his life. Erin felt guilty not following up with him when she could've called. She'd call when she got home.

At 5:00, her doorbell rang. Erin willed the butterflies in her stomach to settle down. She gave herself a once-over and wondered if jeans and a button-up were the best look.

"Hey, Erin." Cody's eyes roamed down to her feet.

Erin glanced down at herself and realized she should've given herself a *twice-over*. She stared at her bare feet.

"Hey. Come in while I find my shoes." Erin offered a sheepish grin. "Want some iced tea or coke?"

"Coke?" Cody laughed. "Southerners crack me up. Where I come from, coke is illegal. We drink soda."

Erin tried to think of something witty to say, but nothing came to mind. "I suppose down here, soda means baking soda."

"Don't think I want any baking soda," Cody said. "Iced tea is fine."

Erin pulled a pitcher from the refrigerator and pushed the cup under the ice dispenser. "It's sweet. That okay?"

Cody smiled. "It's fine. I've adapted."

"She handed him the cup and went in search of her shoes. Five minutes later, Erin was ready to leave.

They stopped at Texas Roadhouse where Erin enjoyed grilled salmon, and Cody ate the biggest steak she'd ever seen. The packed place echoed with the laughter of customers.

A short time later, Cody pulled his SUV into the Show-time Bowling parking lot. Erin stared at the sign. *Yeah, we're about to have a show, all right. A comedy.* She shook her head and reminded herself to relax.

Once the attendant handed them their ugly shoes, Cody and Erin weaved in and out of the crowd to find their assigned lane. Erin couldn't help but notice some middle school kids occupying a couple of the lanes. Several bowling teams took up the other lanes.

One man on a bowling team threw a perfect strike, and Erin thought he could make a YouTube video. Someone should make one of her and put it on America's Funniest Videos.

Erin swapped shoes and began the challenging process of locating the perfect ball. Walking from rack to rack, she tried to decide. After picking up several, she discovered the finger holes were either too small or the balls too heavy.

"How much do you weigh?"

Erin straightened up and slowly turned to find Cody staring at her. His inquisitive expression didn't match her wide-eyed *I cannot believe you just asked me that* expression.

He held up both palms in an apologetic gesture. "Sorry. Finding a ball about ten percent of your body weight is best. I'd guess you weigh about...."

The color drained from Erin's face. Was he about to guess her weight?

Cody flashed an embarrassed grin.

The next ball Erin picked up fit. It felt right. "I've watched a YouTube video, so you're about to see a—"

"You what? You watched a video?"

Erin blew out a breath and held the ball to her chest. "Yes, on how to bowl correctly."

Cody smiled and turned to walk back to their lane. His shoulders dipped and appeared to be shaking.

Was he laughing at her? *Little snot.* Erin watched him pass another man. *Big snot.*

Erin handed her ball to Cody and noticed a middle school boy staring at her. *You may want to turn away, kid, or you could hurt yourself laughing.*

"You know how to keep score?" Cody asked as he returned to the table near the chairs.

"I don't know anything about bowling. I have a feeling that if we're going to keep score, it will be up to you."

Cody put his hands together under his chin as if he were about to pray. "By the time you leave, Erin, you'll be an expert. We don't have to keep score. The computer does it for us. I was just wondering if you understood it."

"Can't say that I do. I suppose ignorance will have to be bliss."

CHAPTER THIRTY-ONE

Genius Scheme

James Williams picked up his drink from the bar at Trackside and strolled to an empty booth. The last thing he wanted was to see someone he knew. When he opened the file he'd been carrying around, the divorce decree fell out onto the table. He wanted to shout or cheer, but he had to settle with toasting himself.

Remembering the shock on his wife's face when he gave her the Country Club house brought a smile to his face. Once he convinced her that giving her the place was the best decision, the proceedings moved forward. Charlene walked away with the house and a tidy sum of money that should take care of her for the rest of her life. No one contested the clause about denying access to future earnings or capital gains. Wouldn't she be surprised when he became the majority owner of Envision Pharmaceuticals with an accompanying stack of millions of dollars?

The whole scheme was genius, but a lot was at stake. This idea had better work. Success was his only option. The divorce settlement he'd agreed to left him the tiny townhouse he'd be moving into and his minimal retirement account. In time, however, he'd have enough money for ten lifetimes as long as everyone performed.

Bob said he had the perfect young man for the job, but James wanted to do his own research. He pulled out his pay-as-you-go phone and texted Bob.

"Just wanted to clarify that all is in order. Has your boy agreed to take on the project?"

Williams had been careful not to identify himself in previous messages, and he'd purchased a throw-away phone for Bob. Using burner phones would keep the authorities from being able to connect him to whatever Bob had cooked up for the Douglas girl.

His eyes roamed the bar, stopping on a beautiful young woman on the other side. So young and beautiful while he was old and broke. Once this deal was over, he'd have young women at his disposal. He looked at his phone and cursed under his breath. No response.

Come on, Bob. Check your phone.

This plan had to come together. So far, social media had been a little treasure-trove of information. Erin wasn't as active as he wished, but she'd posted a few nuggets. Pictures of walking on the campus of Perimeter College and her first day working at Barnes & Noble flashed through his mind. He'd managed to put together a solid bio on the girl by studying Erin's posts, and he passed it along to Morrow. Bob didn't seem to understand the urgency of their situation, however.

Williams reached for a napkin and listed all the variables related to this scheme. Some were out of his control, but other outcomes were within his power to manipulate, like hiring this young man. A lot would be in the boy's hands, so he'd better be perfect for the job.

Was Bob trustworthy? He'd better be. The plan was already in motion, but Williams desired some sort of guarantee, some assurance the boy would do the job. How could he ensure no one else knew of his involvement? He might even have to do away with Bob once the money was safely in his hands. The thought of Bob's million dollars made him smile. Bob may have a fatal accident before he could pick up his cut.

His phone buzzed. "I told you everything is fine. Don't worry about it."

"I'd also like to do my own background check of the young man. Too much riding on this project."

"Do you have other alternatives?"

Williams cursed again. Bob had a point. He had no alternatives and had no idea how to find someone else. Learning everything he could about the guy was still a priority. Bob's boy needed to know what was at stake if he failed.

"Send me his name, phone number, and home address," Williams replied. "And let me know where he'll live once he moves."

"Ok. We're working on some angles. I'll get as much information as I can to you shortly."

That evening, before getting ready for bed, Williams checked his email and found something from Bob. What an idiot! What was he thinking? They may as well contact the FBI and tell them every detail of their plan.

He sent Bob a blistering text telling the fool never to contact him again through his email. When he opened the email, it was clear Bob had done his homework. The email included a photograph of the young man and his girlfriend, addresses, emails, phone numbers, and several paragraphs offering information about his background.

His eyes studied the picture of the boy's girlfriend. What a knockout. Having details about this girl offered useful options. James copied the information, pasted it into a Word file, and deleted the email. He didn't know much about technology, but the authorities could still find emails on a server even if they had been deleted.

The guy was good-looking. Athletic. He'd played football in college until he injured his knee. Of course, he had a girlfriend back home.

So far, so good.

Somehow, he had to ensure the boy would function at a high level of efficiency. The kid had to be an excellent actor. Charming. Above all else, he had to be loyal to Williams.

But how to inspire that level of loyalty? Another variable. It clicked.

The answer slapped him in the face.

The girlfriend.

She'd be an ideal incentive.

* * * * *

"Ladies first," Cody said as he waved his hand toward the bowling balls.

Erin wiped the sweat from her palms and picked up her purple ball. The thing felt twice as heavy as it had earlier. Everyone in the place had to be watching her, but when she looked around, only Cody seemed to know she was about to make a fool of herself.

Come on, Erin. Get a grip on the ball—and yourself.

"Do you want some help?" Cody came toward her.

"Uh, well, I don't exactly know what I'm doing."

He had Erin spread her feet a little and swing the ball back and forth a few times to get a feel for what it would be like to release it. Next, he pointed Erin toward the pins. Reaching around her, he placed his hand on hers.

"In a minute, you'll take a few steps forward and bend at the waist a little. Put your left foot forward and release the ball toward the pins. You'll want to follow through with your right hand so it almost points at the pins."

Cody's proximity had her in knots, and she really liked his musk cologne.

"Look at the guy beside us. Watch how he does it."

Erin watched the man, a pro, no doubt. He launched the ball with unbelievable force and massive spin. All the pins toppled with a loud crack. The man turned and sauntered back to the seats like he threw strikes all the time.

Full of bravado, Erin tightened her grip. "Okay, I'm ready." Without pausing to give any more thought to what she was about to do, she marched a few steps forward and swung the ball back.

A thud and grunt sounded behind her. Not good.

Turning around, Erin gasped when she saw Cody doubled over. He'd been standing behind her. She brought her hands to her mouth to stifle a scream and dropped the ball, which rolled three lanes down through the middle schoolers.

"Cody, Cody. I'm so sorry. Are you okay?"

"I'm fine," he said through gritted teeth. "I should have moved out of the way."

"It's so my fault. I'm such a klutz."

"I'm fine," Cody said, catching his breath. "Guess we should both be a little more careful."

A young boy, working to maintain a solemn expression, walked up with her ball. Erin looked over to see his friends not bothering to hide their delight and amusement.

"Here you go, ma'am," the kid said and turned to rejoin his friends.

"Thank…" *Wait, what? Ma'am? Are you kidding me?*

Cody guided her through a few more practice throws from a safe distance. The first few were gutters, but then Erin knocked down a few pins.

"Great job!" Cody shouted as if she had just won the world championship.

He insisted she practice a little, and after a few tosses, Erin began to get the hang of it. Although her score wouldn't reveal any strikes, she managed to minimize her gutters. Sometimes, she even knocked down more pins than were left standing.

Cody's first toss went into the gutter, an obvious attempt to make her feel better.

"Come on, Cody. I know you're not trying. You don't have to make me feel better. I want to see your best effort."

Erin felt like her third-grade teacher. Her teacher's words came to mind. "Erin, I want your best effort today. You're going to be an outstanding student."

Cody got serious and resembled the professional bowler Erin had watched on YouTube. The ball crashed into the pins, and all ten pins flew up and dropped out of sight.

Cody was a bowling beast. Erin smiled and relaxed. The score didn't matter and how many pins she knocked down was insignificant.

She was having a good time.

* * * * *

Ryan boarded the plane for Dallas and connected to the inflight internet. He first looked at Gatner stock and saw, once again, it had dropped. The bleeding had to stop.

By the time the plane leveled out, he'd finished scanning the business section of the news and reached for his file folder.

He reviewed all the notes he'd made from his visit with Joe Miller and reflected upon the plant tour.

Ryan had seen the Gatner plants many times but had never considered them from the perspective of production flow. His time in Chicago revealed several flaws, so now, he had to confirm some things at the Dallas office. Lori, his assistant, called ahead to schedule a meeting with a couple of company engineers first thing in the morning.

Going to Dallas might not be so bad. He just hoped to arrive in time to go to his favorite Mexican steakhouse. Erin enjoyed Mexican food, too, and would adore this restaurant.

He wondered what she'd be doing on a Wednesday night. If she weren't working, she'd be sitting at home reading *Gone With the Wind* to her cat.

Earlier, Ryan had called Chris, a single guy that worked in Receiving. He was perfect for Erin. He had been interested at first but then got cold feet. Ryan didn't know too many more single guys who were available.

Erin seemed to be losing her nerve about this whole thing, anyway. Who could blame her? This decision would affect the rest of her life. Still, he hated to see her lose out on so much.

Ryan leaned back in his seat and closed his eyes. In just a few days, Erin would be down to eleven months. She had to find a man, get married, and have a baby. Solving Erin's problems made the issues at Gatner seem like a walk in the park.

CHAPTER THIRTY-TWO

Butterflies or Fear

E rin studied the bathroom mirror. The happy woman staring back nearly floated with joy. Her hand touched her cheek where he'd—.

I can't believe he kissed me. Tyler had kissed her cheek before he drove off into the sunset, but that had been a have-a-nice-life kiss.

It seemed obvious now, so why hadn't she seen it coming? Butterflies or fear? Both. She closed her eyes and relived the moment.

Cody had thanked her for going out with him. Erin had been processing the words "going out." The outing had been a date and not just two friends hanging out.

The kiss came out of nowhere. Well, maybe not nowhere. He was standing pretty close. The scent of his masculinity had been more than a little intoxicating, a mixture of his cologne and…and what? And Cody.

She needed to get over it. He kissed her on the cheek, that's all.

The silly grin seemed to be plastered to her face.

Her mind raced back through the events of the evening. They had a great time, and Cody behaved like a gentleman. Humble. The way he bowled, he could've beaten everyone there, but he didn't flaunt his skills.

Erin knew she couldn't let his good looks and charming personality sweep her into a relationship she'd regret.

What about the will? Should she lose all the money and the business?

Erin washed her face and got ready for bed, but her heart continued to race. Falling head over heels for this guy would not be a good idea. They were friends, that's all.

He was just a handsome, friendly guy who kissed her on the cheek. It happened all the time—NOT!

Too wired to sleep, Erin started making chamomile tea and turned on her computer while waiting for the water to boil. Scanning the house listings, she saw the cute little house she'd visited a couple of weeks ago still listed. But she'd have to fix it up, pay rent while making the house livable, and make the house payments. On top of that, she didn't know anything about remodeling houses. She'd have just as much chance of buying Buckingham Palace.

The teapot whistled, and Erin prepared her tea before returning to her computer. She opened another tab, checked her social media page, and saw a posting from the new girl, Emily Simpson. Was she at a birthday party? Her birthday? Erin went to Emily's page, saw it was her birthday, and sent her a birthday greeting.

Her messenger icon revealed she had a message. A smile spread across her face when she saw Tyler's name. How about that? He said he'd stay in touch. After scanning his message, she felt relief for her friend. It looked like the reunion with his father was going well, and he seemed to be settling into his new life. Knowing the following months of his life would be a significant challenge, Erin bowed her head, thanked God, and asked Him for grace and strength for Tyler.

When she looked back at her screen, a message from Emily had popped up.

"Thanks :) It's been a fun day with my family."

Erin tried to remember Emily. One of the negatives of attending a large church was that you only knew a small group of people.

Returning to the real estate page, Erin scanned the pictures of the house and reflected on her recent visit to the property. She opened her note app and started listing things to do to the house. Although she couldn't buy the house, it wouldn't hurt anything to figure out how much it would cost to remodel the place. It would be an educational experience.

She remembered seeing the things under the floor, the wood things that held up the floor. What did you call that? She'd have to spend some time on YouTube later.

Chip and Joanna Gaines, watch out—I'm coming for you.

Her mind started to wander, and she touched her cheek again. The smell of his musk still lingered in her memory. She opened her social media page again and entered his name into the search box. Cody Wilson had to be a popular name, but none were from Wisconsin. Maybe he didn't use social media, which would be another positive thing about him.

James Williams popped back into her mind, and her stomach knotted up when she remembered her day in the lawyer's office. Will or no will, she'd take this relationship with Cody slowly. If it was meant to be, OK. She'd have to let God work out the details in His timing.

* * * * *

Ryan pulled out his phone as he left the hotel gym early Thursday morning. Although sweat dripped from his forehead, he felt refreshed and ready to tackle the day.

He typed a message to Chris. "What do you think about going out with Erin? We could double tomorrow night." He could double, but who would go with him? Melissa was no longer an option. If Chris were willing to take Erin out, he could find someone.

His eyes focused on the phone while willing Chris to reply and agree to take Erin out. Nothing.

It was still early, so even though he planned to make it to the Dallas Gatner office by 8:30, he had plenty of time. He remembered something Erin said about reading the Bible in the mornings. He'd never thought much about reading the Bible and didn't know where to start.

After dressing, Ryan found a Gideon Bible in the bedside table drawer. He opened to the first chapter, "In the beginning, God created the heavens and the earth…" After making it through the creation, he read through several more chapters, which ended with Cain killing Abel. *Wow. Brutal.*

The sin in his life felt heavy, and he wondered if he was responsible for killing Sarah's baby. His baby. How could he overcome the guilt of encouraging Sarah to have an abortion? He'd even paid for it. Maybe he should talk with a pastor. The Bible talked about forgiveness. He once heard a preacher say that when we confess our sins, God buries them in the deepest sea and remembers them no more. How deep would the ocean have to be for God to forget Ryan's sin?

He checked his watch and hurried for his rental car. Dealing with this issue today meant he had to bring his A-game to this meeting. Fixing Gatner's problems would be a milestone-type accomplishment and might secure a promotion.

Driving toward the offices in Irving, Ryan thought about his motives for trying to fix his company's problems. These thoughts led him to consider his reasons for helping Erin. Being friends was a good enough reason. He wanted the best for her, and she deserved the best. Sticking her with the wrong guy couldn't happen. He'd find the right man.

When he pulled into a parking place and turned off the car, his phone buzzed with a text from Chris. Chris had been working on a friendship with someone else and didn't think going out with another woman would be a good idea. Ryan blew out a slow breath.

But what if this other woman could make you a multi-millionaire? Too bad Ryan couldn't mention that to him or anyone. Erin did not need some greedy sleaze to marry her just for the money.

He retrieved his briefcase from the back seat and hurried toward the office building.

* * * * *

Williams ripped open another box he'd packed in an effort to find his hammer. A string of curses spilled out when he cut his finger with the utility knife, and he got up to do something to staunch the bleeding. This packing thing was about to do him in. When he decided to give Charlene the house, he hadn't thought about the pain of getting his stuff out. A moving company was coming the next day, but he had decided to go ahead and pack a few items. But now, he had to get rid of the phone he'd used to call Bob.

Be smart, James.

Too bad he had to destroy a brand-new phone, but they were called "burner phones" for a reason. He had contacted the boy, which meant the key suspect in their little scheme had this number, so the phone had to go.

Placing the phone in a plastic bag, he pounded it with the hammer. While holding the broken phone over the trash can, he paused. Mistakes would get him caught. The trash can at the QT he'd pass on his way into town would be a better option. Then again, gas stations had video cameras aimed at the pumps, so he better choose a different place to discard the crushed phone. Metro Atlanta offered a billion possibilities. He'd also need to pick up another burner.

His conversation with the soon-to-be groom had been enlightening. The boy better be putting a wedding ring on the Douglas girl's finger soon. He'd seemed a little too cocky for James' liking. The lawyer reached for the coffee cup he'd left on the end table and considered what Bob's boy said. He'd been calm and confident, which were useful qualities, but the kid may need more convincing.

The picture in the Word file came to mind, and James had a brilliant idea. All he'd need would be a few photos of the girlfriend, the real girlfriend. A shot through the girl's bed-room window would be convincing. A little threat never hurt anyone; it would let the boy know how high the stakes were.

Did he have enough skill to take the shots himself? Prob-ably not. He'd need a professional if he were going to get closeups. A closeup photo of this girl inside her house would speak volumes. Williams smiled as he imagined the boy getting a picture like that of his girlfriend.

A friend had consulted with him about a case up north a few years ago, and one particular man had been quite useful in helping to win the case with his talent behind a camera. Williams made a few phone calls and got a number for Mac Salazar. Too bad photographers on the take didn't put listings in the Yellow Pages. Were Yellow Pages still a thing?

After gathering a few items and placing them into the car, Williams stabbed at his phone and waited until he heard

Salazar's voice. "Is this James? A friend told me to expect your call."

"Hello, Mac. You may not remember meeting me, but I remember you quite well. Are you available for a little photography job?"

"Depends. What's it paying?"

They agreed on a number and decided to meet in a couple of days. Williams hated flying up there, but this job was too important not to handle it personally. Once this affair was all over, Mac might need to have a fatal accident. No need to risk exposure.

Then again, this venture could be messy. Keeping Mac around might prove helpful. A man like Mac would be accustomed to keeping his mouth shut. James decided to tip him an extra thousand. Paying extra should persuade the knave to cooperate to the fullest.

What about the girl? Would he hurt her if things went sideways? Williams would have to make plans on the fly. The girl would be fine if her man cooperated to the fullest. Memories of the picture of the beautiful girl caused his heartbeat to quicken. She was fine, and hopefully, she'd stay that way.

He searched his smartphone for a phone number for Delta Airlines. Within moments, he made a reservation for a flight to Chicago.

CHAPTER THIRTY-THREE

A Picture's Worth...

"**I** enjoyed last night. Would you like to get dinner after work?"

Erin read the message a second time while pouring water into her coffee maker. Her mouth opened with a yawn. How could she be sleepy after riding nearly ten miles on her bike?

Cody wanted to go out again. Unbelievable. Tonight wouldn't work because of self-defense. Would Ryan be there? She hadn't heard from him, so hopefully, he'd made it back from Chicago. Maybe she should call him.

Erin thought about British Lit and the homework due by midnight. It was going to be a crazy full day. Writing the paper on Tolkien would be a breeze, but it might take a little time.

Her phone buzzed again. "Sorry. I forgot about school and your gym class. How about tomorrow night?"

Erin contemplated the text, unsure how to respond. For starters, Cody got points for remembering she took self-defense, but of course, he thought it was a fitness class. Maybe a little white lie wasn't so bad.

Did things seem to be going a little fast? Erin grinned as she thought about what Ryan would say. "If you're going to be married by next week and pregnant by the week after, you better get crackin'," Erin said in her best Ryan imitation.

She got up and poured fresh coffee into her thermos. Of course, marriage and having a baby were significant, and if she were a betting woman, she'd bet motherhood was not in her near future. Becoming a wife was a big deal, not to mention a mother. As for tomorrow night, why not? She enjoyed being with Cody. Another date wouldn't be the worst idea. He was probably lonely.

She was a little lonely, too.

Erin had Ryan, but he had every girl in the county. And there was Daphne.

Hours later, Erin hustled into the gym's locker room with a few minutes to spare and changed into her sweats. Tim told the group Tuesday night they could sign up for further martial arts training. The whole experience had been a lot of fun, and she'd learned a lot. Moving into general karate might be a good idea.

Hurrying out to the rubber mat, Erin looked around for Ryan. Where was he? Surely, he didn't bail again.

She found a spot next to Rachel, a sweet girl she'd met the previous week. Rachel turned toward Erin and smiled.

Tim led the group through the normal warmup period and asked them to practice some moves they'd previously learned with a partner. Rachel's moves were swift and smooth. Impressive. Erin hoped she'd be as good when her turn came. They spent the rest of the evening focusing on an introduction to karate.

When the instructor finally bowed at the end of the session, like he did each night, Rachel and Erin grabbed their water bottles and headed toward a small table in the corner.

"I have school tonight, online, so I can't stay too long," Erin said.

Rachel smiled and nodded. "So, where's Ryan? Did he quit on us?"

"No, he didn't quit. I'm not sure why he's not here. He had to be in Chicago this week, so maybe he didn't make it home yet."

"I thought you two were an item."

Erin laughed at the thought. "If we were an item, I'd probably be in prison for murder. I've known Ryan my whole life, but we could never date. I don't think of him that way."

Rachel grinned. "Good to know."

Erin tilted her head and studied Rachel. "Go for it. I don't think he's dating anyone right now, but he's a player."

"Oh. Hmmm. I don't know if I like the player types."

"Someone's got to make him settle down. He's a good guy, once you get to know him."

When Erin eventually reached her car, she told her phone to text Ryan Jeffries.

"Hey, lazy bones. Why weren't you at the gym?"

As she buckled her seatbelt, her conversation with Rachel came to mind. Rachel had asked if they were a couple. Why couldn't she and Ryan be "an item?" Oddly, the thought had never crossed her mind. The women he typically dated were in a different league, and she'd never qualify. But did Ryan qualify for her list?

If she had a list, it would be short. Who'd be on it? Cody? Tyler, for sure. Most guys wouldn't want to be included.

Guys sure weren't knocking the doors down to go out with her. Well, except Cody. He seemed interested. He'd eventually meet some other girl and forget Erin existed.

When Erin pulled into her driveway, her phone buzzed. "Sorry I missed your text. I just got out of a meeting."

"You sure are meeting late."

"Well, I'm an hour earlier than you, but still late."

"Oh, yeah. Chicago's in Central time."

"I'm in Dallas now."

"Oh. World traveler. Well, I'm not the only one who missed you. Remember Rachel?"

"Rachel?"

"Pretty brunette next to you a couple of weeks ago. She's got a thing for you."

"I'm supposed to be fixing you up. Not the other way around."

Erin smiled as she imagined Ryan, wherever he was. Thoughts of Ryan and Rachel together came to mind, and her smile faded. The petite brunette wouldn't be a good fit for him.

"Working on another guy," Ryan texted.

Erin shook her head; she didn't need another one of Ryan's friends.

"Don't bother. Had a date last night. Going out again tomorrow."

"??? You're kidding."

"I know. Hard to believe I can find a guy, but yeah."

"Not what I meant."

What did he mean? Why would he think she was kidding? Ryan had every reason to be shocked.

"I'll be home tomorrow," Ryan replied. "Want to go to breakfast Saturday?"

Did she want to go to breakfast with Ryan? "Have to be at work at 10."

"No problem. We'll go early. Cracker Barrel at 8:00! See you then."

Cracker Barrel was a little...well, old. *Why do I let him decide everything about my life?* Erin shoved the phone into her pocket and slammed the car door.

* * * * *

The balding man walked toward the corner booth, and James Williams thought of his pistol in the glove box of his car back home. Was it legal to carry a gun in Chicago?

Mac sat down across from him. "Hello, James."

Williams closed his laptop and reached across the table to shake the man's hand. "Mac. Thanks for meeting me. Do you have anything for me?"

Meaty fingers reached into a pocket, pulled out a flash drive, and held it up for Williams. "Got a USB port on that laptop? You may want to turn your screen so no one can see."

James reached for the flash drive, but Mac pulled it back.

Mac shook his head. "I think there's a little matter of re-muneration first. Five g's?"

The lawyer checked to make sure they weren't being watched and reached into his inner coat pocket. He slid the envelope inside the menu and placed it in the center of the table. "Let's say you can study the menu after I've seen the photos. Deal?"

A waitress walked over with coffee for Mac as the two men sized up each other. Williams had played this game before, and he was no idiot.

Once the waitress walked away, Mac nodded and handed over the flash drive. The small light on the tiny drive turned bright blue, and James eventually found four files. When he clicked on the first one, a picture of a beautiful blonde girl walking into an office building appeared on his screen. The following photos showed her in a grocery store, walking down a sidewalk, and sunbathing beside a swimming pool. He ogled the last one before pushing the menu toward Mac.

Mac pulled another thumb drive from his pocket. "I've got a few more on here that might interest you. They'll only cost another ten grand."

Williams raised an eyebrow at the thug. The guy was smart but still a thug.

"I think these four will work just fine, " the lawyer said before pocketing the small drive. He gathered his things and slid out of the booth, intent on leaving.

"Suit yourself," Mac said as he reached for his coffee. "But I used a telephoto lens."

A closeup of the girl would be invaluable, especially if the shots were taken in a place her boyfriend thought private.

"How do I know they're worth it?" Williams asked.

"Oh, they're worth it. I found an empty apartment across from hers. Get the idea?"

"That a fact?"

"Oh, yeah, and I've got a powerful lens. You might even think...Well, you'll want to see for yourself."

Returning to his seat, Williams tried to calm his racing heart. How could he stall for time? The swindler knew he had him, and James just had to figure out how to access more cash.

"You know I can't pull $10,000 from my account without the authorities being notified. How about $9,500?"

"$9,900 will work," Mac said with an evil grin. "I'll wait."

When Williams returned thirty minutes later, Mac ate breakfast calmly as if he had nothing else to do the entire day. Why would he have anything to do? The man was about to make nearly $15,000. Williams sat down to repeat the enve-lope-in-the-menu action, but the waitress had taken the menu. The folded newspaper worked just as well.

The pictures on the second thumb drive left Williams speechless as he stared with open mouth. He would have paid twenty or thirty thousand for these shots, especially the last one. What would this girl's boyfriend think? He slid the newspaper over to Mac. The photographer pocketed the envelope and left the restaurant without a word.

Williams had already created a bogus email address and figured he'd find a public library somewhere in town. If he sent these pictures to the boy one at a time from different public computers, no one would ever be able to track the emails to him.

He spent several hours moving from computer to computer to send the emails. As he sent the last one, a big smile spread across his face, and he wished he could have been a fly on the wall to watch the guy. Each email offered threats along with select photographs.

Williams checked to ensure no one was watching, even though he'd intentionally chosen a computer that faced a wall. He pulled up the final picture from the file, the most convincing of them all. He scrutinized the beautiful girl and knew Bob's boy would be convinced to cooperate. *I think I already hear some wedding bells in Georgia.*

CHAPTER THIRTY-FOUR

Plans to Prosper

E rin spotted Ryan's black BMW sitting far from other vehicles as she pulled into the Cracker Barrel parking lot Saturday morning. Thinking about Ryan babying his car brought a smile to her face. She pulled beside his empty car and considered telling him someone had keyed it. He'd have a stroke.

Ryan sat near a window in the restaurant with a cup of coffee, his iPad open in front of him. The man never stopped.

Erin hung back at the dining area's entrance and took in the sights and sounds. Conversations from early-morning diners provided an ambiance of friendship as country music played through the speakers, offering the final touches for a relaxing dining experience. The smell of bacon and fresh biscuits had Erin salivating. Her stomach growled. She loved coming to this place.

Her gaze fell on the massive stone fireplace with a giant checkerboard nearby. A memory flooded her mind. She'd sat at that checkerboard with her brother a week before he'd been killed.

Her family had been so normal then. What went wrong? Her brother had died, and his death changed everything. She'd always considered the accident her fault. Ryan told her a million times Ricky's death wasn't her fault, but if she'd been the caring big sister she should have been, Ricky would still be alive.

Something else Ryan often said floated through her mind. "Yesterday ended at midnight, and you can't change the past. You can only live in the moment and change the future." He was right. Regret had consumed her for years for not taking her little brother, but she had to let it go.

Ryan looked up from his iPad, saw Erin, and waved her over.

Erin walked through the crowd to the corner table. "Fancy meeting you here."

"Well, if it isn't a little sunbeam floating through the breakfast crowd."

She rolled her eyes and pulled out a chair. A waitress delivered two menus and took their drink orders.

Erin crossed her arms. "So, where have you been? You missed self-defense twice this week. If I didn't know better, I'd say you signed me up and ditched me."

"You know I wouldn't do that. I had to fly to Dallas for another meeting on Thursday. I think I've solved a huge problem at Gatner and plan to share my proposal with my boss on Monday. It'll dramatically change how we do distribution for the whole company."

"That's good news. Maybe they'll give you another promotion, and you can buy another BMW."

"Ah, sass. I like that." Ryan grinned at Erin over the top of his cup.

"Okay, so I'm glad you've figured out something that significant," Erin admitted. "And I'm not upset with you. I did miss you, but I've really enjoyed self-defense. I told Tim Thursday night I want to continue with karate."

"I'm shocked but not surprised, Erin. You were born for this, and you're already in top shape. You make all those other girls look like tubs of lard."

Erin's cheeks reddened, but deep down, the compliment thrilled her. "Don't *shocked* and *surprised* mean the same thing?"

"Um, not following. Anyway, you definitely run circles around those other girls. So, what have you been up to? Read any more good books to your cat?"

"Funny. Actually, I've gone out on a couple of dates this week. Technically, one was just dinner at my house, but the second was bona fide."

"What?" Ryan raised a little from his chair. "You let a guy you barely know into your house? What were you thinking, Erin? He could have—"

"Calm down, Ryan. He's a new guy at work. I had to train him Tuesday, and I had a major plumbing problem that morning. The handle on the bathtub broke when I was taking a shower. It just so happens he used to work for a plumber."

"So, you believe a guy's word that you don't know, and you bring him through your bedroom into your bathroom? Erin, that's not smart."

"He fixed it," Erin continued, unfazed by Ryan's retorts. "I made him spaghetti, and he asked me out for Wednesday night. We went bowling."

"Bowling? Since when did you learn how to bowl?"

"Since Wednesday night. We had a great time. He's a charming guy, and we went out again last night."

Erin observed Ryan's unreadable face. Was he angry? Hurt? He was probably utterly stunned that she could land a date without his help. Every date he'd orchestrated had not worked out. On the other hand, he had nothing to do with her going out with Tyler or Cody, and both guys had been perfect gentlemen. Although she'd only gone out twice with Cody, he'd been a lot of fun so far.

"Two dates in a row," Ryan said skeptically. "Sounds serious."

"I wouldn't say bowling and walking through a cemetery with a flashlight is serious."

"You did what?"

"We went to dinner, and I told Cody I used to love walking through the cemetery at night as a little girl. So, he took me to McDonough Memorial, and we spent two hours looking at gravestones with a flashlight. I know it sounds weird, but I had a great time."

"At least, you're a cheap date. I've never been so lucky."

Erin had always considered the girls Ryan dated as high maintenance. What did he see in them?

The waitress returned with their coffees and took their orders.

When she walked away, Ryan peered across his coffee cup at Erin. "So, where's this relationship going?"

"I don't know. For now, it's going to church tomorrow."

"You're taking him to church?"

Erin knitted her brows. "Why not? He grew up going to church and hasn't found one down here that he likes."

"Down here?"

"He just moved here from up north. Kenosha, Wisconsin. Loves the Packers."

"There's one strike against him."

"You're just sore they got into the playoffs, and the Falcons didn't."

"I'm surprised you know that bit of trivia."

"Cody told me."

"Figures."

* * * * *

Ryan woke early Sunday morning and tried to organize his plans for the day. For one thing, it was Erin's father's birthday. Fred Douglas' birthday would be hard for Erin with the death of her dad being so fresh. The thought of getting her flowers crossed his mind, but what's his name would be hanging around today.

Learning that Erin's new boyfriend would be at church had messed up his plans. He wanted to go to Southpoint with her, but that was out of the question now. The church across town he normally attended was fine, but he wanted to hear the next sermon in the "Identity Theft" series.

The coffee maker dinged to announce a fresh pot, so Ryan filled a mug and went to his favorite chair in the living room. Reaching for his Bible on the end table, he considered reading a few more chapters. The stiff leather revealed how little he picked up this book. Erin's Bible was soft and limp. Maybe his would be well-worn like that one day.

Genesis had been so interesting that he finished reading it Thursday and had plowed into Exodus. He started getting slightly bogged down the previous day but wanted to try again.

Fanning the pages of his Bible, Ryan had no idea what to read next. He'd heard a preacher say every word was important, but what words did Ryan need today? He decided to open the Bible and read whatever caught his attention.

Closing his eyes, Ryan held the Bible up, opened it with his thumbs, and ran his finger down the page. When he opened his eyes, his finger pointed to a passage from Jeremiah on the left side of the page. He read, "Why will you die, you and your people, by the sword, famine, and pestilence?"

Ryan stopped reading. *Wow. Not sure that works for today.*

His eyes scanned across the page, and the word "plans" jumped out at him. Anything about planning would be pertinent anytime. The words from Jeremiah 29:11 seemed to jump off the page, "'For I know the plans that I have for you,' declares the Lord, 'plans for welfare and not for calamity to give you a future and a hope.'"

God had plans for him. Interesting. The idea of God having plans for him had never crossed his mind, but it sounded intriguing. The next verse grabbed his attention: "Then you will call upon Me and come and pray to Me, and I will listen to you."

Ryan had not prayed much, but according to this verse, prayer should be an important part of his life. He'd heard all his life that prayer was talking to God. What should he say? God would probably want him to pray for the most important people in his life. Erin was at the top of his list. He didn't want to see her get hurt or marry the wrong guy.

Bowing his head, Ryan began to pray. He covered several topics but spent most of the time praying for Erin. Gratitude for God's intervention in helping him figure out the problems at Gatner spilled from his heart as well. After saying, "Amen," Ryan wondered if it was right to pray about work and decided that since God loved him, He would be interested in anything on Ryan's mind.

Ryan also considered his prayer for Erin and wondered if his words expressed his thoughts and feelings. His thoughts were jumbled, and he couldn't seem to capture one of them to analyze it.

The ticking of the clock caught his attention. If he wanted to attend early service at Southpoint, he'd better get moving.

The thought of Erin with what's his name crossed his mind again. Going to the later service would be the best idea. He drove toward Starbucks, where he could kill a little time. Working a little more on the proposal for his boss before the service wouldn't hurt anything. As long as he arrived at South-point twenty minutes before the service started, he'd be able to get a seat near the front.

* * * * *

Erin and Cody found two empty seats in the crowded auditorium. She looked around for Ryan before noticing Cody watching her. Heat rose up her neck. Going to church with a guy felt odd.

It wouldn't be a date, just two friends meeting at church.

Was he the right one? It was hard to tell at this point. Hopefully, God would give her wisdom. This decision had nothing to do with a will, a pharmaceutical company, or millions of dollars; it had everything to do with God's plan for her life.

She pulled out her phone to text Ryan but looked up to see the worship band taking the stage. He would have to wait.

As the congregation began to sing, it seemed Cody didn't know the songs. Maybe they sang different songs in Wisconsin. Regardless, the music soaked into her soul, and hope and joy seemed to seep through her pores. No wonder God wanted His people to worship.

Thoughts of divine love continued to fill her soul as the music ended, and the pastor stepped on stage. Wherever Cody fit into her life, God had something special for her that day.

CHAPTER THIRTY-FIVE

Moving In

Ryan pulled into the church parking lot and began searching for an empty space. The landscaping on the small island to his left was all withered grass. No flowers. It looked as barren as his heart felt.

Memories of the way he'd treated women over the years flooded his mind. How many were like Sarah? How many still hadn't recovered from the pain he'd inflicted?

Why do I do that to women?

He could at least change the tense from *do* to *did*. From now on, he would treat women with the respect they deserved. Dating would take a back seat for a while. He had to work on his priorities, and character mattered.

Scanning the parking lot, Ryan couldn't find a single empty space. It was usually packed. Even at a time when many people seemed to have more pressing matters, people who attended this church made coming each week a priority.

Ryan had always enjoyed coming to Southpoint, but his enthusiasm usually centered around meeting women. This morning, his excitement came from a different motivation. Something inside him had changed.

His whole perspective had been wrong. Religion had always seemed like a way for preachers to fleece people for money or for people to fulfill some obligation. Maybe some just attended to ease their consciences.

Maybe that perspective was wrong. What had changed in his heart?

By the time Ryan found a parking space, people began filing out of the building. The early service must be over. A couple walked his way, and he recognized Erin. Reaching for the door handle, he froze when he saw the guy take Erin's hand. Something deep in the pit of Ryan's stomach churned.

Is this how a protective brother feels toward his little sister?

Erin and the guy walked toward Erin's car, parked one row over from Ryan. Ryan noticed a familiar awkward expression on Erin's face, one he'd seen several times through the years. Usually, it meant she was uneasy about something, but she seemed happy. They talked and laughed. She seemed more than happy, maybe even enthralled.

Ryan studied her friend, tall and well-built. He looked familiar, but Ryan couldn't place him. The gym? Home Depot?

He felt like a voyeur watching them interact beside Erin's little blue Toyota. Keith held her hand. Not Keith. What was his name?

Cody. That's his name.

To Ryan's shock, the guy kissed her cheek. Ryan reached for the door handle again but stopped.

Come on, Ryan. That's what you want, isn't it?

If Erin was going to get married, a kiss was bound to happen sooner or later. Too bad he had a front-row seat. Of course, it was just a quick little kiss, but it was still a kiss.

Erin pulled out and drove toward the exit. Cody stuck his hands into his pockets and sauntered toward an older model, white Chevy Blazer. Ryan would have to get the scoop from Erin about this guy later, but he couldn't make it sound like an interrogation. All that mattered was that Erin was okay.

Ryan waited another three minutes, watched Cody pull off, and hurried toward the auditorium.

* * * * *

Erin had so much to do before small group, but she couldn't concentrate. She had just cleaned the toilet for the second time. Where was her brain? The fact Cody had held her hand while walking to her car had unsettled her enough, but then he kissed her on the cheek again.

Her heart had nearly melted. When he leaned in, he smelled strong, musky. His chiseled features remained on her mind. She didn't know what he saw in her, but their relationship was progressing. Seeing him interact with her small group Bible study in a few hours would be a treat. In the meantime, she had to clean her house.

Several hours later, Erin and Cody stood in the apartment of a young, single woman in Erin's church. Cody handled the Bible study discussion well, though Erin wondered whether he'd been familiar with the passage. She wanted him to fit her checklist of the kind of guy she wanted to marry, but the jury was still out.

One thing was sure, the group seemed impressed with him. Even the guys liked him. Erin caught more than one of the girls staring. Cody's square jaw and broad shoulders would draw the attention of any female. Erin had a hard time keeping her eyes off him, too.

The group began leaving one by one, and Erin suggested she and Cody head home. Grabbing coffee would have been nice, but she had a few more things to do before bed. Tomorrow would be busy.

Once Cody started the vehicle, and Erin clicked her seatbelt, she turned toward him. "What did you think?"

"It was good."

"Good?"

"Yeah. I enjoyed it. I've never been to a Bible study group in someone's home, so I didn't know what to expect."

"I guess that means your church doesn't have small groups?"

"Oh, well, I," Cody paused for a second and cleared his throat. "No."

"Do they have Sunday School?"

"Yes."

"I went to a church when I was a little girl that had Sunday School before worship, except we called worship Big Church. We did crafts and sang songs. I always felt a little awkward in Sunday School."

They drove across town and pulled into Erin's driveway. Glancing at her phone, she saw it was nearly 8:30. So much for finishing chores. Going to bed on time had to be her priority, and she still needed to finish a little homework.

Cody walked Erin to the front door, and she fumbled for the keys. After missing the keyhole three times, she finally unlocked the door and turned back toward him. "Thanks for going with me. I hope you'll consider going back next week. I think they all liked you."

"I'd like that very much."

Cody stepped toward Erin and took her hands. "I enjoy being with you a lot. I know you're busy on Monday and Tuesday, but would you be free to go out again Wednesday?"

Erin felt the familiar flutter in her stomach and the heat crawled up her neck. It always turned red when she got embarrassed or nervous.

"Sure. I'd love to go out."

"I suppose we can talk about specifics on Tuesday. I assume we're both working during the afternoon."

Erin noticed he seemed to be closing the space between them. "I work all day on Tuesday."

Cody slowly pressed his lips against hers like something scripted in a dream. The tender kiss tingled all the way to her toes. Not possessive or demanding. She could have avoided his advance, but she didn't.

When Erin opened her eyes, he was pulling away. Her heart was about to beat out of her chest. What was she supposed to say? "Um, well, thanks for keeping…I mean coming, or rather going with me."

Cody stepped toward the front porch steps. "I had a great time. See you Tuesday."

* * * * *

Ryan sat straight up in bed and reached for the light on the bedside table. Sleep had been pulling him under when the image of Erin's boyfriend popped into his subconscious. Of course, it wasn't like the guy hadn't been on his mind all day.

Earlier, he'd tried to review his investment portfolio and study a few new opportunities, but he couldn't think straight. He kept seeing Cody leaning over and kissing Erin's cheek. Did she enjoy it? Did she want it? Ryan couldn't tell. The guy's body had blocked her face, but the kiss had been on her cheek. The scene replayed a hundred times in his mind, and he decided it was the guy's angle that had convinced him.

Wow, Ryan. What's with the obsession?

Sleep was out of the question for now. That guy, Cody. He had seen him somewhere, and it hadn't been at Home Depot.

The clock beside his bed glowed. Eleven o'clock, ten o'clock in Chicago. He scanned his contacts and dialed a number.

"Hey, Sarah. This is Ryan, Ryan Jeffries. Sorry to be calling you so late."

"Ryan? Uh…hey. I didn't expect to hear from you so soon. No, it's not late. Seeing you this week was a shock and a blessing at the same time."

"I'm so glad to hear it, Sarah."

"I think talking over everything with you has helped me take another step toward closure on a dark time in my life. My feelings have been in such turmoil for a while. I think you coming to Chicago was a God thing."

"I hope so. Have you heard from your fiancé since he was deployed?"

"Not yet. He told me not to expect to hear from him for a few weeks. Everything seemed kind of top secret. You know how the military and special ops are."

"Yeah. Hush, hush. Listen, I may go to Afghanistan in a few weeks."

"Really? You're going to Afghanistan? I didn't know you were military."

"I'm not. I'm helping out with a nonprofit that works with soldiers."

"That's really selfless, Ryan. You've changed."

Ryan felt like a creep for blatantly lying to the girl he'd already hurt so badly. "I hope so. I thought I could say hello if I ran into your boyfriend. I figured we could at least get breakfast together or something. Do you have a picture of him you could send me?"

After talking a few more minutes about her boyfriend, Ryan was armed with a useful description and the guy's name. Sarah told him about her plans for the next twelve months and expressed her desire for the weeks to fly by until she and her fiancé could get back on track for their wedding.

"Sorry to bother you, Sarah. I just got word of my potential travel plans and had the idea."

"I'm so glad you called, Ryan. Could you do me a favor?"

"Sure. Happy to."

"Could I send you a framed picture to take to him? He left so quickly that I didn't even think about giving him something to remind him of me."

"Yeah. Happy to take anything along."

"I've got a digital shot of him on my phone. Do you want me to send it to you?"

"Sure. It wouldn't hurt to have that, too."

Ryan gave her his address and said he didn't know exactly when he'd be leaving. She promised to overnight a package, so he'd have it before he left.

Before disconnecting the call, Ryan heard a woman's voice in the background. Sarah said something to her roommate about getting coffee. Coffee at 10:00 was never a good idea in Ryan's world. After ending the phone call, he turned out the light and listened for his phone to buzz with a picture from Sarah, but it didn't happen. Maybe she got distracted by the thought of cappuccino.

His mind replayed his conversation with Sarah as the blatant lie he told her bothered him. It was odd he was so disturbed by dishonesty. The old Ryan lied all the time. Lying would have to be a thing of the past now. This time, however, lying was justified.

Can lying ever be just?

Maybe his hunch was wrong.

CHAPTER THIRTY-SIX

Discovered

Tuesday afternoon, Ryan saw a package on the front porch as he pulled into his driveway. He trotted over, the heat of a summer day nearly taking his breath. A fly landed on his nose and took off again as he bent over, picked up the package, and hurried into the air-conditioned house.

His sharp pocketknife slid through the tape, and Ryan pulled out a framed photograph. Sarah Hardwick's beautiful smile caught his attention first before he focused on the tall, blue-eyed, muscular guy she embraced.

"Bingo!" Ryan said aloud. "I can't believe it. What in the world is going on?"

Sarah's fiancé stared at him from the picture—the guy who had kissed Erin just two days earlier. Ryan knitted his brows and rubbed his face. How was he going to tell Erin? Or Sarah? Both women would be devastated.

He checked his Fitbit and saw he only had forty-five minutes to eat and get to the gym. Tonight would be the last session unless he opted to move into the martial arts course with Erin.

How would he face Erin while knowing the truth about her new boyfriend? Should he call and make an excuse for missing? *No, I can't do that to her. I've already missed the last two. Besides, I'm her friend. I need to decide on the best way to break the news to her. Before doing that, I have to figure out what's happening.*

* * * * *

Erin parked outside the gym later than she'd intended. Pulling the visor mirror down, she looked at her makeup and inspected her teeth before spotting salad dressing on her T-shirt.

Ugh. Slob.

The day had been so rushed. She'd forgotten her lunch that morning and didn't want to pay for Arby's or Chick-fil-A. Besides, there were healthier options. So, after work, she'd gone home and scarfed down some sliced sandwich meat and a leftover salad.

And I'm wearing the evidence of my frugality. Oh, well. A little Ranch never hurt anyone.

After changing into her workout clothes, Erin marched into the main workout room as the wall clock hit 7:00. Ryan sat stretching on the mat across the room, and she hurried to join him.

Erin dropped onto the mat beside him to begin warming up. "Hey! How'd it go with your boss? I'm sure your awesome proposal blew him away."

"Fine."

"Fine? That's it? You mean he didn't give you a promotion, bonus, or two-week cruise through the Mediterranean?"

"Nope. He said he'd look it over."

"I can't believe it. You work your rear end off for that company, and they don't even appreciate it."

The instructor entered, and everyone settled down. He nodded at Ryan with what Erin thought was mental chastening for missing the last two sessions. Then, he reminded the group about the upcoming martial arts class.

Erin looked at Ryan and whispered, "You going to sign up?"

"Maybe."

Ryan barely spoke the whole evening. Something was eating him. Erin figured she'd be irritated too if she'd been treated by her boss the way Ryan had been by his. They didn't seem to know what a fantastic asset he was to the company.

After class, he didn't have time to hang around. Erin thought they'd at least go for coffee. He said he had piles of work backed up from when he'd spent last week traveling.

When Erin reached the intersection where she usually took a left turn to go home, her car turned right into the Kroger parking lot, almost on its own. She'd recently bought groceries and should have resisted the urge. Before her brain took over, she hurried into the store and walked out a few minutes later with Moose Tracks ice cream. *What am I doing? Oh, well. Too late. I've already bought it.*

Daphne welcomed her as soon as she entered the house. Reaching into the cabinet, Erin pulled out a large bowl and spooned in a healthy portion of ice cream. She sat on the couch where the cushion material was worn and discolored.

Erin opened her laptop, went online, and searched the familiar real estate page for new listings. She poured through all the ads and didn't come across her favorite little house until half of her ice cream had disappeared.

"Look at that, Daffy. Our house is still listed."

Daphne jumped down and scampered toward the bedroom as if she didn't want to move to a new home. Erin clicked on the thumbnail of the little gingerbread-looking house and retook the virtual tour. She zoomed in and imagined how she'd transform it into her perfect home.

What would Chip and Joanna do?

She reached for her remote and pulled up the menu of all the episodes of "Fixer Upper" she'd recorded. Picking one she hadn't seen, she closed the computer and leaned back, ready for inspiration.

* * * * *

"What's up with the pics of his fiancée?" Bob wheezed.

Williams sat in his favorite chair with the phone between his ear and shoulder. He pulled his laptop closer and, with a few clicks, had the best photo of the girl open on the screen. She appeared to be almost posing for the camera. The only thing missing from her beautiful face was a big smile.

The pictures ruffled Bob, but he had to realize they didn't have time to play games. The boy would know this venture was important business. James' emails made it clear that whoever employed Bob knew precisely where his girlfriend lived.

"I felt like your boy needed a little encouragement, Bob. That's all." Williams zoomed in.

"One of those pictures was, like…How did you get it, James? You know this isn't right!"

"In my book, anything goes. Your boy needs to put things into high gear and marry Erin ASAP. I'm concerned he's wasting time. I figured a few strategic pictures would convince him his role is critical."

Bob cursed. "He knows it's critical, James. Your pictures have almost caused him to call it quits so he can get home to protect his fiancée."

Williams slammed his coffee cup onto the table, spilling its contents on the floor. "You tell your boy that he won't have a fiancée to protect if he leaves town," he growled. "Do you understand me?"

He listened to silence on the other end. "On top of that, remind him we're paying him quite well. Also, tell him that because I'm such a gracious guy, I'll add another $10,000 to his pay if he has a ring on her finger in the next three weeks."

"That's absurd, James. You can't just meet a girl and marry her four weeks later."

"People do it all the time. Speaking of time, we're running out of it. Erin not only has to get married but must also get pregnant in the next several months. If it takes him four weeks to marry the girl, we'll be down to less than two months. Sometimes, these things take time. You call up the boy and talk him off the ledge. Tell him the emails were to let him know how determined we are and that he needs to move a little faster."

After disconnecting the call, he rubbed his eyes. The boy wasn't the only one on the ledge. Williams didn't like a venture like this that depended on an unknown, and this kid was an unknown.

He reached for his burner phone and called Bob back. "I want to know what the boy is doing at all times."

"At all times? That's impossible."

"Well, I at least want to know his schedule and when he's going out with the girl again."

"Okay. I'll let him know. They're going out tomorrow."

"Where are they going?"

"Early dinner somewhere and then to Nash Farms for some kind of demonstration. The real rodeo's in a few months."

"Interesting. Okay. Bob, tell me where they'll eat as soon as you know. Got it?"

"Sure. What are you going to do?"

"Relax. I want to check on the cute couple to see how things are going."

Once he got Bob off the phone, Williams pulled up the website about the event at Nash Farms. They had demonstrations of calf roping, barrel racing, and bull rides. There'd be games for kids and a petting zoo. BBQ plates, too. *They're probably eating at the event.*

He pulled up his schedule for the next day and emailed his assistant to cancel his last two appointments. Checking on the boy's progress at Nash Farms should be fairly easy.

The encounter at the Omni Hotel had been a total accident. If Erin saw him at Nash Farms, she'd think it odd. Blending in with a bunch of rodeo enthusiasts shouldn't be too difficult.

How does a tall businessman fit in at a rodeo? Williams looked toward his clothes closet. A cowboy hat! While packing up his old house last week, he'd considered throwing his old hat away but, for some reason, chose to keep it. His face broke into a smile as a plan came to mind. *A Stetson hat and sunglasses will do wonders.*

Chapter Thirty-seven

Coming Together

J ames hurried through his last appointment as he listened to Mrs. McBee's familiar story for the third time. Every divorce story had the same theme. They all usually involved selfishness and sex. It was typically the man, but he'd seen more women stepping out of their marriage vows lately.

Mrs. McBee took up every bit of space in the chair where she sat. "I don't know what Don sees in his secretary," she prattled on. "She's just a kid and is such an airhead. I can't imagine my husband wanting to marry such a bimbo. I questioned whether he should have hired her to start with. I think she came from the club across the street from his office, but that's just my suspicion. He'll come crawling back to me in a month, but I'm not taking the jerk back. I want to stick it to him so hard that he's got nothing left. He's crossed a line this time. I should have done something about him a long time ago. Don't you think? Mr. Williams? Mr. Williams?"

Realizing the woman was calling his name, the lawyer looked up. "Uh, yes, Mrs. McBee. I'm sorry. I'll get all the paperwork together and give you a call."

"Don't you want to hear how I found out about his little fling?"

"I'm sorry, Mrs. McBee. I'm due at the courthouse for a deposition. I'll have Angie contact you for another appointment when I'm ready." He stood, walked around the edge of his desk, and stuck out his hand, but she seemed to have difficulty extricating herself from the chair. She finally popped free and grabbed the lawyer's hand with hers.

After she left his office, Williams sat back down behind his desk. He contemplated his situation and how low he had to stoop these days. Why couldn't people get married and stay that way? Whatever happened to "for better or for worse?"

His marriage hadn't gone the distance either. Charlene was probably moving back into their Country Club home at that moment. Of course, it wasn't theirs anymore. It was hers.

After throwing a few files into his briefcase, he headed for the front door. Poor Angie was being held captive by Mrs. McBee, so he twisted his hand in the air like he was locking the door. Angie closed her eyes and nodded.

He hurried to his Mercedes, dreading the inevitable rat race on I-285. After punching Nash Farms into his GPS, his car squealed out of the parking lot.

Nearly an hour and a half later, a cowboy on a horse directed Williams to a parking place. The green, rolling pastures of the massive ranch, now functioning as an event center, was a goldmine. To his right, a flurry of activity around the gazebo caught his eye. They seemed to be decorating. For a wedding, perhaps?

Bringing Erin to a wedding venue would be ingenious. Maybe the boy was smarter than Williams had thought. His burner phone buzzed with a message from Bob. "They're eating at the rodeo."

Of course, they were eating at the rodeo. He pulled up his phone and typed in a message. "What kind of vehicle does your boy drive?"

"White Chevy Blazer. Possibly 2012?"

When the man on the horse rode away, Williams turned his car so he could watch the entrance. He left the engine running and the air conditioning on high. Slipping on his sunglasses, the lawyer got comfortable.

* * * * *

Erin had been excited all day about the rodeo. Of course, this wasn't exactly going to be a rodeo, but a demonstration was even better for her. She'd never been to a rodeo and wouldn't know how to enjoy one. Maybe after attending this event, she and Cody could return for the real thing in a few months.

The ride to Nash Farms had been as relaxing as if she and Cody had been friends for a lifetime. She marveled at how quickly they'd gotten to know one another, but did she really know him after such a short time?

What she did know, she liked. The bouquet of daisies he'd given her at the door had almost won her heart. He had more manners than anyone she knew other than Ryan. Cody opened doors for her and was always concerned about her comfort. Erin smiled.

We shall see.

A cowboy on a horse approached the vehicle and directed Cody to the next open parking place. Erin shook her head in amazement. *Welcome to the rodeo.*

As soon as Cody turned off the ignition, he was out the door and around to Erin's side. He opened the door and extended his hand to her. When her feet hit the ground, her momentum propelled her into his arms.

He didn't back away. His arms encircled her, and he slowly bent down and briefly kissed her, not a passionate kiss, but powerful, nonetheless. As he pulled away, Erin stood frozen, unable to speak or move.

Cody reached for her left hand. "You hungry? I heard they've got the best barbecue in the South."

The spell broken, Erin heard the car doors lock and saw Cody slipping the key fob into his pocket. As they headed toward the main entrance, Erin noticed a shiny Mercedes Benz pull out of its parking place and head toward the exit. *Why would someone be leaving? The show hasn't even started.*

Cody tugged on her hand, and they moved toward the gate where a middle-aged woman in a gingham dress took tickets. This was going to be a fun night.

* * * * *

For the third time in ten minutes, Ryan called Erin, and for the third time, she didn't answer. He rose from his office chair and started pacing. *She must be out with him again.*

The framed photograph of Sarah and Cody lay on his desk, and Ryan glared at it. Cody's smug face made Ryan's blood boil. Sarah looked at her fiancé with expectation and adoration. She had no idea she loved a snake—a liar.

Putting the photograph back on his desk, Ryan wondered how to proceed. Should he call Erin again? He could intercept them when they got back to her house.

Another possibility. He could spare Erin and confront Cody privately. Maybe threaten him and make him leave town.

I sure would like to know what this guy is doing, though, and if I run him out of town, I may never know why he lied to Sarah.

Ryan looked at his calendar to check his schedule. Phil's name leapt from his phone screen. Racquetball at seven. His eyes fell on the previous weeks. Erin's birthday was highlighted. Erin's birthday. It had only been a few weeks ago, but it seemed like that crazy conversation at the mall was years ago.

He sat back in his chair. If Erin got married and had a baby by her next birthday, she'd become a multi-millionaire and primary owner of Envision Pharmaceuticals.

If she gets all this wealth, so does her husband.

Ryan picked up the picture of Sarah and Cody again and surveyed the face of a heartless jerk.

Who could know about this crazy will? Erin, her dad's lawyer, and now Cody. Somehow, Cody planned to return to Sarah in a year. That would only be possible if Erin was no longer around. Was he going to divorce her? If so, he wouldn't get the money.

The blood drained from Ryan's face as he realized the only other option. He jumped to his feet. Erin was in danger.

As he rushed out of his office, he called to his assistant. "Lori, would you please phone Phil and tell him I've got to reschedule? Phil Reese. He's in my contacts. I've had an emergency come up. See you in the morning."

Ryan considered heading toward the sleazy lawyer's office and beating the truth out of the guy, but then the lawyer would call the cops. Besides, Ryan knew his first obligation was to protect Erin.

He should never have encouraged this crazy notion of finding a husband. What had he been thinking? If anything happened to her, he'd never forgive himself.

While racing around I-285 toward the south side of Atlanta, he continued calling Erin. Nothing. Was she safe?

In the distance, a sea of red brake lights blinked back at him, and he growled while slowing for the gridlock. He didn't have a plan to deal with Cody, but thanks to Atlanta traffic, he had plenty of time to formulate one.

* * * * *

Williams' phone buzzed with a text. "Did you find them?"

He thumbed in a response. "Yes."

After pressing another key, he heard Bob's phone ring three times. "James?"

"Who else would it be?"

"So, you found them?"

"Sure did. They were quite cozy."

"Oh yeah?"

"I saw them in the parking lot at Nash Farms. I watched your boy make a move. He's taken things to a new level and seems to have everything under control."

Williams had almost missed the kiss. He had glanced at his phone and missed seeing the white Blazer pull in two rows across from him. A car driving by caught his attention, which directed his eyes to Erin Douglas in the arms of a tall young man, his lips on hers. It wasn't a big deal kiss, but it was enough. The boy was smooth.

"I told you he could handle it," Bob insisted. "You don't need to worry about anything."

"Well, a kiss is not enough. He's got to get that girl in front of a preacher and then into labor and delivery."

"He knows that, James. Calm down. He'll suggest they run off to Gatlinburg and get married in two weeks."

"That gives them about two months to get pregnant. A little close for comfort."

"Two months is plenty of time. Besides, you offered $10,000 more if he got her to the altar within the next three weeks. He'll have a ring on her finger in one week and marry her in two. Once she has the baby, I'll erase her."

"Whatever you've got to do, Bob. Just make it look like an accident."

"This ain't my first rodeo, James."

Williams remembered the cowboy on a horse earlier at Nash Farms. *Rodeo indeed.*

"Bob, just don't screw me on this one. There's too much at stake. Keep me informed with any updates."

He disconnected the call and stared at the ceiling. His future was definitely bright. Bob's future, not so much. Once this venture was complete, the lawyer had plans for his old associate. As much as Williams appreciated Bob's services, the guy had to go.

Atlanta had plenty of thugs who would knock off someone for the right price. Of course, after this project, he wouldn't need any more thugs. He'd just need somewhere to stash all his money.

CHAPTER THIRTY-EIGHT

Gloves Off

R yan cruised by Erin's house and saw her car in the driveway. Maybe she was inside reading with her phone on silent. He parked and walked to the front door. When she didn't respond to his knock, he located the spare key and let himself in.

The house was as silent as a tomb, and a shiver ran down his back. Daphne darted from under the couch to the bedroom, so Ryan followed the feline. Nothing.

He entered her bathroom and saw dirty clothes in a pile by the shower. *She's probably out with that creep.*

Anger boiled up inside, and he imagined punching Cody. Erin had fallen for this guy, and Ryan had to do something. Once he moved his BMW down the street to the driveway of a vacant house, he settled in to wait on Erin and Cody to return. It might be a long wait, but he'd sit there all night if he had to.

On the drive over, Ryan had tried to decide how to expose this fraud. A bold confrontation was certainly an option, but Ryan had to figure out exactly what was going on. The perfect plan never materialized, but this fiasco would end tonight.

Reaching into his glove box, he pulled out his small Glock 26. Once he checked the clip and chamber, he placed it on the seat beside him. When he applied for a permit to carry a weapon, he never imagined having to shoot someone.

At nearly eleven o'clock, headlights approached Erin's street, and the vehicle slowed and turned into Erin's driveway. Ryan tucked the pistol into his pocket, took a deep breath, and stepped out of the car.

A large tree in Erin's front yard offered him cover, and he watched the sleaze pull his best friend in for a passionate kiss. Ryan staved off his rage and forced himself to wait.

Kudos to Erin for not inviting the jerk into her house. Ryan waited until Erin had closed the door, and Cody started walking back to his car.

"Cody," Ryan shouted as he stepped out from behind the tree. "Cody Wilkerson."

Cody froze in mid-stride. He slowly turned and focused on Ryan.

"I'm sorry," he stammered. "What did you say?" He took a couple of steps toward Ryan.

Ryan leaned against the tree, crossed his legs, and slipped his hands into his pockets. His right hand wrapped around the Glock. "Your real name isn't Cody Wilson. You're Cody Wilkerson from Chicago. I saw you there recently with a dear friend."

"I've never been to Chicago."

"Oh, don't start lying now, Cody." Ryan pushed off from the tree and spread his feet. "Not only do I know Sarah Hardwick, but I have a picture of the two of you together. She's swooning over you because she doesn't know what a creep you are."

Cody closed the distance between them. Ryan reacted, too, but not fast enough.

* * * * *

Erin added water to Daphne's bowl and set it down. Cody's kiss had both stunned and troubled her. What did it mean? Was she ready for that kind of relationship?

Returning to the door to lock it, she cocked her head and listened. Voices. *Who could be in my front yard? Cody? But who's he talking to?*

She opened the front door in time to see Cody swinging his fist at someone.

"Ryan!"

She heard a sickening thud of bone on bone.

Cody reared back for another blow, but at the last moment, Ryan ducked, and Cody's fist smashed into the tree trunk. He groaned and grabbed his now bloody hand.

Ryan seized the opportunity and landed two punches, one to his ribcage and another to his face. Cody fell to the ground, blood gushing from his nose.

Ryan pulled a pistol from his pocket.

Erin jumped down and ran into the yard. "Stop!" she screamed, waving her arms in the air. "What are you doing?"

"We should ask Cody what he's doing," Ryan suggested as the bigger man wiped blood from his face and staggered to his feet.

Erin looked at Cody, his hands raised defensively and head bowed. Other than the sounds of nature and heavy breathing, the night was still. When Mr. Rakestraw's porch light came on, Ryan and Erin looked toward the neighbor's house.

With the speed of a coiled snake, Cody reached for Erin and pulled her against him. Locked in a vice-like grip, she struggled to breathe. Her heart pounded, and her eyes widened in horror as Cody held up a knife.

"Cody, Cody. Please…no," she choked out.

"Quiet, Erin." Cody jerked his head toward the house. "Throw your pistol toward that bush." When Ryan hesitated, Cody moved the blade to Erin's throat. "Now."

Left with no choice, Ryan complied with the ultimatum.

Terror shook every part of Erin. Her heart raced, and she couldn't move, or breathe. So, she prayed. Peace flowed through her like a soothing balm. She felt protected...and something else.

She'd been in this spot before. It came to her. Strong arms. Bear hug. It seemed both odd and familiar. Erin rehearsed the scene in her mind while filling her lungs with air. She blew the air out in a rush and stomped Cody's foot. At the same time Cody moved the knife away from her throat, Erin slid from his grasp and grabbed his right wrist.

Erin yanked Cody's arm back and jammed her left palm into his elbow in one fluid motion. A sickening crack split through the night air as he screamed in pain.

Ryan leaped toward Cody and delivered a blow to the side of Cody's head. Cody fell to the ground like a rag doll. Out cold. His arm lay at an unnatural angle. Ryan jumped on top of him and pulled his arms behind him, though it seemed his right arm had completely snapped.

"Erin, do you have duct tape?" Ryan panted.

Erin stood frozen. Lost. She had just broken a man's elbow.

"Erin? Listen to me. I need you to find a roll of duct tape."

Cold sweat beaded on her forehead. Unable to remove her gaze from Cody's prone form, she began to tremble.

"Erin, I know this isn't easy," Ryan prodded.

Erin still didn't move.

"Erin! I need duct tape!" Ryan shouted, trying to break through her fog.

She looked blankly at Ryan and turned toward the house. Thoughts of duct tape registered, but the sound of Cody's bone snapping rang in her mind. Had Cody planned on hurting her? Why would he hold a knife against her throat? As though still in a trance, Erin trudged across the yard and into the house.

The roll of tape was tucked away in a cabinet above her washing machine. While taking it to Ryan, she tried to process what had happened. Tried but failed.

Why was blood on Ryan's clothes and on *her* clothes?

Ryan wrapped the tape around Cody's wrists, and Erin thought she saw something protruding from Cody's arm. A bone? Her stomach churned, and she turned away and wretched.

* * * * *

Ryan layered the tape around Cody's wrists as tightly as he could while monitoring Erin out of the corner of his eye. She stepped back onto the porch and into the house.

"Erin?"

Moving to Cody's ankles, he began to secure them with tape. He looked up to ensure Cody was still out when a crash inside the house propelled him onto the porch.

"Erin?" Ryan ran through the front door.

Erin lay sprawled on the floor with a cut on her forehead. *Did she faint?* Ryan glanced toward the front yard, where his captive remained unconscious.

Ryan cradled Erin in his arms. "Erin? Can you hear me? Are you okay?"

He brushed hair out of her face and gently rubbed her cheek. Her face looked as white as the dining room tablecloth.

Erin's eyes fluttered open. Her gaze roamed the room before focusing on Ryan. "Wh…what's going on?"

Ryan exhaled, not realizing he'd been holding his breath. "You fainted. Are you all right?"

She squirmed as a bit of color returned to her cheeks. Then she sat straight up, panicked. "Cody! What about Cody?"

"Still unconscious in the front yard, his hands and ankles taped up. He's fine for now. He'll be in a lot of pain when he awakes. You broke his elbow, Erin." Ryan's voice had a trace of pride. "Unbelievable."

Erin started to tremble. "You called the police, right?"

Ryan patted his pockets. "I must have dropped my phone. Where's yours?"

"In my purse, I think."

"Do you feel like sitting up in a chair? I need to get back outside and make sure Cody's secure."

As Ryan helped Erin into a chair at the kitchen table, a vehicle's engine cut through the night. Ryan bolted onto the front porch in time to see Cody peeling away, his Blazer fish-tailing.

Ryan jumped off the porch, ran into the road, and watched the SUV speed off into the night. He jogged back into the yard and found his phone on the ground beside a wad of duct tape. The tape had been torn and sliced.

He must have gotten to his knife and somehow cut the tape loose.

Just a few feet away, Ryan noticed his Glock glinting in the pale moonlight. Why didn't Cody grab the gun and take it with him?

A creaking sound caught his attention, and Ryan saw Mr. Rakestraw stepping cautiously across his porch. The old man raised his hand in a half-wave to Ryan.

Ryan picked up his phone and Glock and hurried back into the house.

"He's gone," Ryan said as he returned to the kitchen. "He managed to cut the tape from his wrist. I don't think I had his hands bound tightly enough."

"I can't believe I fainted. I've never fainted before."

Ryan sat and placed his hand on top of Erin's. "You scared me to death."

Erin still looked off. Her hair was disheveled, and though she'd regained some color, she seemed pale.

"I'm okay now." Erin insisted.

Ryan snatched a cup from the cabinet and filled it with water for Erin. "You were so amazing. I doubt his arm will ever be right. He'll need surgery, for sure."

Erin sipped water and gazed into the distance. She still didn't seem to be acting normal. Did her fall give her a concussion? She may need to go to the hospital.

"We need to call the police," Ryan insisted. "I don't know what they can do other than look for a guy driving a white Blazer. Do you know where he lives?"

Erin shook her head. "I have no idea. He may have told me, but I don't remember."

After making the call, Ryan ran down the street to his car. He stored the gun in the glove box and moved the vehicle to Erin's driveway. When he returned to the kitchen, Erin still sat at the table.

"I'll make coffee," Ryan said. "I have a feeling we'll be up a while."

"Fine."

"You feeling better? You look a little better."

Erin dropped her head into her hands. "Yeah, just embarrassed and confused. Why'd you come over?"

Ryan told her about seeing Cody and Sarah in Chicago and related how he'd contacted his friend for a picture. "I guess Cody's working with someone who knows about the will. I think the plan may have been to marry you."

"Marry me?" Erin gasped. "Would he do that? Why?"

"Millions of dollars. The question is, who knew about this will? Did you tell anyone else about it?"

Erin shook her head. "No. I haven't breathed a word to anyone." Her words trailed off to almost a whisper.

"So, your dad's lawyer is the only one who knew. He must have been part of some scheme. I'm sure the police will speak with him."

The doorbell rang, and Ryan hurried to answer it. "Maybe the police can help us make sense of all this."

CHAPTER THIRTY-NINE

Aftermath

The police officers closed their notebooks after making notes about every detail Ryan and Erin could remember. They promised to do everything possible to find Cody but agreed it would be difficult. A detective agreed to talk with James Williams the next day.

One of the officers asked to see Ryan's permit to carry a weapon. After scanning the card, he said, "You know, Mr. Jeffries, you're fortunate this man didn't pick up your weapon and kill you both."

Ryan nodded and admitted he'd already considered that possibility. Erin stiffened at the reminder, and he wished he could put her at ease.

One of the officers reached out to shake Ryan's hand. "We'll place a patrol car on the street, just for extra protection."

"Thank you," Ryan said. "We appreciate your help."

Ryan walked the officers to the door and returned to the living room. "Did you see how those policemen reacted to you breaking Cody's arm? They couldn't believe it. I still can't believe it, and I saw the whole thing. I can't wait to tell Tim. You're going to be his star student for sure."

Erin didn't move. Ryan wondered if she'd fallen asleep.

"Hey." He knelt beside her. "You okay?" He took her hand in his. "You probably bumped your head pretty hard when you fell."

Erin didn't open her eyes. "It's just all so hard to take in, Ryan."

Ryan rubbed his thumb over her knuckle. So vulnerable. His beautiful best friend, a warrior who had broken a guy's arm, was still delicate and needed him.

He pushed a strand of hair from her face and examined the cut on her head. After retrieving a washcloth from the bathroom, he held it under the hot water, and returned to Erin. The cut on her forehead was no longer bleeding, so he cleaned it and applied first aid cream.

"This Band-Aid really makes you look like a ninja."

Erin remained quiet with her eyes closed. Ryan didn't know what to do or say, so he held her hands and sat in silence.

The image of Cody kissing her flashed through his mind, and something stirred inside him. Anger? The jerk needed another fist to the face.

"Listen, Erin." Ryan broke the silence. "I, I don't know what to say. I'm sorry. I'm sure having your boyfriend pull a knife on you shook you up."

Erin's eyes shot open. "He's not my boyfriend."

"Could have fooled me. I'd call that a passionate kiss."

"You were watching?"

Ryan looked down at their intertwined hands. "I was worried about you, Erin."

"So, you were hiding in the bushes watching me come home?" Erin stood to her feet. "Ridiculous, Ryan. He's not my boyfriend, and that wasn't a passionate kiss."

Ryan stood, and his temperature seemed to have risen ten degrees. "Yes, I watched you because I knew Cody was not some new, innocent, handsome guy you met at work who had stolen your heart. And if that wasn't a passionate kiss, then I don't know anything about passion."

Erin's hands balled into a fist as she put them on her hips. "Don't get angry with me, Ryan Jeffries. I didn't ask you to hide in my bushes, and I didn't know you were so clueless. Cody Wilson has not stolen my heart!"

"Wilkerson," Ryan corrected.

"Fine, Wilkerson! Whatever. A passionate kiss should be between two people who are intensely in love. A passionate kiss is never one-sided, and that kiss was about as one-sided as a one-way street headed to…to downtown Peoria."

She growled and dropped her fists to her side. Tears overflowed from her eyes. "He's, he's not my boyfriend," she stammered, "and never would have been my boyfriend. I didn't want him to kiss me, and I never would have married him. I'm sick of this dating thing, and I wish my father had never made this stupid challenge."

Erin began to cry, and Ryan pulled her into his arms. Her tears turned into sobs, and her body shook against his chest. He held her until she stopped crying.

"I shouldn't have pushed you to date those guys," Ryan said into the silence. "I put you in danger. If something had happened to you, I never would have gotten over it."

Silence. Erin wiped her nose with the back of her hand. She pulled away, grabbed a tissue from a box on the end table, and blew her nose.

"I've got to take out my contacts."

Ryan sat at the kitchen table, and after a few minutes, Erin returned, wearing her glasses.

"I think I need to be alone, Ryan. Tonight has been…" Her words fell away.

"Sure. I understand. I'll leave."

The refrigerator made a few popping sounds in the awkward silence. On impulse, Ryan pulled Erin back into his arms. Holding her close, he breathed in her scent, and whispered, "Are you sure you're going to be okay? Do you need to go to the hospital?"

Erin stepped back. "I'm fine, but your cheek looks awfully red."

"I'm all right. Do you want me to spend the night? I can sleep on the couch."

"No. I'm fine."

Ryan kissed her on the cheek. "Okay. Call me if you need me. I'm only a few miles away. I'll check in tomorrow."

* * * * *

Erin watched Ryan walk out the front door and listened as his sleek, luxury car purred to life. She reached up, placed her hand against her cheek, and stood motionless.

Oblivious to the cat rubbing against her leg, she entered the kitchen, bumped into the table, and poured coffee. Images of Cody's elbow snapping replayed in her mind. Lifting the mug to her lips, she nearly gagged on the sweet, hot liquid. How much sugar had she put in her coffee?

She dumped the cup into the sink and poured in fresh coffee, adding cream and only three spoons of sugar.

The lighthouse painting she'd taken from her father's office caught her attention. The lighthouse keeper stood in the lighthouse entrance in the middle of a raging storm, the ocean's fury lashing around him. What had her father seen in this photograph? It wasn't just the life-threatening, crashing waves that captured her attention. It was the man. It almost made her angry to look at him, so calm, while the world around him appeared chaotic.

Something about it seemed—.

Erin turned on the overhead light and moved in closer. The corners of the man's mouth were lifted just a little. Was he about to smile? He stood in the storm's epicenter, drinking coffee, and seemed at peace. How was that possible?

The epicenter of her storm had to be when Cody held a knife to her throat. She hadn't smiled, but she had acted. Her actions resulted in breaking his arm. How did she pull that off? And who was Cody?

A car squealing down the street startled Erin. Coffee sloshed onto the floor as she turned toward the front door and looked through the small window. Her driveway was empty, except for her little blue Toyota. It must have been the kids from the next block. She opened the door and peered down the street and saw the police car.

After locking the door, she turned the deadbolt. Moving from window to window, Erin checked the locks. Her bathroom window had been the only one unlocked.

The man in the painting flashed through her mind again. He seemed secure and peaceful in his storm. Where was her peace? She felt lost, like a child at the mall who had become separated from her parents.

Wandering back into the kitchen, she considered the possibility of James Williams devising a scheme to steal her inheritance. The thought of someone stalking her and conspiring with others to take her money made her shiver.

How did Cody think he'd get the money? Maybe he thought she'd put the money in a joint account, and he could withdraw it and flee.

The coffee cup halfway to her lips, she froze. The only way he would have gotten the money and the business would have been by inheriting it, which meant she would have to die.

As she dropped into the kitchen chair, it scooted a little on the floor. Anger and fear overtook her as she considered Cody's deception. How had she fallen for his kind manners and fake tenderness? Could he have killed her?

Thinking back to numerous times when someone had purposely tried to hurt her, a nagging thought kept pulling on her mind. In every instance from her past, Ryan Jeffries had always factored into the story. Ryan was the one constant in her life. He always showed up and made things better. Tonight was no exception.

Erin jumped as Daphne pressed against her leg. "Oh, Daffy, poor thing. I'm sorry I've been ignoring you. You must be traumatized, too. I'm sure you're starving, though it looks like your shadow would weigh ten pounds by itself."

A glance at the cat's food bowl showed it had been licked clean. Grabbing a can from the cabinet, Erin turned back to the large cat. "How's fish?"

The room filled with a horrible smell, and Erin wrinkled her nose. *How can she eat this stuff?*

"Okay, Daff. You eat, and I'm going to sleep. I'm exhausted. Brush your teeth before coming to bed." She smiled at the image of her cat with a toothbrush.

The shock and stress of the day nagged at Erin as she lay in bed, desperate for sleep. Cody had seemed so sweet and considerate. Of course, he had. He wanted millions of dollars, even though it meant marrying her and fathering a child. Thoughts of that possibility terrified Erin.

And then, there was Ryan. Her best friend in all the world. The one person she could call any time of day or night. He always cared about whatever she was going through, and he was always there for her.

And he kissed me and held me while I cried...and got snot all over his shirt.

The day's ugliness kept forcing its way back into Erin's mind. Cody. The knife.

Fear.

Erin got up and looked out the window. The cop car stationed on the street should make her feel secure. *You're safe, Erin. Go to sleep.*

She crawled back into bed and pounded her pillow into submission.

It was going to be a long night.

* * * * *

Ryan looked at the clock and groaned. Only twenty minutes had passed since the last time he'd ventured a peek at the clock. He craved sleep but knew it was hopeless.

Erin. Poor, sweet Erin. This whole episode could have ended so differently. He rubbed his eyes and breathed in deeply.

Was he relieved the crisis was over or that Cody was no longer around? Erin was safe, and they didn't have to worry about that lunatic for now. But was that the only thing?

The memory of holding her and smelling her hair caused a smile to spread across his face as something stirred within him. He'd kissed her cheek, but what if he'd kissed her lips?

In his imagination, he held her and kissed her, really kissed her.

Sitting up in bed, Ryan rubbed his hands through his hair. "I didn't kiss her, but I want to," he said aloud. He dragged himself to the bathroom, turned on the light, and looked into the mirror. His hair stuck straight up, and dark bags high-lighted his eyes. "Who are you kidding, Ryan Jeffries?"

The light from his bedside clock glowed into the night, 3:05. He pulled on his clothes, brushed his teeth, and retrieved his keys. Erin always rode her bike first thing. She wouldn't be up for a while, but he could sit on her porch until she came outside. He couldn't sleep tonight.

Ryan approached Erin's house and knew something was wrong. Her car was gone. He slipped out of his vehicle and approached the police officer getting out of the car.

"Where's Erin?" Ryan asked

"And you are…?"

"I'm Ryan Jeffries. We're friends. I was with her earlier this evening."

The cop looked at Ryan's car. "Yeah. I remember your car. She went somewhere but didn't tell me where. My job is to stay here in front of her house; not babysit her."

Ryan got back into his car. "Okay, Erin. Where are you?" Her mother's house? He drove to where her mother lived, but the place was dark. No blue Toyota.

Where is she?

He dialed her number. Voicemail.

One other place came to mind, a place that held a sweet spot in her heart. It was a little bit of a drive, but the more he thought about it, the more confident he became that's where he'd find her.

He headed toward the Interstate.

CHAPTER FORTY

Finding Home

Erin's car sat alone in the parking lot of the Stone Mountain Human Resources building. Ryan knew that while the gates to the park would be closed at this hour, people could always enter through the walkers' gate. He remembered Erin often speaking about climbing to the top to watch the sunrise, and his hunch had been correct. She once told him that watching the sunrise from atop Stone Mountain was a spiritual experience for her.

He parked his car and jogged toward the hiking trail. Although he'd been to the park several times, he'd never seen it so still and quiet. His heart, however, was far from quiet and nearly beat out of his chest. Erin had to be on top, and every step took him closer to her.

What would she do when she saw him? What if he missed her somehow? Was there more than one way down from the top?

As he crossed the railroad track, Ryan quickened his pace and ran. Halfway up the mountain, he twisted his ankle and crashed onto the stone.

Stupid! What was I thinking?

He massaged his ankle but decided to leave his shoe in place. His foot could swell, and he'd never get his shoe back on. The last thing he wanted was to hop up the mountain with his shoe off. He stood, put weight on his injured foot, and gingerly limped toward the top.

What would he say to her? Clueless. He just had to see her.

Finally, coming to the top of the vast granite rock, he scanned his surroundings but didn't see Erin. Of course, she could be anywhere—or somewhere else in the park, for that matter. The park had miles of hiking trails.

What had she told him about climbing the mountain? If she were going to watch the sunrise, she'd have to be on the east side.

Why haven't I ever done this with her?

The sky began to show the hint of a new morning as bright red streaks shot across it. Ryan limped under the sky lift cables and spotted the lone figure of a young woman facing the eastern sky. He moved toward her. In the growing light, he could see her right hand resting on a particular spot.

It looks like a heart carved into the stone.

* * * * *

A tear slid down Erin's cheek. *Why are you crying, Erin?* She took her glasses off and wiped her eyes.

Earlier, while climbing the mountain, her tears flowed freely. She had begun to think about her parents coming up here to watch the sunrise. They'd been so happy at first. Life had been good, and the future was so bright. Who could have known tragedy awaited them and their lives would fall apart?

Had the tears been about her parents? No, these were her tears. Her life. Confusion clouded her mind. Having a knife held to your throat brought a lot of things into proper perspective.

While her job was necessary, and school was a significant priority, those were not the most essential parts of her life.

They were just things. Stuff. The only things that mattered in life were not things at all but relationships. Her relationship with God was vital, but also her relationship with—.

Erin froze as she heard a pebble rolling over the smooth granite toward her. Someone was behind her. Cody? Had Cody managed to find her? Fear seized her heart, and she couldn't breathe. She slowly turned and let out the breath she'd been holding.

"Hey," Ryan managed.

"What are you doing here?" Erin asked as she pushed up onto wobbly legs.

"I was going to ask you the same question."

"I wanted to be alone."

Ryan took a few steps toward her, closing the distance to mere inches, and took hold of her hands. "I can leave if you'd like."

"No." Erin shook her head. "I don't want you to leave."

His gaze held her captive. His eyes were like dark pools of liquid hope. She stared deep into his soul, and something within her stirred. His hands felt like warm strength in hers, and his smile lit her world greater than the rising sun.

"I don't want to leave, Erin Douglas. Ever."

Erin looked down at their clasped hands. Together. She let go with one hand and wiped her face as tears slipped from her eyes.

"Are you okay?" Ryan wiped another stray tear. "Why are you crying?"

"I don't know. I cried the whole way up the mountain, and I've been crying ever since sitting down. It's just—well, I'm confused. I'm horrified Cody wanted to kill me. I figured out that he was planning to murder me so he could inherit my money and business, but that would mean we would've gotten married and had a baby. And then your kiss. I know you just kissed my cheek, but—"

She looked up at him and knitted her eyebrows. "Did you say *ever?*"

Ryan's smile broadened. "Yes. Ever. I don't ever want to leave you."

He slowly lowered his face toward hers and paused, offering her a choice. Erin wrapped her arms around his neck and closed the gap. Electricity shot through her as their kiss deepened. She pressed into him, and it felt like their hearts beat as one.

Ryan pulled back and framed each side of her face. "I love you, Erin Douglas. I realized tonight that I've always loved you. I couldn't bear it if anything happened to you, or if you decided to spend the rest of your life with anyone but me."

Was he serious? He wanted to spend the rest of his life with her? Erin searched his face. He'd been her best friend her entire life. Why couldn't they be more than best friends forever?

"I love you, too, Ryan. It probably started just after I helped you up from the bathroom floor in fifth grade. I didn't think love was an option, so I never opened that door."

"I've been too blind and stupid to see it, but it is an option, Erin. The only option for me."

Erin's fingers pushed through Ryan's hair as she considered his statement: the only option for him. He was the only option for her. Not Tyler. Definitely not Cody. Just sweet, loyal Ryan.

Ryan shifted and winced in pain.

Erin looked down at his foot. "What happened?"

He told Erin about his fall, and she insisted they sit. Ryan pulled Erin against him and wrapped his arms around her.

They watched the sun inch over the horizon as birds dipped and darted in the distance, the sky painted with pink and orange as though by the hand of the master artist. Sounds of morning blended into an intoxicating symphony of joy.

Ryan kissed her forehead. "So, that kiss a few minutes ago…Using your definition, I think it qualifies as a passionate kiss."

Erin smiled up at him. "No doubt about it."

She leaned her head against Ryan, and he tightened his arms around her. He kissed the top of her head and lifted her face toward his. Their lips met again briefly, but even that short kiss held promise.

Ryan suggested they start making their way down the trail and go home.

Erin smiled up at Ryan as his strong arm tightened around her.

No hurry. She *was* home.

What's Next?

Deadline Book 2 – Coming Late 2025:

What happens next? Surely wedding bells are in Ryan and Erin's future, or are they?

Do you want to stay in touch so you'll know when Book 2 is released? Download Judah's free book here, and we'll send you an email update on the release of *Crucible*.

From the Author

I hope you enjoyed this first book of my Deadline Series. If you did, will you please take a moment to leave a review on Amazon?

I enjoy crafting stories about life, its challenges, opportunities, and victories. This genre has become especially enjoyable to me as I write about the kinds of relationships my readers want to experience while creating suspenseful circumstances that hopefully cause you to want to continue turning the pages to see what happens next.

This is the first book in a six-book series. If you are one of my early readers, you'll have to wait a few weeks for the next books in the series to come out. While you are waiting, I'd like to offer you a gift.

I wrote a novella to accompany a previous series called "The Davenports." It could serve as Book 7 of the series, but it can also be read as a standalone book. You can access this free book.

My inbox is always open, and I'd love to hear from you. Please visit the contact page on my website and send me a note.

I look forward to hearing from you soon. Thank you again for reading my book, and I look forward to seeing you in the next adventure.

Judah Knight

Judah Knight's...

The Davenport Series

Scuba Diving, Treasure Hunting, Intrigue
Through the series, you'll journey from the Bahamas, to Spain, to Denmark, and to Mexico on this exciting tale of adventure, danger, discovery, and love.

Learn more at: **Judahknight.com/books**